The
Vesuvius
Club

The Vesuvius Club

A BIT OF FLUFF

by

MARK GATISS

POCKET
BOOKS

First published in Great Britain by Simon & Schuster UK Ltd, 2004
This edition published by Pocket Books, 2005
An imprint of Simon & Schuster UK Ltd
A CBS COMPANY

Copyright © Mark Gatiss, 2004

Illustrations by Ian Bass

19

Simon & Schuster UK Ltd
1st Floor
222 Gray's Inn Road
London WC1X 8HB

Simon & Schuster Australia
Sydney

A CIP catalogue record for this book is available from the British Library

ISBN-13: 978-0-7434-8379-7

Typeset by M Rules
Printed and bound by
CPI Group (UK) Ltd, Croydon, CR0 4YY

*For Ian
My love, my life*

ACKNOWLEDGEMENTS

Huge thanks to Ian Bass, John Jarrold (who lit the first Lucifer), Clayton Hickman, Darren Nash and my editor Ben Ball – honorary English gentleman.

I

MR LUCIFER BOX ENTERTAINS

HAVE always been an appalling judge of character. It is my most beguiling virtue.

What, then, did I make of the Honourable Everard Supple whose likeness I was conjuring on to canvas in my studio that sultry July evening?

He was an imposing cove of sixty-odd, built like a pugilist, who had made a fortune in the diamond mines of the Cape. His declining years, he'd told me during the second sitting – when a client begins to thaw a mite – were to be devoted entirely to pleasure, principally in the gaming houses of the warmer and naughtier parts of Europe. A portrait, in his opinion (and his absence), would be just the thing to hang over the vast baronial fireplace in the vast baronial hall he had recently lavished a hundred thou' upon.

The Supples, it has to be said, were not amongst the oldest and most distinguished families in the realm. Only one generation back from the

Honourable Everard had been the less than honourable Gerald who had prospered only tolerably in a manufactory of leather thumb-braces. Son and heir had done rather better for himself and now to add to the title (of sorts) and the fake coat of arms being busily prepared across town he had his new portrait. This, he told me with a wheezy chuckle, would convey the required air of old-world veracity. And if my painting were any good (that *hurt*), perhaps I might even be interested in knocking up a few carefully aged canvases of his ancestors?

Supple blinked repeatedly, as was his habit, one lid lingering over his jade-irised glass eye (the left one) as I let myself imagine him tramping into the studio in doublet and hose, all in the name of family honour.

He cleared his throat with a grisly expectoration and I realized he'd been addressing me. I snapped out of my reverie and peeped around the side of the canvas. I've been told I peep rather well.

'I do beg your pardon, I was absorbed in the curve of your ear-lobes.'

'I was suggesting dinner, sir,' said Supple, flipping a half-hunter watch from his waistcoat. 'To celebrate the successful conclusion of me picture.'

'I should be delighted,' I lied. 'But I feel it only right to warn you that I have a peculiar horror of artichokes.'

The Honourable Everard Supple rose from the doubtful Louis Quinze into which I'd plonked him, sending a whisper of paint-flakes to the dust-sheeted floor.

'We might try me club, then,' he suggested, brushing the sleeve of his frock-coat. 'Or do you have somewhere you artistic-types favour?'

I rose and ran one of my long, bony hands through my hair. They *are* long, white and bony, I cannot deny it, but very fine. Waistcoat and face flecked with paint, I shrugged.

'As a matter of fact, I do,' I said. 'Charming little spot in Rosebery Avenue. Come back at eight and we'll drive over.' So saying, I suddenly turned the easel on its squeaking castors, revealing the portrait to the golden light washing through the skylight. 'Behold! Your immortality!'

Supple creaked forward on his expensive boots and fixed a monocle, rather unnecessarily, into the orbit of his false eye. He frowned, cocked his head to left and right and grimaced.

'Well, I suppose you get what you pay for, eh, Mr Box?'

My name is Lucifer Box, but I imagine you know that. Whether these scribblings eventually form the core of my memoirs or are found secreted in oilskin wrappers at the bottom of a lavatory cistern years after my demise, I have no doubt that, by the time you read this, I will be most terribly famous.

I handed Supple his soft kid-gloves with as much brusqueness as I could muster. 'You don't like it?'

The old fool shrugged. 'Just not sure it's terribly like me.'

I helped him into his overcoat. 'On the contrary, sir, I believe I have caught you.'

I smiled what my friends call, naturally enough, the smile of Lucifer.

Ah! London in the summertime! *Hellish*, as any resident will tell you. Even in those first few innocent years of the new century it smelled of roasting excrement. So it was with 'kerchiefs pressed to mouths that Supple and I entered the dining rooms I had selected. They were alarmingly unfashionable but, in the long light of dusk, the white-panelled plainness could have been called Vermeeresque. Not by me, you understand. A flypaper above the hearth twisted lazily, amber and black like a screw of ear-wax.

This place, I told Supple, was owned and run by a woman called Delilah whose crippled daughter I had once painted as a favour.

'She was not, perhaps, the bonniest thing,' I confided as we set-tled down to eat. 'Lost both hands to a wasting disease and had them replaced with wooden ones. And – oh! – her little legs were in horrid iron rings.' I shook my head despairingly. 'Ought to have been exposed at birth, her father said.'

'Nay!' cried Supple.

'Aye! But her dear mother loved the little mite. When I came to paint the portrait I did my best to make little Ida look like an angel. Prophetically enough. Though it turned out she had some pluck.'

Supple wiped soup from his pinkish lips. Sentimental old Victorian that he was, a tear sprang to his one good eye. Most probably the Death of Little Nell had been like mother's milk to him.

'Poor Ida,' I sighed, picking idly at a chicken leg. 'Grabbed from her bath-chair by a gang of dacoits and sold into bondage.'

Supple's shook his head mournfully. No doubt an image of the doe-eyed cripple had flashed into his silly old brain. His fingers tightened on the fish-knife. 'Go on. What happened?'

'She made a bolt for it, God bless her,' I continued. 'Took off across the rooftops with the fiends in hot pursuit.'

Blink-blink. The jade glass eye regarded me steadily. 'And then?'

I closed my eyes and steepled my fingers. 'She got as far as Wapping before her brittle little legs gave out. She fell through the roof of a sugar merchant's and into a vat of treacle. Of course, with those wooden hands she could get no purchase on the rim and she drowned. Very, very slowly.'

Drinking the last of an indifferent burgundy with an air of finality, I clapped my hands and turned the conversation towards more cheerful matters. Now I had Supple's trust, it was time to betray that of others. I wanted the practice.

I regaled Supple with what I know to be an inexhaustible supply of anecdotes (not many of them true, certainly not the best ones) concerning the greatish and goodish who have paid yours truly not nearly enough to be immortalized in oils.

'You are very indiscreet, sir,' laughed the old man, cheering up. 'I am glad not to have confided any of my secrets in you!'

I smiled my wide smile.

Supple, for his part, talked at length about his time in South Africa and the great adventure a young man like me might have there. He told me about his own daughter – a great joy to the old man by his account – and I nodded and smiled with the air of sagacity I like to assume for such occasions. I put on a good show of being fascinated by his colourful account of dawn over the Transvaal as I took out my watch and stared at the second hand racing over the porcelain dial. I could hear the soft action of the tiny spring.

It was midway between the fish course and the pudding, as Supple opened his mouth to begin another interminable tale, that I did the decent thing and shot him.

A stain spread across the breast of his stiff white waistcoat like poppy petals emerging through the snow. How I wish I'd had my sketch-book with me! The scene was a riot of crimson possibilities.

There, now. I've shocked you, haven't I? What the deuce can Mr Box be up to? Are customers in such abundant supply? Well, you'll just have to be patient. All good things et cetera.

Supple's face, never particularly smashing as you may have gathered, froze in an expression of pained surprise and a little bubble of red spit frolicked over his lips. He slid forward on to the table where his teeth met the rim of his pudding bowl with a shocking crack, like the knees of an out-of-practice supplicant.

I watched smoke curl from the end of the snub-barrelled pistol I'd used, then replaced the weapon under a jelly mould – silver and shaped like a sleeping hare – where it had been until recently ensconced.

Lighting a cigarette, I re-pocketed my watch and, rising, dabbed a napkin at the corners of my full-lipped mouth (it's a very pretty mouth – more of it later). Taking up a dessert spoon, I dug it into Supple's left socket and carefully removed the old fellow's glass eye. It popped out with just a little poking and lay nestled in my palm like a gull's egg. I looked at the iris and smiled. It was just the shade of green I had in mind for a new tie and now I had a match for my tailor. What a happy accident! I slipped the eye into my waistcoat and draped the napkin carelessly over the dead man's head.

A large and ugly mirror hung over the fireplace of the dark little room. I checked my appearance in it (*very* acceptable), adjusting my stance to avoid the mottled edges of the glass, which tended to obscure the wonderful cut of my best tail-coat and pulled the tatty bell-rope that hung close by.

The doors were opened almost at once by a huge woman in a daffodil-coloured frock. Her gin-flushed cheeks, abutting a long, blotchy nose gave her face the appearance of bruised knackers in a harness.

'Good evening, Delilah,' I said, with just the slightest turn from the mirror.

'Hevening, sir,' said the drudge. She shuffled a little awkwardly, glanced at the table and cleared her throat.

'Heverything in horder, sir?'

I turned, cigarette between teeth, adjusting my white tie with both hands.

'Hmm? Oh yes. The burgundy was deadly and the partridge a trifle high. Other than that a most satisfactory evening.'

Delilah nodded her massive head. 'And the hother gentleman, sir?'

'Will be leaving us now, thank you.'

Delilah thrust both mitt-like hands under the armpits of the Honourable Everard Supple and dragged the one-eyed corpse with apparent effortlessness towards the doors. I hopped athletically over the dead man's legs, sweeping up my cloak and topper from a chair.

'How's little Ida?' I asked, clapping the hat to my head.

'Very good, thankyou for hasking, sir. No doubt be seeing you soon, sir,' grunted Delilah.

'No doubt,' I replied. 'Ta, ta.'

I stepped over the threshold of the mean little dwelling and out into the sultry evening. Thinking I deserved a little treat, I hailed a hansom.

'The Pomegranate Rooms,' I said to the driver. Work was over for the moment. Time to play.

Twenty minutes later, I was dropped a short distance from said night-spot and made my way towards its mouldering wedding-cake façade. The slattern on the door opened it a crack and treated me to a quick view of her form. Poured carelessly into a garish oriental gown she had the look of a pox-ravaged sultana – both the potentess and the dried fruit.

I slipped through the grimy doorway.

'Any riff-raff in tonight, my sweet?' I enquired.

'Plenty,' she gurgled, taking my hat and cloak as persons on doors are wont to do.

'Splendid!'

The Pomegranate Rooms were small, sweltering and poorly lit by gas sconces stained tobacco-yellow, lending the whole a colour not unlike the bitter pith of the titular fruit. Rickety wooden tables littered the crimson carpets; spilled champagne formed great fizzing puddles in every shadowed corner. Each table was occupied by rather more patrons than was good for it; the majority of the sweating men in evening dress, or the remains of it, with a quantity of backless white waistcoats slung over the chairs; the women, and there were many of them, less respectably dressed, some scarcely dressed at all. It was all quite ghastly and I was very fond of it.

Such establishments erupt on to the bloated body of the capital with the unerring regularity of a clap-rash but the Pomegranate Rooms were something of a special case. A hangover from the fever-dream that had been the Naughty Nineties, I had once, within its stuffy, cigar-fume-drenched walls, espied our present monarch being 'attended to' by a French noblewoman of uncertain virtue.

I dropped into a chair at the only free table and ordered up some plonk. A fat bawd close by, rouged like an *ingénue* under-taker's first case, began at once to make eyes at me. I examined my nails until she lost interest. I cannot abide the obese and in a whore it is surely tantamount to unprofessionalism. Her chums were not much better.

I ate something to take away the taste of the champagne and then smoked a cigarette to take away the taste of the food. I tried not to make it too obvious that I was on my lonesome. It is a ter-rible thing to dine alone. One stinks of desperation.

With as much nonchalance as I could affect, I examined the play of the light on my champagne glass whilst surreptitiously sneaking looks at the patrons in the hope of spotting something pretty.

And then, without any ado whatsoever, a young woman glided into the seat opposite me. In a white satin dress with pearls at her throat and rather gorgeous blonde hair piled high she looked like one of Sargent's slightly elongated females. I felt a stir down below that could have been the beginnings of indigestion but probably had more to do with the way her dewy eyes were fixed on me.

7

I lifted the plonk bottle and my eyebrows enquiringly.

'You're rather out of place here, my dear,' I said, as I poured her a glass. 'I should say the Pomegranate Rooms rarely see the likes of you.'

She inclined her head slightly. 'Got any fags?'

A little taken aback, I nodded and took out my cigarette case. It is flat and well-polished with my initials in Gothic script upon it, yet it has never been called upon to save my life by absorbing the impact of a bullet. That's what servants are for.

'Armenian or Georgian?' I enquired.

She took out one of the long black specimens that cram the case's right-hand side and struck a match off the heel of her elegant shoe, lighting the cigarette in one rapid movement.

Her brazen behaviour delighted me.

'Lor, I was dying for that,' said the vision, taking in great gulps of smoke. 'Mind if I take one for later?'

I waved a hand. 'Be my guest.'

She scooped up a dozen or so cigarettes and stuffed them inside her corset.

'You're full of surprises,' I managed.

'Ain't I, though?' She laughed and gave a hoarse cough. 'You on your own?'

My performance had been penetrated. I poured myself another drink. 'Alas.'

She looked me up and down with what I can only describe as sauciness. 'That's a shame. You're a looker.'

I could not deny it.

'I like a tall gent,' she continued. 'You a foreigner?'

I ran a hand through my long black hair. 'My complexion owes much to my Franco-Slavic mama and little to my British papa. My waist is all my own work.'

'Hm. They must've been proud of having such a bonny babe.'

'A baroness once told me that she could cut her wrists on my cheek-bones.'

'Lot of girls died for you have they?'

'Only those who cannot live for me.'

She rested her chin on a gloved hand. 'You got cold eyes, though. Blue as poison-bottles.'

'Really, you must desist or I shall consider running away with myself.' I placed my hand on hers. 'What's your name?'

She shook her head, blowing out a cloud of smoke and smiling. 'I don't like mine. I'd much rather hear yours.'

I fiddled lightly with my cuff-link. 'Gabriel,' I said, adopting one of my *noms de guerre*. 'Gabriel Ratchitt.'

The nameless lovely took this in. 'That's an angel's name.'

'I know, my dear,' came my murmur. 'And I fear I may be falling.'

II

ON THE EFFICACY OF ASSASSINATION

OTH the night and my blood were far too hot to waste time journeying home, so I got to grips with my new acquaintance in a slimy alley at the back of the Pomegranate Rooms. I have a vivid memory of her raised skirts brushing against my chin and the feel of her very lovely bosom beneath my fine, white hands (I've mentioned them). As I plunged on, my eye caught a bill pasted haphazardly to the wet brickwork. Nellie Best was playing at the Collins Music Hall. I might just have time between this coupling and my next appointment to make the second house.

Nellie was on fine form and so was I, hearing her belt out 'Who Were You With Last Night?' as I strolled into the upstairs bar-room and topped myself up on hock. Groping for a seat and tripping irresponsibly over the fetching white ankles of a dozen young ladies, the hall became one great wonderful blur of gaseous colour and light. I felt as though I had tumbled head-first into one of Sickert's delightfully *déclassé* canvases. The hollowed shadows enveloped me in grimy red plush, Nelly Best's canary-yellow crinolines flaring before my grinning phiz like sunbursts.

After several choruses too many of 'Oh What a Silly Place to Kiss a Girl', I tottered out into the balmy night and a cab.

'Piccadilly,' I cried, banging my cane rather unnecessarily against the roof.

Shortly afterwards, I was deposited in front of the Royal Academy of Art. By day I am naturally used to entering premises by the front door but, that night, I took care descending the treacherously corkscrew steps down to the tradesmen's entrance.

Delilah, having finished her work at the dining rooms, was there to greet me with her broken-toothed smile; she ushered me through into a corridor tiled in black and white parquet. I threw off my cloak and hooked my hat carefully on to the horns of a stuffed ibyx head, whose startled expression was not at all dissimilar to that of the late Everard Supple.

At the very end of the room was a small and awfully discreet door, inlaid, quite exquisitely, with blond marquetry in a pattern of peacock feathers. I went through the door and into a panelled hall lit by sputtering gas-jets. There had been some excitable talk about having the electricity laid on but I had used my meagre powers to veto this. I liked the atmosphere of the little journey. Somehow the flames in their bold brass stanchions felt like primitive torches in a secret tunnel. We all know the attraction of secret tunnels. When I was a boy, there was nothing in the world I wanted to discover more. It's quite rewarding finally to have one at the office.

I stuffed my hands into my trouser pockets and whistled a few bars of Nellie Best's best as I reached the end of the silent corridor. It terminated in a kind of ship's wheel, studded at the tip of each spoke with a porcelain button rather in the manner of bath taps. I tapped in a little sequence of letters corresponding to some code or other and span the wheel to the left. Another discreet door, though not nearly so prettily carved, sprang open just to my right. Why they couldn't just let me knock, I'll never know.

I passed through into a gentlemen's lavatory. Planting my rump (avec trousers, you understand) on the cold seat in one of the cubicles, I folded my arms and exhaled impatiently. It was a further five minutes before I heard the sound of footfalls and the opening and closing of the cubicle door next to mine. Finally, with a grim protesting shriek, the metal wall dividing the cubicles began to rise.

Sitting on the next po along, impeccable in frock-coat and imperial collar, was the dwarfish form of Joshua Reynolds. My boss; three foot something in his stockinged feet and ever so jolly.

'Hello, Lucifer,' trilled the little fellow. He wriggled on the seat of the lavatory and pumped my hand. His tiny patent leather shoes glistened in the gas-light.

'Evening,' I rejoined. 'Still can't run to a proper office, eh?'

Reynolds gave an impish laugh. 'No, no. You know how we like it. Cloak and dagger, my boy. That's what we thrive on. Ha-ha. Smoke and mirrors.' His eyes were bright and black in his face like raisins in dough. 'Now then,' he continued, rubbing his pudgy hands together. 'The . . . er . . . business is concluded?'

I nodded and smiled my wide smile. 'It is.'

'And the . . . er . . . package has been . . . sent to . . . Sebastopol?'

'Ye-es.'

'And was the . . . transaction . . . er . . . accomplished without undue . . .'

'If you mean have I killed old Supple, then yes, I have,' I cried. 'Shot him in the chest and watched him die like the filthy dog he was.'

The little man sniffed and nodded. He seemed to suffer an eternal cold in the head.

'A modicum of thanks would not go amiss,' I ventured.

Reynolds laughed explosively. 'What would you like me to say, my boy? That England owes you a great debt?'

'That would do to begin with. Hmm . . . "The nation will be forever and profoundly grateful." That sort of thing. But will the nation ever know it? To them the Honourable Everard will remain a gallant servant of the Empire –'

'Shot defending his own home by a vicious gang of roughs,' put in JR.

'Is that what we're saying?'

'So I gather.'

I shrugged lightly. 'Yes, he will remain every inch the gallant lad rather than the atrocious anarchist with plans to explode bombs under the foreign secretary that we know him to be. To have *been*.'

'Well, well, my boy,' said Joshua Reynolds with a twinkle. 'That is why we call it *secret* service.'

Ah, now. The cat's out of the bag. There you are, having paid your few shillings at Mr Smith's emporium at Waterloo Station (if my memoirs ever make it out of the cistern), fully expecting the entertaining ramblings of the great Lucifer Box, RA, foremost portraitist of his age (a man must have ambition) and what do you discover? That in between my little daubs I was living a double life!

It was a connection humble enough in origin. For reasons that are too painful and private to relate I'd ended up owing a favour or two to our family solicitor. Joshua Reynolds (for it was he), despite being small, turned out to be something very *big* in His Majesty's Government. Strictly behind the scenes, you understand, and most secret. I liked to flatter myself that he really couldn't manage without me.

He peered at me now with a strange expression somewhere between a smile and a grimace.

'You're looking positively consumptive, dear heart,' he said at last.

'How you wound me! The Beardsley style is *so* unfashionable.'

'Eat a little more!'

'I find it difficult to manage on the pittance you pay.'

The little man sniffed back a drop of moisture from his nostril. 'Oh, now you're being cruel. Your late papa would never forgive me if I let you starve.'

'Were I more at liberty, I could get by very well on my artistic commissions.'

He reached across and patted my hand. His own was dimpled fatly like that of an overfed baby. 'Of course, of course. But my little problems do provide a more regular salary, eh? And not too much effort required on your part.'

I smiled, admitting his point. 'Effort only in the service of pleasure.'

It may have seemed rash of them to give the job to an aberrant character like me but I cannot deny how much I relished it. The world was my studio, and they laid on the apprentices to clean the brushes. Say there was a visiting Turkish despot to be bumped off. Furnished with the dry details, the artistic part would be left to me. I'd formulate a little plan with the Domestics (Delilah, she of the daffodil frock was one of the best) and off we'd toddle. The Ottoman offender would be taking a stroll in some pleasure garden and, if the night were a dark one, a swift dagger through the ribs might be enough. I would go off on my merry way and the Domestics would move in, eradicating any trace of my presence. A day or so later, the *stabbee* would be found a hundred miles away (in, let us say, Newcastle-under-Lyme), the victim of a 'crazed malcontent'. The malcontent – usually the body of a vagrant retrieved from the local mortuary, dressed up with a dagger clasped in his rapidly stiffening digits – was sometimes found there too. Within twenty-four hours both corpses would be under-lime themselves. Oftentimes, though, something a shade more baroque was called for and Delilah and I would roll up our sleeves and embark on a coffee-fuelled plotting session that was rather cheerfully like cramming for an examination. It was all terribly well done and it lent one an immunity from even the vaguest threat of prosecution that was quite giddying. Artistic licence to kill, you might say.

Joshua Reynolds, who really was the most frightful old woman (well, no, he *really* was a dwarf, but you follow me?), glanced at me as I sank back against the cold lavatory wall and grinned at him. For once there was a flicker of something less pleasant in those bright black eyes.

'Enthusiasm is all very well, my dear Lucifer, but we mustn't get sloppy, must we? We must always remember that nasty business of the Bow Road.'

I bristled at this but held my tongue. As I say, some things are painful and private.

I was a bit done in after all the evening's excitement, but it was clear the boss had more work for me. He blew his button nose and retrieved a file from his case. As he examined its contents, I examined my fingernails. In the morning, I thought, I would take a steam bath.

'You got my note?' he said at length.

'I'm afraid I haven't checked my correspondence. I was running late, you see, what with the murdering.'

The dwarf gazed in a puzzled fashion at the contents of his handkerchief. 'Do you know Poop?'

'Poop?'

'Jocelyn Poop. Our man in Naples. We received a wire from him some days ago.'

He tossed me a square of buff paper. I read it over swiftly.

VERDIGRIS SASH. MOST URGENT.
DETAILS FOLLOW.

I looked up. 'Instructions to a curtain maker?'

'Verdigris and Sash were both highly respected scientists.'

'*Were?*'

'They died. Within a day of each other.'

'Did they indeed?' I tapped the telegram against my chin. 'And what more does Poop have to say?'

'Not a great deal. He's vanished.'

'Like me to look into it?'

Joshua Reynolds batted his eyelids. 'I'd be so grateful.'

I took a file of papers from my erstwhile employer and, with a curt nod, stepped out of the lavatory. Out of habit, I washed my hands.

Once back out into the humid night, I made my way towards Downing Street. I bade the bobby on duty outside Number Ten a cheery 'goodnight' then let myself into Number Nine.

I know, ostentatious, isn't it? But somebody has to live there.

III

THE MYSTERY OF THE TWO GEOLOGISTS

Y occupancy of Number Nine is a long and not particularly edifying story. Once upon a time, my late papa's people owned the land whereon Downing Street was built and though HMG grabbed most of it, they couldn't get their mitts on that one house which, through some stubborn whimsy of the Boxes, was to remain in the family in perpetuity. And now, as last of the line, Number Nine had come to me. More than anything I wished to be shot of the place but the terms of my inheritance were strict and so impecunious old Lucifer occupied three rooms, more or less, on the ground floor of one of the grandest houses in London. The rest of the pointlessly huge edifice was shuttered, sheeted, quietly rotting and likely to remain so unless I started to sell a lot more pictures. On the positive side it was awfully handy for town.

I awoke to find myself fully dressed and on top of the bed, surrounded by a litter of files on the missing Poop and the late Professors Sash and Verdigris. I must have drifted off in either a haze of data or a haze of hashish, I really cannot recall.

I was about to call for my man Poplar, when I remembered that he had taken a bullet in the back three weeks before on the southbound platform of a Serbian railway station (no silver cigarette case, you see). I sighed hugely. I'd certainly miss old Poplar and his passing left me in the unfortunate

position of requiring a new manservant. Taking a small propelling pencil from my waistcoat pocket, I scribbled the words 'Get Help' on to my shirt cuff as an *aide memoir*. It was to be hoped that my laundress would not interpret this as the desperate plea of a kidnapped heiress hidden amongst my evening clothes.

A manservant was one of the perks of the job, yet Joshua Reynolds seemed in no great hurry to furnish me with a new one. If things didn't improve soon

I was faced with the grisly prospect of getting in Delilah to rinse out my undergarments.

I bathed in preparation for my Turkish bath and sent a note round to one of my pals expressing the desire that he join me there. The pal in question was a fiercely handsome, unfailingly cheerful lad called Christopher Miracle. To look at, you would think him one of those fellows who go stamping off around the world in a pea-coat having peninsulas named after them. In fact, he was one of the most famous portraitists in England and was said to possess an extraordinary patience and delicacy of touch. He had not been born into wealth but had *earned* it (imagine!) and the gulf that existed between our financial situations resulted in the kind of slow-burning resentment that fuels the best friendships. As a result of his status, he was quite staggeringly well-connected and I had a fancy he might know something of my missing professors.

The summer day was bright as a flare and stultifyingly humid. I was hard pressed to notice any change in atmosphere between the outside and the interior of the Wigmore Street baths where I later found myself.

As blond and enthusiastic as a Labrador puppy, Christopher Miracle bounced startlingly out of the wreaths of steam and thumped me on the back as a token of his affection.

'Box, old man! How are you? Looking distinctly peaky, I'd say. You getting enough nosh?'

I made a place on the warm marble beside me. 'You're not the first to speculate.'

He extended his long legs before him, the white towel around his waist pulling as taut and neat as a tablecloth.

'Is there tea?' he cried, smoothing back a lock of wet blond hair. 'I must have tea!'

He snapped his fingers with the assurance of a born team captain, face already reddening in the heat, and sat with one leg up on the marble, as solid and impressive as the Velázquez Mars (having mislaid his helmet). Next to his frame, I did seem positively emaciated.

We sipped at small glasses of sweet-smelling tea brought to us by a capaciously girthed Turk and fell into happy conversation (or gossip if you prefer), denigrating the pompous and the talent-less who we felt were being preferred over us. Merely assassinating someone's *character* made for a pleasant change.

'By the way,' said Miracle suddenly. 'I'm having a party. Or a ball, if you want to be grand. In honour of the return of Persephone, goddess of the summer. Possible you could come? Or are you over-committed?'

'I collect invitations on the mantelpiece behind a bust of the late Queen. Just now I fear Her Majesty will be pitched forward into the fireplace. I'd never miss one of your parties, though, Christopher. I trust there will be a superabundance of flesh?'

'I'm counting on it. I may invite one or two from my drawing class.'

'Drawing class?'

'Didn't I tell you? Oh, I've been taking a class for ladies in one of those mechanical institutes down in Chelsea. A weekly thing. Requires little effort on my part and has several benefits. Perhaps you should give it a bash.'

I sank back on the seat and rested on my palms. 'Benefits, eh? Let me guess,' I mused. 'Firstly, hmm, yes, it keeps you in regular contact with just the kind of idle rich who are liable to commission pictures from you.'

'Excellent.'

'Further enhancing your laurel-strewn reputation,' I said gazing thoughtfully at the steam-clouded ceiling. 'Secondly, every now and then one such patron turns out to be a real stunner and game for a lark.'

Miracle laughed explosively. 'Now, really, Box.'

'Thirdly, it allows you to put a little back into society by encouraging the artistic endeavours of those less talented than yourself.'

I smiled broadly. 'I have, of course, put these benefits in order of priority.'

'Your reasoning, Box, is perfectly sound,' said Miracle with a grin. 'I allow twelve of them in at any one time,' he said. 'Probably for no better reason than it makes the occasion feel vaguely like a coven.'

'With you as the presiding daemon?'

'Naturally. They have tea and there's a little chatter and not a little swooning around yours truly, then my pupils set to work scrawling away quite appallingly with their charcoal at whatever I place in the centre of the room. It seems they have come to regard my classes as the highlights of their existence.'

I nodded to an orderly who came forward with a brass bowl of cold water. I splashed my face and ran a hand through my hair.

'What a shining light you are, Miracle!' I ejaculated. 'How come that booby Holman Hunt never did your portrait in that hideous style of his?'

Miracle chuckled.

'Speaking of pictures,' I said, 'didn't you once paint a scientist chap called Verdigris?'

Miracle thought for a moment. 'Believe I did. Great fat fellow. Eyes spaced too wide like a flat-fish. Come to think of it, I heard he's vanished. Along with some old pal of his called Sash.'

'I too had heard something of the kind.'

'Don't know much about the other. Seems they both suffered a sort of seizure. Are you digging for something?'

I shrugged. Alone amongst my friends, Miracle had some idea of my 'other life' but even then thought it no more than the hobby of an over-diligent gossip.

'Geologists, I gather,' I said at last.

Miracle nodded. 'Old Cambridge chums. Verdigris died the day after Sash. Very rum.'

'Life is full of coincidences.'

'So they say,' laughed Miracle. 'Do you think these events are connected? I'll see what I can root out.'

For a while, we sat in silence, steeped in the lethargy induced by the chamber's broiling heat. Occasionally, the mists cleared, revealing the green-and-red tiled arches of the roof. The baths hummed with human traffic; the hissing of the coals, the distant *ploosh* of patrons in the plunge pools, the heavy sighing of thickset, red-faced gents, towels wrapped like swaddling around their hard bellies.

After a time, Miracle smiled, thrust out his lower lip then patted my leg and rose. 'Shan't be a moment. Nature calls.'

I watched him stride away through the billowing steam-clouds and was so engrossed by the progress of a great heavy drop of sweat down my face that I almost failed to notice a veiny forearm suddenly clamp itself around my gullet.

With a gasp, I sank my fingers into the flesh of the arm. Struggling to stand, I found myself hauled backwards by a wild strength. My back struck the slippery marble steps and for a second or so my head swam.

'Blackguard!' hissed a voice in my ear. 'Scoundrel!'

Well, I had been called worse. I twisted my head wildly to one side, attempting to catch sight of my attacker, but the clouds of steam showed only glimpses of glistening flesh and a pair of goggling, enraged eyes beneath thick black brows. His arm tightened around my throat.

I kicked out at the brass bowl in a desperate effort to attract the attention of the attendants but, with lightning speed, my assailant began to drag me towards a neglected niche. The towel slipped from my waist and I felt my buttocks sliding over the seat.

I croaked frantically. Would one of the elderly gentlemen in their steamy shrouds notice and raise the alarm? But a ruddy hand with hairy knuckles was quickly planted over my mouth. I was completely helpless. Salty sweat stung at my eyes.

'Now, you villain! Now I have you!' The fellow's breath was stale with tobacco. I was on my haunches, my senses whirling.

Yet, at the very moment of defeat, I snatched a chance of victory. Using the brute's heaviness to my advantage, I shoved backwards against him and drove my elbow savagely into his midriff.

He gave a startled cry, fell lumpenly against the tiles and momentarily slackened his iron grip on my head and neck. It was all I needed.

Springing to my feet, I whirled around and kicked him in the throat, my leg extended with the grace of a dancer – even if I do say so myself.

His hands flew to his Adam's apple but I gave him no quarter, pummelling his face with my fists and then, after taking a handful of his wet hair, cracking his face off the wall.

'What is this?' I gasped. 'What do you want with me?'

The fellow was revealed now, a great hirsute middle-aged creature, with long, oily moustaches and a face as red as brick. Where *had* I seen the ugly bastard before? In the criminal archives of the Viennese police, perhaps? Or was he one of the brotherhood of blind assassins who had sworn revenge on me after the Affair of the Prussian Martyrs?

Those enraged eyes glared at me still. With a snarl he put his head down and charged at me. I stepped swiftly to one side but he caught me round the waist and together we stumbled back into the main chamber.

By now, of course, we had been noticed. As we whirled about, feet slithering on the wet floor, I had a confused impression of white towels and scarlet faces, mouths opened in wide 'o's of astonishment. The Turk who had brought Miracle's tea hovered around us, arms flapping, like the referee in a wrestling bout.

'Can't we . . . discuss this . . . like gentlemen?' I gasped.

He rose from my naked waist and jabbed a fist at my face. I side-stepped clumsily, feet skidding.

'*Gentleman?* You?' he spat.

The Turk was at his elbow, his face a mask of misery. 'Please! Please, sirs! If you have business, let it be concluded in the –'

He said no more, as my attacker laid him out with a swift right to the underside of his swarthy jaw and he fell to the tiles like a sack of coal.

I cracked a fist against my assailant's cheek-bone. 'Christ!' I yelled, sucking my knuckles.

He screwed up one eye in pain and jabbed at me again. 'Lucifer Box! Ha! Was ever a rascal so well named? You are the devil, sir. The very devil!'

I ducked from his fist and managed to land a serious wallop on the side of his head. He staggered and almost fell on the treacherous floor.

'Bringer of light, I assure you!' I cried. My blood was up and so were my fists as I circled the monster. 'Lucifer was the brightest and most beautiful of the angels. Till that old margery of a deity got so jealous that he cast him out!'

He snarled at this and succeeded in punching me, with sickening force, in the ribs.

Crying out in pain, I dropped, winded. My knees smacking on the floor with a snap like wish-bones.

The fellow stalked up to me and grasped a great hunk of my hair. 'Bringer of light! What have you brought to my household but misery and scandal? My God, sir, I shall thrash the life out of you before I'm done!'

I shook my head miserably. 'Who . . . who are you?'

He sneered at me, his moustaches hanging limply around his red mouth like those of a Chinaman. 'I am Pugg, sir. Major Strangeways Pugg.'

'Oh,' I said, simply.

'And it is my daughter, my sweet little Avril who you have despoiled and ruined!'

I winced as he tightened his grip on my hair. Remembrance swept over me like cold water from the Turk's brass bowl. A party, some months previously. Whey-faced poets, frayed-cuffed artists; all the splendid flotsam of bohemian London life. And a girl. A girl with a dog's name and the body of a goddess. Avril Pugg. There'd been a balcony, starlight, whispered words then something very cheeky in the rhododendrons.

Now there was a father. He raised his great fist and drew it back. I watched it swing towards me through streaming eyes.

Then there came a strange, bright clang and Pugg crashed to the floor, his addled eyes rolling up in his head like those of a doll.

I looked up and saw my friend standing over the unconscious major, a filigreed Turkish tea-urn still swinging in his right hand.

'Miracle,' I groaned.

'Too bloody right!' he cried, grasping my hand and pulling me to my feet.

IV

THE VISITOR

THAT night, still as humid as the steam-rooms, I swaddled my bruised carcass in a Japanese dressing gown patterned with embroidered sunflowers and purchased with money I should have spent on oil-paints. Or food. Or tickets to the Continent avoiding enraged fathers.

After leaving the baths, Miracle had seen me right then I had swiftly made contact with the Domestics. Delilah, always the soul of discretion, assured me that, although it didn't come quite within the purview of Joshua Reynolds's department, she would 'sort fings out' and Major Strangeways Pugg would be 'hencouraged' to drop the matter forthwith. Well, it's pointless having power unless you can abuse it, don't you think?

I then wrapped up the portrait of the Hon. Everard Supple (a present for his grieving family) and began to ponder Chris Miracle's suggestion of giving art instruction. He was making a

killing off all these lonely old horrors in need of a little thrill to while away their afternoons. Why shouldn't I? In fact, why shouldn't I *more*. The prestigious address! The handsome young artist! The showers of sovereigns I could squeeze out of the gullible nitwits! And then I could afford to replace Poplar without waiting for Reynolds's patronage. Of course, I'd have to do a little clearing up, but think of it!

The upshot was I placed a small advertisement in *The Times*, *Pall Mall Gazette*, *Budget* and a few other rags, making the arrangement sound thoroughly wholesome, with just the faintest whiff of *la vie bohème* to attract those craving excitement.

I then engaged a char to spruce up Downing Street. I had intended to supervise her work but couldn't bear the looks of disapproval and endless 'tsk-tsk's as she peeled old collars and unwashed dishes from the debris of my studio, so off I went to invest money I didn't have in new curtains. I collected some interesting bric-a-brac that my pupils might find amusing to draw and added Everard Supple's glass eye to the pile as a little touch of the Gothic.

After that, with rather impressive zeal, I assumed the disguise of a dour-faced newspaperman (all it takes is a dreadful suit, bowler and false moustache) and called at the home of the late Professor Eli Verdigris in Holland Park.

It was a house plunged into mourning; black crêpe blossoming from every niche and banister, a wreath of some stinking violet flower encircling friend Miracle's rather bad portrait of the great man. He had indeed been a corpulent fellow with curious wide-apart eyes and a dimpled chin of such prominence that he resembled a Hapsburg.

Under the pretence of preparing a eulogy of the professor for the *Pall Mall Gazette* I was shown into a cluttered study for an audience.

'I'm afraid you'll have to make do with me,' said a tall young man, as fat as his father, ushering me into a chair. 'My poor mama is quite beside herself.'

'It was very unexpected, then?' I whispered, laying on the sympathy as thick as impasto.

'Entirely.' He rubbed absently at the black arm-band around his sleeve. 'My father has not had a day's illness in his life.'

I nodded and scribbled in a little note-book. 'The doctors' opinion?'

Verdigris Junior shrugged. 'They seem at something of a loss. A seizure of some kind followed by coma and . . . well . . . death.'

'Dear me. The *Gazette* offers its sincerest condolences.'

The young fellow sniffed and looked up at me. 'Everyone has been quite marvellous, though. The family. His colleagues and friends.'

'And the funeral . . . ?'

'The day before yesterday. It was . . . well . . . It is over now.'

I gave him a sad smile. 'Could you give me some idea of the nature of your father's work?'

Verdigris's mouth tugged downwards. 'Not really, I'm afraid. Frightful dunce where papa's stuff is concerned. I can root out some literature for you, if you'd care to wait.'

'That would be most helpful, sir.'

Whilst he was out, I made a quick inspection of the fire-grate and the desk. There was no evidence of anything being burnt in the grate but on the desk I spotted a large appointments diary. I flicked hastily through the pages. What was I looking for? Well, anything out of the common, I suppose. But I found nothing save evidence of Verdigris's dreary affairs and the rest of the study proved equally barren. The walls were lined with books and very indifferent landscapes in need of cleaning. I closed the diary carefully, brushed off a dusty purplish residue from the desk that had adhered to my sleeve and dashed back to my chair.

Young Verdigris came back in and handed me a thick, dust-jacketed volume. 'Here is it. Papa's magnum opus. Tried my damnedest to get into it but . . .'

I turned the book over and looked at the spine. The title was picked out in gold.

Magnetic Viscosity, I read, *with some notes on volcanic convection*. More light reading seemed on the agenda.

Sans moustache, I lunched in the domino room at the Café Royal, studying the coroner's report on the deaths of both men. There were no traces of toxins. Nothing at all to indicate that death had not been due to some freak seizure. But what connection was Poop's telegram driving at? And why had Poop himself disappeared?

I resumed my disguise as Fleet Street's finest and took an underground train to meet the wife of Professor Frederick Sash, the second of the late scientists. I had tried to make some sense of Verdigris's book but could not get on with it. It seemed terrible nonsense, or terribly clever.

Mrs Sash, a good-looking piece with a swan-like neck, received me graciously enough, although she had the infuriating habit of cutting one off in mid-sentence. As I sipped my tea, I glanced around the darkened drawing room. 'I see you have a copy of Verdigris's seminal *Magnetic Viscosity*,' I said blithely. 'Was your husband acquainted with –?'

'Oh yes. From their Cambridge days. Eli seems to have passed away the day after Frederick. What in heaven's name can it mean?'

I nodded sympathetically and scratched at my false moustache. 'Of course, there was no . . . ill feeling between –?'

Mrs Sash shook her handsome head. 'There was some rivalry, naturally, both being in the same field but no more than that. They were always on very good terms, though they had seen little of one another since their Continental adventure came to an end.'

'Continental –?'

'They once worked together in Europe for some little time.'

I scribbled in my note-book. 'No previous illness –?'

'There had been nothing out of the ordinary.'

I was hoping to persuade the lady to absent herself briefly as I had with Professor Verdigris's son, to facilitate a quick nose around the room, but my request for refreshment was answered by a delicate pull on the bell rope and the appearance of a dour-faced flunky.

I paused with my pencil hovering over the paper. 'This was your husband's –?'

'Study? No, no. He has a room on the first floor. Claimed it was too noisy down here.' She passed a hand over her face. 'He was at home all day, working up a theorem. The late post had just come when –'

She sniffed back a tear. 'You must excuse me for now, sir. We are somewhat upside-down at the moment. There is so much to do.'

'One final thing, Mrs Sash. Have I missed the funeral?'

I had. It had taken place only the previous day in Southwark.

Mrs Sash glanced down at her neat little hands. 'There again I was vexed. We were unable to use the firm my husband's family had always relied upon.'

'Firm?'

'The undertaking firm, sir. Tulip Brothers. Retired, it seems, without so much as a note! The business has been taken over. I suppose it all passed off well enough . . .'

'But?'

'But there was something a little . . . *queer* about them.'

'What makes you say that?'

She sighed. 'Well, whatever good-will they inherited has been squandered, I can tell you. It was a rather amateurish display.'

'And what is the name of this curious firm?'

Mrs Sash crossed to a small bureau and produced a black-edged card. 'I'm not saying it's necessarily worthy of a newspaper investigation,' she said, handing it over. 'But I found their attitude most peculiar. I'd be easier in my mind if someone were to do a little . . . um . . . digging.' For the first time, she smiled.

I held up the card.

TOM BOWLER. SUPERIOR FUNERALS.
188 ENGLAND'S LANE. LONDON N.W.

I had changed and was stretching a canvas in my studio that afternoon, wondering how to infiltrate an undertakers without a cadaver to present, when I heard a knock at the door.

Still expecting old Poplar to answer it, I ignored the summons for a full minute before heading through into the hallway with a muttered curse.

A singularly lovely personage stood on my doorstep, clutching a folded newspaper in her lace-gloved hand.

'Mr Box?'

'I am he.'

She stepped forward and the sunlight cast a glow over the russet-coloured dress that clung so charmingly to her figure. Tall and elfin-featured, with a tumbling fall of Mucha-like curls, she held up the newspaper and flashed me a lovely smile. 'I came in response to your advertisement.' The voice was lightly accented – Dutch? – and tinkled like a music-box.

'Advertisement? Oh! Oh, yes of course! Come in, please, Miss . . . ?'

'Pok.'

'Pok?'

'Bella Pok.' The delectable creature crossed the threshold and looked inquisitively about the hallway.

'Would you care for some tea?' I asked.

She looked me straight in the eye. 'Do you have anything stronger?'

'My dear, I daresay. Please, come through.'

'Number Nine, Downing Street,' she said, entering the drawing room. 'You have trouble with your neighbours?'

'Only once every four years.'

She smiled and took a seat by the window whilst I hurriedly looked about for refreshment. 'Such a curious place for an artist to live . . .'

'Sherry?' I offered.

'I like a little vermouth at this hour.'

I nodded, rather pleasantly shocked. 'Geographically, I am at the very beating heart of the Empire, Miss Pok. In other respects, I am as much an outcast as the greatest of my calling have been . . .' I gestured around the room. 'You must forgive my current situation but my servant is . . . *servants* are away.'

'I have learned never to judge a gentleman by the cleanliness of his doilies.'

'Then I feel we shall get on splendidly.'

I slipped through to the kitchen and began to hunt around for where the char had put clean glasses. 'Now tell me,' I said, calling through. 'What drew you to my advertisement? You have had some training in draughtsmanship?'

'Not at all,' she cried. 'It is only that I have always longed to draw and paint, Mr Box, and currently find my self with the time and the resources to fulfil my daydreams.'

'Capital!' I said, returning with two fairly respectable cut-glass vessels, a bottle of vermouth and a rather sad-looking seed cake.

'Speaking of capital,' she said, reaching for her beaded bag, 'the advertisement said a guinea per lesson.'

I held up my hand. 'Let us not concern ourselves with these bothersome details just now. Tell me a little more about yourself.'

'What could a dull little creature like me possibly have that could interest you?' she trilled. I could think of several things and made a mental note to treat Chris Miracle to dinner for his splendid suggestion.

Miss Bella Pok and I had, it transpired, a great deal in common. A mutual loathing of the frightful El Greco and veneration of the sainted Velázquez, a suspicion of Titian and an unhealthy regard for Caravaggio. As we drank our vermouth I thought how pretty and charming was my potential pupil. The sunlight pouring through the window crowned her lovely face, illumining her eyelashes as she angled it towards me.

I showed her into the studio. She crossed at once to the centre of the room and began to examine the body of a spelter Napoleonic lancer I'd picked up in a junk shop off the Edgware Road. It was a cheap thing, just a fellow in britches on horseback, but she seemed taken by it. Perhaps it was the way he brandished his lance. I rested my shoulder against the wall, one hand in contemplative attitude on my chin.

'When can I begin?' she asked brightly.

I shrugged. 'Why not at once? Will the lancer do?'

So saying, I drew up a chair and fixed a rectangle of good-quality paper to a wooden board. Miss Bella unpinned her hat and sat down. I handed her the board and some sticks of charcoal then stood behind her in silence, listening to the sound of her breathing and the sweet, liquid *tick* made by her lips as they parted.

I grinned happily to myself, deriving curious satisfaction from the quiet, methodical way she worked.

'Have you had many answers to your advertisement, Mr Box?'

The charcoal swooped and scratched over the virginal paper.

'You are the first.'

The horse's head, caught swiftly and surely. She was rather good.

'Then perhaps we can make this a . . . private arrangement.'

Steady. I felt a little flip in my heart and a distinct throb in my britches. I thought of Avril Pugg's father and the sensation lessened. A little.

'Perhaps.'

Miss Bella had caught the heavy fullness of the spelter lancer's thigh with one, decisive stroke of the charcoal. With equal boldness I now crossed the room towards her and took hold of her drawing hand. I guided it to the paper, moving myself until I was almost pressed against her back. She did not demur as I slid the charcoal over the surface of the paper, shading the lancer's legs and bottom with what I knew to be forthright sensuousness.

'You are doing very nicely, Miss Pok,' I cooed. 'You have an extraordinary grasp of military anatomy.'

I carried on with the drawing without taking my eyes from the figurine.

'A bottom is a bottom, Mr Box,' she said, 'whether a soldier's or a parlour-maid's.'

I suppressed a smile. 'True, I suppose. Tell me, are you town or country born?'

I pressed myself closer to her. There could be no mistaking the broom-handle in my trousers. With a slight dip of her lovely head Bella Pok moved away from me a little and released her hand from my grip. 'I am a farmer's daughter, Mr Box,' she murmured.

I held up my hands in supplication and backed away. *And you know a fox when you see one*, I thought.

Turning in her seat, she gave a little gasp. I looked to where she looked and saw that she was staring at the glass eye I had placed near the lancer.

'How ghoulish!' she cried, with her musical laugh.

'Isn't it?' I said. 'Shall I put it away?'

'No, no. I am not so squeamish as you might think. But it does, as they say about the *Mona Lisa*, rather follow one about the room!'

She turned back to me, grinning and presented the drawing board. 'Well, then. What is the verdict?' she said.

'Guilty!' I cried.

She gathered up her things. 'Is there any hope for me?'

I folded my arms and smiled. 'I sentence you to commence your classes on Monday next. And may the Lord have mercy upon your —'

I stopped very suddenly. My attention had become riveted on the newspaper that Miss Bella had brought through into the studio. I plucked it from her grasp. 'Mr Box?' she said with concern. 'Are you quite all right?'

In a column adjacent to my advertisement was a small item of news.

BRITISH DIPLOMAT MURDERED

Terrible discovery in Naples.

A body found in the harbour at Naples on Monday last has been positively identified as that of Jocelyn Utterson Poop of His Majesty's Diplomatic Service. Mr Poop, who was thirty-three years of age, had been stationed in the Italian city for over four years. The Neapolitan police say that the unfortunate man had been the victim of a murderous attack, leaving his skull crushed, probably by a stick or some such blunt instrument . . .

'Mr Box? *Mr Box?*' The lovely Miss Pok placed a hand on my arm.

'I'm very sorry, my dear,' I said quietly. 'The lesson is over for today.'

V

A CURIOUS UNDERTAKING

'O clue?'

Joshua Reynolds, sitting in his accustomed place on the pan, raised his little hands, palm upwards. 'The Italian police have it down as a robbery gone awry. We shall have to wait and see. The body has been packed in ice and arrives tomorrow.'

'Poor devil,' I said, leaning back against the pleasantly chill wall of the lavatory. 'Saw Naples and died, you might say.'

'So much for Poop,' said Reynolds glumly. 'Have you made any progress with the dead professors?'

I thrust my hands into my trouser pockets and kicked idly at the cubicle wall. 'Some, I think. They were both concerned with the same branch of Geological Physics and had known each other of old. In addition, there was something odd about Sash's funeral.'

Reynolds frowned. 'Not much, all told.'

'I had precious little chance to

investigate Professor Sash's effects,' I continued. 'So I plan to return for a . . . root about.'

The little man gave a sigh. 'How I envy you your adventures, Lucifer. What is left for me but a dull retirement spent in the cultivation of ornamental carp?'

'One man's fish is another man's *poisson*.'

'Ye . . . es. Now then, there's someone I'd like you to meet.'

So saying, he pulled at the toilet chain and, with a screeching, grinding sound, the wall behind me rose up and another lavatory bowl glided into the room.

Sitting on it was a gangling young man in quite the most horrible piece of tailoring I'd ever seen. The sleeves of his suit crept over the knuckles of slim, feminine hands with which he was kneading his hat like a widow with her rosary.

'Mr Box,' said Reynolds, pulling his handkerchief from his pocket and pressing it to his reddened nose. 'This is Mr Unmann.'

The blond man shot a hand to his crown in order to doff his hat and then remembered it was doffed already. A stupid smile made his nose crinkle in the middle.

'Sorry,' he began.

'Whatever for?' I asked.

'Oh, sorry. Don't really know why I said that. It's a great honour to meet you at last, Mr Box. Cretaceous Unmann.'

'Cretaceous?'

'Yes,' he muttered, looking down at his hands. 'Fact is, Papa was an amateur dinosaur-hunter. Never got much further than the Isle of Wight but, hey-ho. Took it upon himself to name me in honour of his favourite epoch. Sorry.'

I smiled pityingly. 'I suppose it could have been worse,' I said. 'He could have named you after his favourite dinosaur.'

'Ha, ha! Yes!' Unmann exploded in a shrill laugh. '*Iguanodon* Unmann, eh?'

Thankfully, Reynolds cut in at this juncture. 'Mr Unmann has been lined up to succeed Poop in the Naples office.'

'I see. Remarkably expeditious of you.'

'Yes. Shocking business,' bleated Unmann. 'I knew old Jocelyn. Sometimes acted as his deputy. Dreadful, dreadful.'

He looked down at his squashed hat and then put it to one side of the lavatory bowl.

The dwarf handed a buff folder to me.

'Someone fired his rooms,' said Unmann, miserably. 'But those few fragments escaped.'

'Our people in Naples sent them straight over with Mr Unmann,' said Reynolds.

I opened the file. A smell of charred paper hit me at once. A couple of documents were enclosed within, tied up neatly with waxed string. I released them and swiftly read them over.

The first was a scrap of good-quality notepaper. On it was written the legend:

K TO V.C.?

'Looks like hotel stationery,' I said. 'Shouldn't be too difficult to trace.'

The next was a long white envelope containing a sheet of slightly singed foolscap.

To Joshua Reynolds
Sir. It is important that you know all that is afoot. I am
certain I may rely on you above all persons, even poor
Unmann, bless his heart, who has been such a brick and who
means so well.

I glanced across at the young man. His face twisted into a shy smile.

If all goes well, I shall return to London as planned and there
relate to you the story of my adventures. It is a tale so fantastic
that you will scarcely credit it. I do not lie when I say it could
shake the pillars of the Empire! If I can but thwart these men's
schemes, then I will be Poop the Civil Service mouse no more
but Poop the Lion of the Foreign Office! If I am unlucky then it
will fall to others to pick up the threads. All that I know of this
affair is contained in the trunk marked with my name. I pray
you will never have to read this. JP

I folded the letter on my lap and replaced it in its envelope.

'The trunk of course, did not escape the flames,' muttered Joshua Reynolds miserably. 'Foolish youth! Such wilful egotism has more than once cost us dear. If a conspiracy is discovered then simple candour is absolutely essential!'

I could only agree. I recalled the Shanghai Balloon Incident – which so nearly did for one of our lesser PMs – and the fatal damage caused by one fellow's refusal to share what he knew with his colleagues. I should know. That fellow was me.

I tapped the envelope. 'Any suspects in the Poop murder?'

'They've rounded up the traditional pretty lot. Smashers, thugs, vitriol throwers, extortionists . . .'

'A veritable catalogue of vice!' I cried cheerily. 'Now isn't that a good idea? The kind of catalogue I'd instantly subscribe to.'

'Lucifer,' said Joshua Reynolds, warningly.

I tapped my fingers against my chin. '"Shake the pillars of the Empire", eh? What the deuce could he have meant?'

The next morning found me on a train rattling through a muggy north London. Dreary villas streamed past in a blur of hideous brightness. As soon as I reached the nearest post office, I thought, I would send a wire to Miss Bella Pok apologizing again for the hasty termination of our lesson and looking forward to another meeting soon. What would it be like to flee this baking wen of a city and run barefoot through a field of ripening green corn with that lovely girl? I pictured us laughing gaily, tumbling into the undergrowth, the cyan sky blazing above us . . .

I ran a finger under my collar and sighed, horribly stifled by my summer rig. Surely the cause of Men's Dress Reform must do most of its recruiting during the interminable London Augusts? I longed to throw my straw hat from the carriage and toss my cream waistcoat into the Thames as the Reformers are wont to do. Leafy Belsize Park was not, I reasoned, quite ready for the sight of yours truly in the buff, so I hopped from the train still fully clothed and, after contracting my business at the post office, found myself outside the offices of Mr Tom Bowler Esq. – the undertaker who had so disquieted Mrs Sash.

I began by taking a quick look around the yard at the rear of the premises. A dog-cart with a sad-looking horse in its shafts stood squarely in the centre but it was otherwise empty, save for a heap of dead flowers and wreaths that might have been the beginnings of a bonfire. I crouched down and picked through the wilted debris. Here was a wreath for the late Professor Sash. Here was a bouquet of flattened lilies, reeking dreadfully. And here – aha! A wreath for Professor Eli Verdigris! Both funerals had been taken care of by the same firm! And with a similar want of respect for the trappings of grief. I made my way around to the front.

The door was ajar and the rooms within lit. I adopted my most doleful expression and made my way inside.

It was a bare-looking suite of rooms with frosted windows and a long, dark counter that occupied half its width. Framed mezzotints of cherubs and angels crowded the green walls. There were pots of lilies everywhere and motes of orange pollen drifting from them through the dim gas-light. I wrinkled my nose at the faint smell of brackish water.

There seemed to be no one about. I rang the brass bell on the counter and, after a time, a door opened somewhere in the rear of the premises and footsteps sounded on bare boards.

Black curtains parted and out stepped a burly man with oily hair the colour of wet slate. He seemed a very jovial chap for one of his profession, grinning all over his face and, rather surprisingly, tucking into a chicken leg with gusto. Closer to, I noticed his bluey, poorly shaved chin and the spots of grease on his tie.

'Hello,' he said brightly.

I made a small bow. 'Do I have the honour of addressing Mr Bowler?'

'You do, sir!' he said, wiping his greasy fingers on his coat.

Incredibly, he dropped the chicken leg down on to the counter and rubbed his hands together. 'Now what can I do for you?'

I fiddled coyly with my tie-pin. 'I was recommended to your predecessors' excellent firm by a family friend.'

'Ah, yes! We bought the old fellows out! So, you've had a bereavement?' His brows drew together and his mouth turned down like some operatic clown. 'Aww.'

'Indeed.' I managed to hide my astonishment at his behaviour and made a quick grab for my handkerchief. 'My dear wife,' I croaked, stifling a sob.

Bowler inclined his head slightly but still smirked. 'Please accept the firm's sincere condolences, Mr . . . ?'

'Box.'

'Mr Box. I regret to say, however, that we are currently over-whelmed with . . . um . . . clients. Dying, you see, being one of the few things that never really goes out of fashion! Ha, ha!'

I blinked and returned my handkerchief to my pocket.

Bowler's gaze strayed longingly to the greasy meat he had laid on the counter and he wiped his wet mouth with the back of his hand. 'It would be rather wrong of us to take on your wife's funeral at this time.'

'Well, I'm . . . delighted to see you are prospering.'

'Very much so,' grinned Bowler. 'I can recommend another firm if you like? They're really very reasonable.'

'Expense is not the issue.'

'Of course not, sir. Ha, ha. I would further add that they are dis-creet and most respectful.'

I nodded. 'You are very kind.'

Bowler brushed a stray hair from his eyes. 'If you just wait here, I will furnish you with the details.'

I smiled weakly. He disappeared back behind the curtain.

I glanced about and then, looking down at the counter, ran a gloved finger down its length, scoring a mahogany-coloured groove in the patina of dust that covered it.

The scrape of curtain rings announced Bowler's return. He handed me a bit of paper upon which he'd written the name of another firm in a bold hand. The black ink was smudged by his greasy thumb-print.

I thanked him for his kindness.

'Not at all, sir. Good day.'

Then, without a second thought, he picked up the chicken leg and sank his teeth into it. I made my way out. Bowler watched me until I was through the door. Through the frosted pane I distinctly saw him wave.

I stepped out on to the street and crossed the road, pausing under a shady lime tree. The state of the counter alone told me that the firm of Mr Bowler was not prospering. So why had he turned down my business and recommended a rival? And, more revealingly, why had he signally failed to comment on the fact that, despite my recent 'bereavement', I was dressed head to toe in white linen?

Just then, a loud creaking close by drew my attention and I stepped closer to the tree so as to remain unobserved. I realized that I was at the entrance to the undertaker's yard. As I watched, both the rickety gates swung open and the dog-cart rattled through and on to the street. At the reins was a hard-faced fellow in a rust-coloured coat with a great scar across his nose.

In the back of the cart lay a long wooden crate of similar dimensions to a coffin. I could see that it had some kind of shipping label plastered over its planking.

I strolled from my hiding place as nonchalantly as I could and managed to get myself into the path of the cart as it clattered into the road. Scar-Face glared at me. I doffed my hat.

'I do beg your pardon. Could you direct me to the underground station?'

He scowled at me for what seemed like a full minute before grudgingly jerking his thumb over his shoulder. Whipping up the horse, the vehicle lurched ahead.

'Most kind,' I rejoined, stepping out of its path before it ran me down.

For a brief moment I was aware of nothing but the label shuddering its way into the distance.

Then I crossed to the pavement, made my way past the yard and didn't look behind me until I had reached the station. Once there, I stood with my back to the gingerbread-brown tiles, deep in thought. According to that shipping label the crate was heading for Naples.

*

43

That afternoon, I found myself standing on the jetty of a grimy wharf in the East End. The day remained unbearably humid and the tarry black warehouses loomed over me like overcoated giants. As I watched, another crate was hauled up from a small rowing boat.

It was a scene far from the dreamy river-scapes of old man Monet. A noxious haze drifted over the drear Thames, insinuating its way like smoke into the nearest doorway where three stout fellows and the even-stouter Delilah now dragged the crate. I followed at a distance and doffed my straw hat. Respect for the dead, do you see, because inside that narrow splintering box were the mortal remains of the unfortunate Jocelyn Poop, would-be lion of the foreign office now little more than ten stones of rapidly deteriorating flesh.

The interior of the warehouse was dim. I stepped back into the queasy green shadows of the gas-lamps as Delilah planted her feet firmly on the floor and, jemmy in hand, began to wrench the planks from the improvised coffin.

"Ave 'im hart hin just ha jiffy, sir,' she grunted, tossing broken planking over her shoulder. Her three thickset fellow Domestics, meanwhile, prepared the butcher's slab on to which Poop was to be conveyed.

Melted ice was already pooling about Delilah's boots and I heard it cracking and splintering as though in a gin-glass as the brutish female began to lift Poop's body out by the shoulders.

'Cor! What ha stink!' cackled Delilah. 'They don't know 'ow to pack hem, those bleedin' heye-ties, do they sir?'

I clamped my glove to my mouth and shook my head. The stench was vile and almost overpowering. Hastily, I gestured to the Domestics to get on with it and, within a moment or two, the dead man lay before me, his skin waxy, pockets of ice plastering the soaked fabric of his linen suit. There seemed nothing much to be gleaned from the reasonably intact torso. Poop's head, however, was quite a different matter. It was little more than a football-shaped outrage, black with congealed blood and matted with weed-like hair.

Stepping gingerly forward I peered at the gory mess and risked taking away the glove from my mouth.

'Contents of the clothing, Delilah,' I barked.

'Right haway, sir.' She returned to the wharf to collect the rest of the delivery.

I nodded towards the other Domestics. 'Get me a jug of water and a scrubbing brush.'

One of them nodded in acquiescence. By the time Delilah returned with a small leather satchel, I had cleaned up Poop's shattered noggin somewhat, exposing a hook nose and a rather unprepossessing moustache. Above the bridge of the nose, the whole of the forehead had been stoved in.

'It was more than a cosh that did this,' I mused to myself. Taking up the jug, I poured water into the wound. Particles of skin and brain matter floated away over Poop's cheeks in ghastly rivulets like congealed crusts of oil-paint.

I bent closer, holding my breath against the stench of corruption. Anticipating my needs, Delilah stepped forward with a lantern that I took from her fat hand. There was something very odd about the wound in Poop's head.

I probed with my fingers for some little time then, sucking my teeth thoughtfully, stepped away from the corpse and folded my arms.

'Delilah, I should be most awfully grateful if you could fetch me some plaster of Paris.'

'Plaster of Paris, sir?'

'Yes. Though where you'll lay your hands on some all the way out here . . .'

She smiled her dreadful smile and gave a little bow. She was back within twenty minutes. As I said the Domestics were without peer.

While the others prepared the mixture, covering themselves in floury clouds in the process, I laid out the contents of Poop's pockets that had been thoughtfully documented by the Neapolitan coppers. It was a sad little bundle. A daguerreotype of some ugly tart – probably his fiancée, two tickets to *Rigoletto* dated the night of his disappearance and a quantity of soggy paperwork, all depressingly mundane. I searched in vain for any reference to VC. What had his note said? 'K to V.C.?' Sounded like a chess move. People do play these agonizingly long-winded games over continents and decades. 'K' corresponding to 'King' . . . but to 'V.C.'? Could be an accumulation of medals. Knight of the Garter to Victoria Cross? No, no. Nonsense. Perhaps those opera tickets? *Verdi's Cabal?* Was there some link to the renowned tunesmith and his *Rigoletto*? Had Poop been done to death by a vengeful hunchback dwarf?

I decided to leave it there for the time being (a good idea as you can probably tell) and turned to the bowl of wet plaster prepared for me by the Domestics. I took off my coat, rolled up my sleeves and then carried the mixture over to the slab. With Delilah and one of her pals holding Poop's shattered head steady, I carefully poured the plaster into the great gaping wound. After setting down the bowl I smoked a cheroot and waited for the stuff to dry.

It is not a pleasant thing to make a mould from a fellow's dead bonce but between us we managed to prise the set plaster from the sticky ooze of Poop's skull. I turned the impression upwards and dragged the lantern towards it.

'Ah!' I ejaculated. 'Do you see it? Do you see it?'

Delilah ambled closer and screwed up her eyes at the plaster impression made by the object that someone had so unsportingly smashed into Jocelyn Poop's brain.

'Well, Hi'll retire to Bedlam!' breathed Delilah. 'Hit's a *face!*'

VI

THE WOMAN IN THE VEIL

 FACE it was. Clearly discernible were waves of hair above a noble brow and hollow eyes; the bridge of an aquiline nose and a suggestion of lip completing the picture. It was either the most forceful head-butt in history or the impression of some kind of bust or statue. I took a rough guess that Poop had been attacked with a relic of the grandeur that was Rome, though precise dating was beyond me. I despatched the plaster cast with the Domestics, confident of a speedy identification by one of Joshua Reynolds's other agents and also passed on a note to the little man himself recommending that a watch be kept on the strange undertaking firm of Mr Tom Bowler.

As for me, it was time for that rooting around I had promised myself.

Back at Downing Street, to change togs, I found I was in receipt of a charming note from Bella Pok. *I look forward immensely to our next assignation*, it ran. *I feel there is much we shall do together.*

Rather!

I changed into a dark costume and pumps, bundling my other clothes into a heavy bag, then waited for Delilah to arrive in a brougham.

There is a limit, you see, to what can be gleaned through what the yellow press like to call 'the proper channels'. As you can imagine, it is only the *im*proper channels that turn up matters of real interest. Having been unable to instigate a thorough search, I prepared, as promised, to have another  look inside the home of Professor Frederick Sash.

I am a practised housebreaker and had done my best to look over the layout of the missing scientist's residence during my interview with his wife. I had myself dropped off a few streets away from the Sash residence and then lay skulking in a clump of hydrangeas until the lights in the place were extinguished.

It was another sweltering night, heavy with patches of unhealthy-looking mist so that the shrubberies glowed oddly like spider-webs. I slipped on a half-mask and, with a heavy jemmy in one hand and a dark-lantern in the other, padded across the lawn, keeping low until I reached the shelter of the house. Once there, I flattened myself against the brickwork and paused for breath.

The easiest point of entry to the villa, it seemed to me, was through a small, diamond-paned window in the porchway. I crept around the wall until I reached this, then began an examination of the window. I had the jemmy all ready to prise open the woodwork but then discovered that it was already ajar, no doubt left so due to the heat. I gently pushed the window open to its fullest extent and slid my terribly lithe and nimble frame through it.

The porch led straight through into the great hallway, its ceiling made up almost entirely of skylights.

I made my way stealthily past majolica pots stuffed with exotic plants and rows of walnut cabinets, crammed willy-nilly with quantities of blue china.

I examined each cabinet in turn but felt sure that it was Sash's study that I needed to explore. I made for the broad staircase, my rubber-soled pumps making not a sound as I ran swiftly upwards. A series of rooms led off a walkway that looked down directly on to the hall below.

I was making for the first door with great urgency when I heard the unmistakable creak of a floorboard.

I froze. After a moment, I edged slowly and silently back to the panelled wall, secreting myself in the shadow of yet another cabinet. I peered across the space, struggling to make out anything in the darkness. Yes there, yes! There was a shape, undoubtedly human, moving stealthily up the stairs I had come up.

It was difficult to be certain from the way it moved whether or not the stranger was an inhabitant or intent on something nefarious. Either way I was in danger. I slipped my hand into my Norfolk and pulled out my revolver, then raised the dark-lantern and prepared to slip back its metal door.

A loud cough stopped me. The figure stepped into a patch of starlight, revealing itself to be Mrs Sash, her long hair tumbled down over her neck, a glass of milk carried in one hand.

She cleared her throat again and, oblivious to my presence, moved silently along the corridor to what I presumed was her bedroom. Once the door had closed behind her, I breathed a sigh of relief and moved on.

Four doors led off the walkway. One I could now eliminate. With the utmost care, I opened the dark-lantern a crack and then, silently, the first door. Within I could make out lumpen black shapes, in all probability the sleeping forms of Sash's overfed children. One faced the ceiling and was snoring, the other had her hands tucked beneath her face like a child in a nursery picture.

I stepped back on to the landing and gently closed the door.

The next room revealed itself to be merely a linen cupboard; I made swiftly for the third. It was locked.

I bent down to the lock and rammed the jemmy into it. With a fearfully loud crack, the old door sprang open. I glanced swiftly about but no one seemed to have stirred.

Once inside, I moved to the wall and discovered it covered by thick curtains. I checked to ensure I would remain unobserved and then opened the lantern to its fullest extent. The room smelled of old leather. Books lined the walls.

This looked rather promisingly like Sash's study.

I swung the lantern around the room. The light picked out a bureau and a tall cabinet filled with curiosities. Moving on, I crossed swiftly to the bureau and pushed up the rolled top. Three or four envelopes lay there, in all probability the late post mentioned by Mrs Sash. The professor would never open them now. I opened each of the drawers in turn. Nothing of interest caught my attention – they seemed merely to contain reams of dry scientific discourse. I plunged my hand into the back of the drawers and felt about in case there were any recessed panels or buttons. Real life rarely fails to disappoint and I found no such thing.

As I turned, however, I noticed on the desk a portmanteau photograph in a tortoiseshell frame. Of the three panels, the facing portraits were of Sash and his wife. The middle picture, though, apparently taken some time in the sixties, showed four men standing in stiffly formal pose. I recognized two of the men at once as younger versions of Sash, whose study I was rifling, and his colleague Verdigris whose portrait I had studied earlier. The next man – willowy and ascetic-looking – I did not know but the fourth seemed very familiar. Swaddled in a blanket and looking prematurely ancient he sat in a wheeled chair and scowled down the decades at me.

'Aha!' I exclaimed. The man in the wheeled chair was a stranger no more. In a flash I recognized him as none other than Sir Emmanuel Quibble, chief fellow of the Royal Society and the foremost scientific mind of our age. It was well known that he had long ago retired. To, of all places, the Amalfi coast . . .

I was musing on this information when the distinctive odour of burnt paper caught my attention. I swung the dark-lantern around and brought its feeble light to bear on the fire-grate, which was revealed to contain a quantity of blackened paper. Had Professor Sash laid a fire in the middle of summer? Or had he – or one of his family – destroyed something of a compromising nature? In my experience nothing is ever incinerated in a grate unless it is of a *deliciously* compromising nature.

I almost jumped out of my skin as the door was thrown open and the room illuminated by the yellow glow of an oil-lamp.

'Hold hard!' yelled some burly chap, whose outline was just discernible in the gloom. At his side, Mrs Sash twittered and wailed in distress. Clearly I would have to retake Advanced Breaking and Entering. Without a second thought I thrust the portmanteau photograph into my jacket, leapt towards the bookcase and brought it crashing down between my discoverers and me. Then I hopped nimbly on to a leather chair, smashed the study window with my jemmy and jumped into the night, hitting the lawn in a neat ball and rolling to my feet. As I pelted away from the place hell for leather, I could hear the household rousing but they were too tardy to catch lucky old Lucifer.

That next morning, I ran myself a bath. Really, I had to do something about replacing Poplar. The service had dug out a chambermaid to do this sort of thing but although I *am* one of those johnnies who delight in lording it over their inferiors, I've always found that one, indispensable manservant is worth a whole retinue of girls in mob-caps whose presence can only lead, in any case, to babies being left on doorsteps and photogravures in the *Police Gazette*. I lay steaming for over an hour, my hair pooling above me like weed. How Millais would have loved me then!

Reluctantly, I dragged myself from the bath and crossed the bare boards to my dressing room. Here, among my treasured wardrobe of fabulous apparel, I would prepare for the work of the day. A note from Miracle had told me he had news on my late professors. I glanced at my watch on the dresser. My appointment was for eleven. I had only two hours to dress!

I reached Miracle's studio only a few minutes late and was about to pull at the bell when I remembered that today was the day he took his drawing class. I had passed the Mechanical Institute on the way and returned to it now – a big, black ugly building, concealed behind scrubby bushes and gold-tipped railings – where stood an expensive-looking carriage with two glossy horses at its head. The creatures seemed restless, stamping at the cobbles, inching the carriage forward by degrees despite the best efforts of the groom clutching at their bridles. A sharp, ammoniac smell assailed me.

Sitting in splendid isolation against the upholstery of the carriage was a thin man, bald beneath his silk topper, his black-gloved hands bulging like burnt sausages as he gripped the head of his cane.

'Can't you keep them still?' he snapped. 'Can't you?'

The groom was profuse in his apologies. The vehicle lurched forward again and the bald man scowled. Then he took out a turnip-sized watch from his waistcoat and, looking at it, scowled again.

Just as I reached the steps to the institute, the door opened, releasing a torrent of ladies on to the street, resembling, in their feathery, chattering finery, nothing so much as the Regent's Park geese. I tipped my hat to them as they rolled by, averting their eyes and giggling. I had almost reached the door when a latecomer emerged and I had to step back to avoid careering into her.

Unlike her à la mode classmates, this lady wore a violet-coloured dress in the fashion of ten years back. A large black hat with a heavy veil, like that of a bee-keeper, completely obscured her face.

She was holding a tan-leather portfolio under her arm and her hands, in long, black evening gloves, fluttered around its handle as though she were in great distress.

'I do beg your pardon,' I murmured.

I stepped to one side to let the curious apparition pass and then turned to see that the bald man from the carriage was standing on the step beneath me, his sour face jutting towards me like that of an angry Mr Punch.

'Come,' he barked, thrusting his arm through the crook of the woman's free elbow and pulling her past me towards the carriage, shooting back poisonous glances the whole way.

'Charmed!' I cried, doffing my boater.

The double doors swung open again, revealing Miracle.

'Hullo, Box,' he cried, rubbing together his big hands. 'Come a-spying, eh?'

Without letting on how close to the mark Miracle was, I pointed my cane towards the carriage. The groom was lashing at the horses as the vehicle turned in the empty road. 'Who the devil was that?'

'Ah,' grinned Miracle. 'The veiled scribbler. She's a curiosity that one. Name of Mrs Knight. Mrs Midsomer Knight.'

'A dream, is she?'

'According to one of the ladies who caught a glimpse of her in the conveniences, more of a nightmare! Poor devil. Husband might be described as something of a brute. Never lets her out in society. She hardly says a word.'

'Why the veils? Does he beat her?'

'Burnt in a fire years back, I gather.'

My friend plunged his hands into his pockets and jutted out his lip thoughtfully. 'It's a funny thing, Box, but my teaching seems to have had an adverse effect on her.'

'What do you mean?'

Miracle shrugged. 'Only that she began well but of late her work has been shocking.'

'Hmm, perhaps school-mastering is not for you, after all. And, Miracle before you fill me in on the nefarious secrets of our missing professors, you should know that you cannot afford to be so ineffective. I took your advice. I now have a pupil of my own!'

We spent the rest of the morning ensconced in Miracle's studio drinking far too much and smoking a brace of cigars. His place was quite lovely, possessing a domed glass roof that let summer sunshine flood the pale green walls. Shadier nooks housed Miracle's super-abundance of landscapes (I abhor landscapes) and still lifes (the Frenchies call them *nature morte* and I can't think of a better description).

As the day wore on, and we began to radiate a mildly tipsy bonhomie, I allowed him to prise out of me the story of Miss Pok.

'You sly dog,' grinned Miracle. 'What is she like?'

I waved a hand extravagantly. 'A delight. Captivating. I was thinking of inviting her to your party. Hope you don't mind.'

'Mind? I cannot wait to meet this paragon.'

'You must promise to behave now, Christopher.' I smoked my cigar contentedly. 'You'll think me foolish, I know, but there is something very particular about her. Uncommon.'

'Such as?'

'Well, she drinks vermouth in the afternoons and has no fear of being in a gentleman's company unchaperoned.'

'Ten a penny at the Café Royal.'

'*Touché*. But she pays to be with me.'

'Pooh! She pays for her *lessons*, not your company!'

'Perhaps.'

'Do I detect more than the usual predatory instinct at work, Box?' cried Miracle. 'Can it be – never! You have fallen for her?'

I did not look him in the eye.

Miracle smiled. 'I shall refrain from tormenting you further. Now! It is high time to get down to something like business.'

'I suppose so,' I sighed. 'What have you to tell me?'

Miracle sat forward in his chair. 'Professors Verdigris and Sash were at the same Cambridge college between 1866 and 1869. Star pupils of their intake, it seems, along with two others.'

'Let me guess. One of them was Emmanuel Quibble?'

'Quite so! How did you –?'

'I have sources of my own,' I smiled. 'The other?'

'Chap called Morraine. Maxwell Morraine.'

I nodded thoughtfully. Was this the fourth man in the photograph?

Miracle leant back on the dark red leather. 'Their chosen field was something rather bewildering to do with the molten core of the earth. They formed some kind of research team. Went out to Italy.'

'Italy, eh? And did they call themselves anything?'

'Hm?'

'The Verdigris Collective. Something like that.'

Miracle shook his head. 'Not as far as I know.'

'Do you know what happened to . . . what-do-you-call-him? Morraine?'

'Apparently he went mad and died out there. Quibble, of course, rose to great heights.'

'Indeed. Terribly hard to get an audience with the old man, from what I hear.'

'Oh, nigh on impossible. Lives in Naples, I gather. Practically a recluse.'

'Hm. I know you won't let me down.'

Miracle gave a little laugh. 'There's a limit to what strings even I can pull, old man.'

'Nonsense. I have the utmost faith in your ability to flatter the most Doric pillars of society to their very capitals. I can be in Italy for – what shall we say? Next Thursday?'

VII

THE VERDIGRIS MAUSOLEUM

RETURNED to Downing Street to find a communication from the Domestics. The firm of Tom Bowler, Belsize Park, was apparently engaged in an unusual amount of activity at the dockside. Enquiries suggested that the firm specialized in the repatriation of Englishmen and Italians who had died abroad. Coffins were shipped over in packing crates (intrinsically valuable, it seemed, as they were returned, empty, to the point of egress, namely the port of Naples). I determined to have another nocturnal poke around, this time at the undertaker's and, after sobering myself up with a pot of coffee, put on a black suit with a waistcoat of burnt-orange to do so. I stepped out into Whitehall where Delilah was drawing up in the firm's cab. For the purpose, she had traded in her signature yellow frock for a cabby's coat and gaiters.

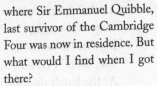

'Evening, Mr Box, hand where is we hoff to?'

I gave the Belsize Park address and we were away.

As we clattered along, I pressed my face to the window and closed my eyes. Night had come and the air was sickly with a yellow smog that covered the city like some monstrous slug-trail.

I tried to make sense of recent curious events. All clues pointed to Naples. Poop had died there and had foreseen catastrophic events. It was the place where that mysterious crate of Mr Bowler had been destined, the place where Sir Emmanuel Quibble, last survivor of the Cambridge Four was now in residence. But what would I find when I got there?

I was jerked from my reverie by the sudden acceleration of the cab. Rapping on the ceiling, I was answered by the Delilah's heavy features peering down at me through the hatch.

'Beg, pardon, sir,' she wheezed. 'Hi believe we his being followed.'

I pulled at the heavy leather strap of the window and peered out. I had no clear idea of where we were but could just make out the silhouette of another cab, swaying alarmingly as it juddered around the corner.

'How long has this been going on?' I demanded.

Delilah coughed into her grubby collar. I could just catch the glint of the street lamps in her eyes as she swivelled round to look back at our pursuers.

'Couple ha mile, sir. Hi've tried to throw 'im off the track but hit hain't no good.'

I dragged the window upwards with a firm tug. 'Do what you can then.'

'Righto, sir,' she answered brightly, relishing the challenge. 'I could try to – look hout!'

I was conscious of a loud report from outside the cab, as though someone had stepped heavily on the surface of a frozen pond.

'What is it?' I demanded, peering upwards.

Delilah spluttered as though mortally offended. ''E bloody well shot hat hus, sir!'

This sounded a bit much. What murderous thug had I attracted now? I pressed my nose to the glass and did a quick reconnoitre as we rattled furiously along. I thought briefly of leaping from the carriage and taking Delilah's place but instead turned my head to address her once more.

'On, then!' I cried. 'Anywhere. Lose him!'

As the hatch thumped back into place, Delilah whipped up the horse with a mixture of endearments and obscenities. We lurched forward with renewed vigour and I was flung against the dark leather. As we tottered leftwards, the cab's wheels gave an horrendous squeal and bumped twice over the kerb.

I tore off my coat and scrabbled at the lining, popping the excellent stitches (how that hurt me!) to reveal the small pistol I knew the Tailoring Domestics had concealed there.

Rocked back and forth by the motion of the carriage, I dropped on to my knees and placed the gun on the floor. In the queasy atmosphere of summer-fret and gas-light, the gun's barrel-less body glowed like a silverfish. I grabbed at my left boot and swiftly removed the long, slim tube secreted in its own compartment within the elasticated side.

As carefully as I could, the cab bucking over the cobbles, I screwed the tube on to the front of the pistol. Within moments, I was in possession of a very effective, long-range weapon.

Delilah's muffled curses and whip-cracks rang out sharply as I rammed down the window with my elbow and leaned out over the sill.

Behind us, the other cab, seemingly all of a piece with its driver, materialized like a ghostly ship. I could see nothing clearly, merely a suggestion of bowler hat and ulster. Then our pursuer's hand flew up, there came a yellowy flash and the report of a gun.

I ducked back into the cab and then levelled my own pistol, loosing off a couple of shots as we careered over a crossroads, almost colliding with a third cab. There were garbled shouts of protest, the whinny of horses, but we tore on past, street-lamps blurring like phantom dandelion clocks.

The pursuing cabman fired twice more, the *crack-crack* of his pistol swamped by the dense curtain of fog.

Suddenly, my cab smacked against the pavement and I was tossed to the floor of the carriage. I swore as my leg scraped the rough surface and I felt the fabric of my trousers rend. Struggling to right myself as we reeled ahead, I managed to get one barked knee on to the seat and, leaning up, pushed open the hatch in the ceiling.

'Try to keep us steady –' I began, then pulled myself up to peer through the hole. Delilah had sunk back, her corpulent face a mask of agony. She gripped her chest with a gloved hand.

''E got me, sir!' she gasped, then suddenly pitched sideways, diving into the fog like an uncertain swimmer into the Serpentine.

I reached out to grab her, but it was too late.

I knew I had only moments before the vehicle would career out of control. I kicked at the door and swung myself out and on to the body of the cab, hanging on for grim death.

Chancing a glance behind me, I saw the murderous driver of the other cab taking aim once again. I gained a quick foothold on the top of the door and then swung myself upwards, falling into the empty driver's seat. At once, I began lashing mercilessly at the horse, keeping my bare head low as another shot whistled past. I turned and replied with a volley of three but still the cab bore down.

We were heading down some endless, snaking high street made tunnel-like by the enshrouding smog. I had a vague impression of the blazing windows of public houses and the blank façades of shut-up shops.

Some young fellow pulled his sweetheart from our path just in time to prevent her being crushed beneath the wheels. I heard her cry out as my assailant fired again, the bullet splintering the wood-work of the vehicle just by me.

An arch of some sort loomed up on my left: two fat pillars, fringed with ivy. I had to get off the main highway to secure the general population. Between the pillars stood a pair of iron gates, thankfully open. With a lash of the whip I urged my horse through and into the gaping darkness beyond.

Looking back, I saw that my pursuer had not been discouraged and was only a hundred yards behind. As he swung through the arch, he too was lost in the black of the night. Nevertheless, I had surprised him and, as I urged the horse onwards, I tried to take stock of my situation.

All through the frantic pursuit, my mind raced. Who was behind this murderous attack? Could this have something to do with the mystery on hand? Or perhaps it was that murderous fool Major Strangeways Pugg, still set on avenging his lovely Avril.

No longer on cobbles I appeared to be travelling over some kind of muddy track or pathway. The road was as narrow as a

footpath and branches lashed at the sides of the cab as I urged it forward.

Jerking round I fired the last of my bullets behind me and then almost fell from my perch as something reared out of the Stygian gloom.

It was an angel.

I fancy my face must have been a pretty sight but I recovered quickly. An angel it was, but stone and sacred to the memory of some poor bastard as far as I could make out. I thrashed and swore at the horse. The rapid appearance of a dozen stone crosses and then a massive, ugly mausoleum confirmed that I had passed into some great municipal cemetery.

The pathway forked right and I drove the coach on, meanwhile feeling in my other boot for the clip of bullets I kept there. It was a devil of a job trying to reload the pistol and still prevent the cab from crashing into the gravestones that projected from the wet ground like scattered dragon's teeth. I had just managed it when I was startled again, this time by the sudden appearance of my enemy right *ahead* of me.

Somehow he had cut me off. Perhaps he knew this necropolis well. It was as though some hellish beast were bearing down on me, the driver's scarf flapping behind him like a pennant in a gale.

I dragged at the reins and managed to steer the cab to the left but it was too late. The two vehicles clashed like galleons and I heard the bodywork rend and protest as we ground against each other on the narrow lane.

But then suddenly I was past him and still going!

The black night exploded into unnatural light as I loosed off another two shots. My assailant seemed to stagger in his seat as his cab retreated but in an instant he had turned and fired too, taking the nose off a rather comely stone cherub in the process.

I now had some advantage in that my enemy's cab was rattling away from me in the wrong direction. There came a frantic whinny from his horse as he flogged at its flanks.

'Hyar! Hyar!'

He was turning, or attempting to. Meanwhile, my own vehicle had not slackened its pace and was thundering heedlessly through the hollows of the cemetery. Mausoleums streamed past like the town-houses of the dead.

What to do? According to the manual – or to Lady Cecely Midwinter's Espionage Academy on the Old Kent Road where yours truly had been apprenticed – I should abandon the cab and secrete myself amidst the thick gorse that enveloped the memorial stones. If my would-be assassin came back this way, I could pick him off from my hiding place among the angels.

These thoughts were flashing across my mind when suddenly the mist thinned and I saw the enormous outline of a grand building only a matter of fifty yards ahead. It was a bleak-looking chapel of some kind, its towers sparkling eerily, its great black doors securely barred against all-comers and I was heading straight for it.

Wrenching the reins until I felt the hot leather tearing at my palms, I tried to steer the carriage away from the chapel. The horse gave a great snorting cry and lurched right. I reeled from the impact as the side of the cab slammed against the old wooden doors of the building. There was a tremendous booming crash and I felt the whole cab splinter and the ground hurtle up towards me.

My chest hit the iron-hard mud and I felt the wind comprehensively knocked from me. Dazed and sick I lay on my front, staring miserably ahead as the pursuing cab drew up alongside the chapel. The figure, swathed in ulster, scarf and brown bowler, seemed smaller now as he clambered down from the driver's seat. In one gloved hand he held his pistol.

I tried to roll over but the breath was only coming back to me with agonizing slowness. Just ahead and out of reach lay my own pistol, the long barrel protruding from a clump of weeds. I flung out my arm and tried to drag myself towards it. The figure advanced remorselessly, cocking his weapon and reaching up with his other hand to pull down the scarf from his face. Was it that vengeful Fury, Pugg? There was a hole the size of a tanner in the shoulder of his cape but no sign of blood. Had I winged him or merely ruined his coat?

Lungs bursting, I tried to sit up and sling myself into cover.

'Damn it,' I gasped. 'Who are you, you ruddy maniac?'

The figure stopped and seemed to consider me.

Then, echoing across the cemetery with the eeriness of a banshee came a cry: 'Hello! What's going on? What are you doing there?'

Two men, holding yellow lamps high above their heads hove into view to my left. Their appearance had a startling effect on my attacker. Swiftly, he slipped his pistol into the folds of his ulster and raced back towards the cab, pulling himself up into the driver's perch. He whipped up the horse and rattled away.

The lamp-bearers ran towards me, as welcome as real angels. 'Good Lord, are you all right, sir?' said one. His companion, heavily bearded and mean-looking was less forgiving. 'What the blazes has been going on?' he demanded.

Ignoring him, I struggled to my feet and grabbed for my pistol. I aimed at the retreating cab, but in moments it was out of range. I turned on my heel and wrenched the lamp from the bearded man's hand.

'Here! What are you doing?'

'His number,' I hissed. 'The cab number. Can you see it?'

Nothing was clear, though, in the sickly yellow light and the cab soon vanished into the murk.

I stood for a moment, swinging the lamp round in an arc and illuminating the devastation I had wrought. My cab was almost cracked in two. The horse stood nearby, placidly chewing grass at the foot of one of those broken columns that tell of life cut off in its prime. Happily, that life had not been mine.

''Ere!' cried my bearded rescuer. 'You was bloomin' shooting! What the hell do you think you're about? This is a place of rest!'

The cemetery watchmen took me to a little cabin where I was treated to a tot of rum by the kinder of the two – Lukey by name – and furious glares from his mate, name of Bob. I assured the good burghers that all expenses would be met. In the morning I would despatch the Domestics to set about hushing things up, not least the body of the faithful Delilah who was probably still lying undiscovered with a bullet between her shoulder blades on some dreadful suburban roadway. I dragged my ragged, filthy and exhausted self to my feet and was moving towards the cabin door when a notice pinned to the wall caught my gaze.

'What is that?' I asked.

'That's the interments list, sir,' said Lukey.

'Is it, by George. And that name, fourth down . . . ?'

'The Verdigris Mausoleum, sir.'

'What a coincidence,' I mused. 'An . . . acquaintance of mine goes by that name. I wonder if it is his family tomb. Would it . . . would it be an awful imposition to ask to see that mausoleum?'

The bearded one positively glared at me and cleared his throat of a noisome expectoration that landed in a hissing green lump on the coals of the fire. 'The Verdigris? Indeed it would! After what you've been up to tonight, you're damned lucky we ain't called the bobbies!'

Lukey laid a hand on the other's arm. 'Now then, Bob. Watch that temper of your'n. You said there was summat funny about that funeral in any case.'

I adopted a sombre expression. 'Gentlemen, I am investigating certain irregularities connected with that funeral. It is more than likely that you have given invaluable service to the Crown. I need you to show me that mausoleum. At once!'

With much ill-grace Bob finally assented and a few minutes later the three of us stepped back out into the humid night.

Our feet crunched on the gravel pathways, the lantern held aloft by Bob throwing a funnel of yellow light into the oily gloom.

I was dog-tired but pressed on, unsure of what, if anything, I might find.

The Verdigris family tomb was about the size of a small cottage, done in the familiarly dreary style of Corinthian columns and arched roof. A pair of massive bronze doors were set in the centre, a thick, well-oiled padlock strung between the door handles like a fob-chain across the waistcoat of a prize-fighter.

'There,' barked Bob the lantern-carrier. 'Can we now get back to our business?'

I moved towards the mausoleum and craned my neck to make out the family name, picked out in black against the white marble.

I assumed the masterful tone that comes so easily to me. 'Quickly, man, the key!'

'Now hold on a moment –'

'Give him the key, Bob!' wailed Lukey.

Cursing, the burly fellow began to fiddle with the huge bunch of keys at his waist.

'Hurry!' I urged.

At last he selected a long, spindly specimen and, grunting with the effort, shifted his belly forward so he could insert it into the lock.

As soon as the tumblers clicked, I dragged at the chain and hauled it to the ground.

'The lantern, Bob!' I hissed. 'Give it to me!'

So saying, I grabbed the thing from his hand and, dragging open the doors, plunged into the mausoleum.

Inside the air was suffocatingly stale. The grim black oblong of a new coffin stood out boldly on its shelf against the homogenous dust-grey boxes that abutted it.

'Give me a hand,' I commanded, pulling at the head end of the coffin.

''Ere!' cried Bob, entering the building.

'No time to explain!' I cried shrilly. 'Get the coffin on the floor and get the lid off.'

'Do as he says,' said Lukey. 'He's on to something.'

Together, Lukey and myself pulled the coffin to the dust-thick floor, then I began to look about for something to prise open the lid.

'My God, if the family find out about this –' murmured Bob.

'Never mind that,' I barked. 'Hold the lantern high.'

I swung round and then stopped as my eyes alighted on half a dozen wooden chairs, stacked in the corner and presumably for use at funerals. Without hesitation I grabbed at the top chair and smashed it to pieces on the floor. From the debris I retrieved a chair leg and with this began to hammer away under the coffin lid. After ten or twelve blows, the lid gave with a nasty squeal and splintered across.

'Pull it apart!' I cried. 'Open the thing!'

Lukey stepped forward and, grasping at the wood, wrenched the lid away. Bob glided forward from out of the shadows, the queasy yellow lantern light flooding the macabre sight before us.

'Well, bless my soul!' whispered Lukey.

For within the coffin was revealed a cloth dummy, its innards stuffed with straw, its eyes and mouth merely crude stitching like that on some common scarecrow.

'Ha!' I cried triumphantly. 'Exactly what I expected to find!'

Which was a bloody lie but there you are.

VIII

THE MAN IN THE INDIGO SPECTACLES

KNOW what you're thinking. Resurrectionists! Body-snatchers once more at work in old London town! Had the good professor (and his erstwhile colleague – for a search of Sash's tomb the next day revealed the same result) been made away with by wall-eyed, whisky-breathed anatomists to be displayed and skewered at the Whitechapel Hospital? Well, no. Very probably not. At least, I shouldn't have thought so. This was the twentieth century, after all.

No, it seemed altogether more probable that Tom Bowler Esq. lay behind this bizarre enterprise. The Belsize Park premises were immediately raided but somehow the jolly mortician had avoided the Domestics and stolen away like a street-Arab in the night. I was sure I knew where to run him to earth and booked passage on the next departing vessel to Naples without waiting to hear whether Miracle had worked his

charms on old Quibble. I would leave at once. Well, almost at once. There was still the little matter of Miracle's summer ball. Business, of course, as I needed to confirm my appointment with Miracle, and perhaps a little pleasure.

My friend's parties were something of a legend. In fact, Miracle's gorgeous Belgravia house had been the scene of my poking of Avril Pugg the previous December. Christmas is a time for giving, after all. I found I was looking forward to this ball immensely. It would be a welcome distraction from the problem in hand but I would also be escorting the delectable Bella Pok and could impress her with statements of the 'I fear I must away to the Continent this very night!' variety.

There had been no time for another drawing lesson but we had been in constant communication via letter and cable. I had broached the ball and she had been delighted to accept. Might I be permitted to call on her? No, she would prefer to call at Downing Street. Would eight o'clock suit?

I spent much of the late afternoon selecting a flower for my lapel. Joe Chamberlain had made orchid-growing awfully fashionable and the delicate purple flower I selected as a button-hole set off my pale complexion most appealingly. Not quite ready to admit I was still without a servant of any kind, I opened the door to Bella myself – a delirious vision in crimson – turned her round immediately and helped her back into the cab.

As we clattered along I could see how thrilled she was at the prospect of the party. Her eyes blazed and her expression was almost wild as she turned to me.

'Will I not be awfully out of place, Mr Box?'

I took her gloved hand. 'My dear, you will outshine them all.'

'And Mr Miracle. What is he like? They say he's very handsome.'

'No doubt they do. You'll like him, I'm sure.'

Curiously, though, when we arrived at Miracle's house, of our host there was no sign. Instead, the party seemed to be under the direction of Lady Constance Tutt-Haffenschafft, a friend of Miracle's and quite the old hand at throwing a function like this.

Lady Constance – of Austrian stock and the widow of someone awfully grand in trans-Atlantic telegraphy – was one of London's more unusual hostesses. She was a genuinely warm and congenial old soul who had survived the Tay Bridge disaster and, as a consequence, had developed a morbid fear of railway engines. To everyone's eternal embarrassment, she was wont to impersonate steam trains at the most inopportune moments. It was like Miracle, who didn't give a fig for convention, to take her under his wing when the rest of society had shunned her.

Glittering with jewels, Lady Constance barrelled towards us, swathed in taffeta. 'Ach! How delightful to see you, Lucifer!' she gushed. 'Do you know where young Miracle is hiding? He is not here! *Choo! Choo!* I arrive early, yes? To help in the preparations, but where is the boy? I do not know. So – *Choo! Choo!* – I have to take charge! But who is this? Who is this flower?'

'Lady Constance Tutt-Haffenschafft,' I said. 'Miss Bella Pok.'

'Miss Pok! Enchanted. En – *choo-choo*-chanted.'

Bella stepped back a little, blinking in surprise. Lady Constance gave a quick little smile. 'You are in your choice of companion most fortunate, my dear Lucifer,' she enthused in her guttural croak.

'And I in mine,' said Bella, glancing in my direction.

I glowed with pleasure.

'I had no idea you would be accompanied,' said Lady C, teeth glinting. 'Pok. An unusual name. *Choo! Choo!* You have come far?'

'Tonight, no. But I am Dutch by birth.'

'I trust you did not come to London by one of these steam trains?'

Bella shook her head. 'No. By boat.'

'Thank God! The train is the devil's play-thing! Even now I hear them! *Chuff! Chuff!*'

Lady Constance pressed her hand to her forehead for a moment then exhaled as though steam were forcing its way out of her big nostrils. The moment, it seemed, had passed.

'Forgive me. Now do go off and get yourself a little drink. I'm afraid I must make free with Mr Box for a moment.'

I bowed to Bella and, with an amused smile, she plunged off into the ballroom, soon lost to sight amongst the miasma of silken gowns and black cut-aways.

'You are very naughty,' said Lady Constance, pinching my arm.

'I am?'

'You know very well that your being London's most alluring bachelor is the principal reason why so many unattached young ladies come to Christopher's parties. *Choo!* You are meant to come alone.'

She giggled and it ran like a tremor through her portly frame.

I patted the old sow's hand indulgently. 'I am still very much unattached, my dear Lady Constance and, besides, you know there is only one woman in the world for me.'

I gave her the kind of saucy look that would keep her enthralled for another twelvemonth. Eyelids fluttering bashfully, she batted her fan lightly against the silk-faced lapels of my suit. 'Ach! You flatterer! *Choo! Choo!* You know I have purchased the most glorious new gown. Perhaps I could sit for you again . . . ?'

This was good news. I had painted her perhaps a dozen times, all for excellent remuneration. During our sittings, for some reason, the railway mania abated and she fell into glorious, blissful silence.

Looking towards the crowd in the ballroom, Lady Constance took my arm and began leading me in. 'But you have done wonderfully, Lucifer. This girl Pok. She is like a flame. So beautiful!'

'I must concur with you there.'

'And you *are* fond of her, yes? I could see it at once when the two of you stood together. I must have every detail! I am starved of gossip! *Huff!* Now, we must hurry and disengage your Miss Bella from those old goats in there before her virtue . . . *choo!* . . . is entirely compromised.'

The ballroom was hung about with paper lanterns and summer flowers. Chattering faces, reflected to the infinite by the huge quantity of gilt mirrors, looked out at me as I sauntered towards Bella. I stepped across the threshold and the old thrill lit up my innards. What did these blandly respectable folk know of me? Could they tell that beneath my crisp white gloves were fingernails that had so recently scrabbled in grave-dirt? Could they guess for even a moment that I was about to embark on a perilous mission that might save their very way of life? Of course not, but what did that matter? At that moment, the guilty pleasure that comes from leading a double life coursed through me like salts.

I caught sight of Bella once more.

She sat: a splendid curl of long scarlet silk, wrapped about with a stole of Arctic fox. An ugly young pup with unwashed hair hanging to his collar stood to her right, jabbering away.

She gave a little start as I appeared and clicked my heels.

'Bella,' I said.

The greasy fellow swung towards me with a questioning look.

'Do forgive me,' I said. 'Lucifer Box. I have come to rescue my friend Miss Pok from your miserable attentions. Shall we, my dear?'

I extended the crook of my elbow. She took it and rose with a small smile, leaving her beau blustering in fury.

'You are rather a terrible person, Lucifer,' she said.

'You're the second person to say that this evening.'

'And certain to have a bad end,' she added.

'It comes of having a bad beginning. You didn't need rescuing?'

'Of course! He was so dreary and had breath like a spaniel.'

'Well, it was my duty. And my right. You are, after all, my partner for the evening.'

She glanced towards me and the chandeliers glittered in her violet eyes. 'Indeed.'

'Then let's have some cham and then a dance. Quickly, now, I can see Lady Chuff-chuff heading our way and the band have struck up a polka.'

So, in the sweet heat of the evening, we whiled away a very pleasant hour or so, conversation and blood quickened by Mumm. Bella's gaze was locked on mine, and as we swirled effortlessly around the ballroom, I fervently wished myself free of all responsibilities. Must the dread burden of saving the Empire always fall on me?

I was standing with my back to the room when I saw Bella glance over my shoulder. A little shiver prickled up my spine and I turned and saw a queer-looking fellow standing at the hearth.

He was a very tall, barrel-chested man in spotless evening dress, standing with legs apart, thumbs tucked into the pockets of his white waistcoat, nodding and occasionally smiling tightly at some pleasantry. Thick, oily curls, streaked with white sprouted from his massive head. Perched upon his prominent nose was a pair of curious, indigo-hued spectacles. He seemed ill at ease and was constantly flipping his watch from his waistcoat.

Almost as though he sensed my looking at him, the great head flicked upwards, the light turning his spectacles a flashing white.

'Good Lord,' I said. 'Who is that?'

'That is the Duce Tiepolo,' said Lady Constance, appearing at my side with further champagne. 'I met him once before in Biarritz. I had heard he was in town.'

'Who?' I glanced almost furtively at the imposing figure by the fireplace.

'He is an Italian duke,' said Bella. 'I have read about him in the society columns.'

'One of the discoveries – *choo!* – of our oh-so-dear Mr Miracle,' trilled Lady Constance. 'How he dotes on us stray dogs.'

'Indeed,' I said. 'That's why he likes me so much. This one doesn't look like a stray dog, though.'

'Oh, he is, to Christopher, like royalty, my dear boy. Tiepolo is the last of a dying scion. His people, they fought, oh most bravely against the Garibaldi fellow back in the sixties – *chuff!* – but his family were all sent into exile when the . . . what do you call it? . . . the Rissole . . . the Risorgan . . .'

'Risorgimento,' said Bella softly.

'Yes,' said Lady Constance. 'When they came in.'

'He strikes quite a noble figure, does he not?' observed my beautiful companion.

'Oh dear,' I mused. 'Another one with a penchant for hard-luck cases.'

'You would like to meet him, yes?'

'Why not,' I said.

So we were led over and into the presence of the great man.

'Your Grace . . .'

The Duce turned slowly towards us, the deep lines at the corners of his eyes creasing together.

'Aha! Lady Constance! How delightful!'

The train-fearer was delighted to be remembered. After an exchange of pleasantries, I stepped forward and he inclined his head slightly at the sight of me. It was like being observed by some great patient snake. The lenses of the indigo spectacles prevented even a hint of his expression from being visible.

'This is Mr Lucifer Box,' said Lady Constance. 'The famous painter.'

'Oh, you flatter me,' I oiled. 'Your Grace.'

I bowed and clicked my heels. He did likewise.

'Tiepolo,' I said. 'I'm afraid I do not know the province . . .'

'One of the more ancient duchies,' he said, with a smile. The voice was quiet but assured, like a great and well-maintained engine using but a fraction of its true power.

He turned to Bella.

'Miss Bella Pok,' announced Lady Constance.

He took her hand in his great paw without hesitation. 'I'm afraid, your Grace,' she cooed, 'that I know very little of the history of your country . . .'

'Oh, my unhappy country!' said the Duce, raising his hands palms outward and smiling in mock-anguish. 'But now, here, is not the time to be remembering old sorrows. Perhaps if you would do me the honour of dining with me . . . ?'

Bella's eyes flashed.

I moved with the speed of a jealous panther. If you've ever seen one, you'll know. 'Your Grace,' I interrupted, 'I would consider it a great honour if you would consent to sit for a portrait.'

The Duce's mouth pinched in displeasure. 'This is impossible, alas. I am leaving most soon for the Continent. Besides, a *painting* . . .' He gave a little shrug. 'I was saying to our friend Mr Miracle – where is he by the way? – is not painting most . . . old-fashioned?'

Lady Constance leant forward. 'The Duce is a photographic enthusiast.'

'Is he, by George?' I said, nettled. 'Well, in that case I should hate to bother him with such a trifle as a portrait in oils.'

Bella shot me an odd look.

'You are going to the Continent, you say, your Grace?' I said airily.

'Yes.'

'Back to Italy?'

The great man's face darkened.

I put my fingers to my lips as though to hush them. 'Of course not! How silly of me! They wouldn't take too kindly to seeing anyone from the old days, would they? Where *do* you spend your exile?'

'Well, if you will excuse me, Lady Constance,' he began. 'Miss Pok . . .'

'I have myself some little knowledge of those days,' I interrupted. The champagne was, I fear, beginning to tell. 'My father told me all about it. Italy was in a parlous state back then, Bella. Wasn't really Italy at all, to speak of. Ruled by the Frogs, the Spanish, even the ruddy Austrians – saving your presence, Lady C.'

The Duce gazed levelly at me. 'It was a troubled time. But we could have survived as we were. If not for Signor Giuseppe Garibaldi . . .'

'You may know the biscuit,' I said in an undertone to Bella. 'He pulled the country together, didn't he, under King What's-his-name. Yes. I'm off there tomorrow myself, as a matter of fact. I'll send them your regards, hmm?'

The Duce's lips set into a grim line. 'You will excuse me. I must . . . that is, I . . .'

He seemed genuinely put out. Making a little bow to the ladies, he melted away into the crowd.

'Well!' said Bella.

'Hmm?'

'I thought you were rather rude to that poor wanderer.'

I flashed a cheeky smile at Lady Constance and she, giggling girlishly, waved back at me. Then I took Bella by the elbow and steered her towards the balcony. 'My dear Bella, these pompous so-called aristos are all alike. It won't do him a bit of harm to be reminded that he's the ex-Duke of an ex-duchy. He'll go home and kick his valet in all probability, but that's scarcely our concern. Now, I suggest a little air to clear away the fug of his rhetoric. Besides, I found that I didn't take to the idea at all of someone else dining with you.'

She cocked her head to one side impishly and gave me the benefit of her most devastating smile.

We walked through the French windows and out on to the warm terrace. Balustraded steps led down on either side to Miracle's vast gardens.

'It's very beautiful in the moonlight,' said Bella, gazing out at the hedges and fountains.

'Mmm,' I concurred. 'By day this place is a riot of colour. I once painted Lady Constance against the bougainvillaea over there.'

'Did she like it?'

'She was chuff-chuffed.'

Bella giggled, then shivered a little and I slipped out of my coat.

'Allow me.'

She took the coat and draped it about her shoulders. 'Perhaps you would care to paint me one day?'

'You wouldn't prefer the Duke to photograph you?'

'There's no beauty in chemicals and paper, Lucifer,' she murmured.

'Indeed not. I would . . . I would consider it a very great honour to paint you, Bella. How would you like it done?'

'Perhaps I could be Jeanne d'Arc . . . or Helen,' she said, thrusting her shoulders back and lifting up that fine, proud head.

'In Troy? Or being ravished by Zeus? Oh no, that was Leda wasn't it?'

I moved just a fraction closer to her. A tiny pulse was beating in her throat.

'I think I should like that,' she said quietly.

'To be painted or to be . . .'

'Ravished?' She laughed her charming, tinkling laugh. She did not move away as my arm brushed hers. 'Zeus was fond of all that, was he not? Forever appearing as swans or showers of gold . . .'

'I know so little about you,' I said suddenly, 'but I do not wish to pry.'

'Pry away.'

'You really are *Miss* Pok?'

'I really am. I was engaged once. To a count, would you believe?'

I looked at her in the starlight. Her eyes glittered like fragments of amethyst. I could believe princes, kings and emperors might lose their wits over her.

'I must confess that I have posed for a portrait before.'

'Oh yes?'

'Yes. The Count. He paid for a portrait.'

'How did it come out?'

'Indifferently.'

'And what about the Count? How did he come out?'

'Equally indifferently.'

'My dear,' I began, taking her hand, 'I am distressed beyond measure to have to go away.'

'To Italy?'

I nodded.

'Business or pleasure?'

I looked down and contemplated her delicate, gloved hand. 'Oh, business only. Nothing but the most vital business would take me away from you at this juncture.'

'You would rather stay in London?'

'I would rather stay with you,' I said quietly. 'And continue your . . . instruction.'

I reached out and took her hand in mine. She turned, the curve of her cheek illumined like a crescent moon. Her lips parted and I could feel the warmth of her breath.

All at once, there came the crunch of running footsteps on the gravel below and a figure lolloped towards the terrace. Both of us turned at the sight of him, his handsome face flushed, his cravat all askew. It was Christopher Miracle!

He clattered up the steps and stopped, swaying slightly, when he clapped eyes on me.

'Box!' he cried.

'Miracle! Where the devil have you been? Lady Constance has been manfully holding the fort –'

'Thank God you are here! You must help me! Dear God, it is terrible! Terrible!'

I laid a hand upon his arm. 'My dear Christopher! What is it? What has happened?'

He shot a glance at Bella.

'Miss Pok,' I said calmly, 'perhaps it would be better if you returned to the party –'

She shook her head. 'I would far rather be of assistance, if I can.'

Miracle gripped my arm. 'She's vanished and they think I have something to do with it!'

'Who has vanished?' asked Bella with a concerned frown.

'Come, Christopher. Let's get you somewhere warm. Bella, would you check there's no one observing?'

We slipped him back through into the ballroom and, by sticking close to the heavy curtains, managed to steer him into a panelled corridor without anyone seeing us.

I tried a door and we found ourselves in a darkened study.

Bella lit a lamp as I settled Miracle into a chair and pushed a tumbler of Scotch into his shaking hands.

The glass clattered against his teeth. 'They say I was the last person to see her. Now she is missing and – the police don't say it but they suspect some foul play I'm sure of it!'

'Miracle! Calm yourself! Who has gone missing?'

He looked at me with a puzzled expression. 'Have I not said? Why, Mrs Knight, of course. Mrs Midsomer Knight.'

'Who?'

'The woman I told you of. Remember? You must remember.'

'What, the veiled creature?'

Miracle nodded, his head drooping between defeated shoulders.

'Come along, sir,' said Bella gently. 'Drink up and tell us all about it.'

Miracle nodded and rubbed his tired face. 'Yesterday. It was time for my usual drawing class. I arrived early and so, for the first time, did she. Mrs Knight, that is. That spectre of a husband of hers was just dropping her off.'

I nodded. 'And then?'

'I escorted her up the steps of the Institute. She said her husband had some urgent business out of town and so had brought her before her usual time, was this acceptable? I said of course it was, as long as she didn't mind busying herself until the other ladies arrived.'

'What time was this?'

'Nine-thirty. As soon as we were inside, she excused herself and disappeared into the . . . er *conveniences*. And that was the last I saw of her, I swear it!'

'She didn't come back into your room?'

'I went about my work and forgot all about her! At ten, the other ladies came. The Misses Fullalove were at each other's throats. My mind was elsewhere . . .'

'Did none of the others notice her absence?' I asked.

He shook his head. 'No. At least, none of them remarked upon it.'

'And when did the business begin to assume a more sinister aspect?' said Bella.

'Well, at the end of the lesson when the husband arrived. Of course, I had no idea where she might be. There was the most frightful row and the police were called. A glove was then found, unquestionably belonging to Mrs Knight. A blood-stained glove, Lucifer. In the ladies' conveniences!'

'And the peelers suspect foul play?'

'We were alone in the building for half an hour before the others arrived. Knight himself saw us on the steps of the Institute. I don't know where the devil she is but I had nothing to do with it. God help me! I am sworn on my honour not to leave town.'

I exhaled noisily. 'Well, this is a pickle.'

'They've questioned me over and over and only recently released me. I have nothing to tell them!'

'But they haven't arrested you!'

'Not yet. But it can only be –'

There was some kind of commotion in the corridor beyond. Lady Constance's voice chuffed in indignation, then there were footsteps on the carpet. Bella looked at me with a fearful expression as we heard first one, then another door being opened and then firmly shut.

Miracle shuddered, his eyes wide with terror.

The door to the study opened admitting a lively little ball of a man with great shaving brushes of hair projecting from his ears and nose. The rest of his face was concealed beneath a derby hat and a pair of massive, old-fashioned Piccadilly weepers.

'Please forgive this intrusion, sir,' he said, looking at me, then at Bella. '*Miss.* Inspector Flush. Scotland Yard.'

He removed his hat and threw a very serious look at my friend Christopher.

'Mr Miracle, I'm afraid I shall have to ask you to come with me to the Yard. Certain . . . developments have come to light.'

'Developments?'

I held up a hand. 'Just a moment, Inspector. Before you haul my friend off on some spurious charge, had we not best get the facts in order? Mr Miracle was in the process of describing the events to us. You can surely show him the courtesy of allowing him to finish.'

Flush gave a triple-chinned shrug. 'That is a courtesy we should be glad to extend – at the station.'

'What developments?' cried Miracle with some asperity.

With slightly more drama than was necessary (I liked him at once), Flush removed his hat, and held it to his breast. 'We've located the missing woman.'

'Safe and well, I trust,' said Bella.

'No, miss,' said the inspector. 'Dead.'

IX

THE HORROR IN THE CARDBOARD TUBE

ELL, there it was. *Dead.* A bloated body had been pulled out of the Thames and though rats had made short work of her face, the dress, reticule and certain papers found on the corpse had led the husband to a positive identification. How tiresome it was.

The wretched Miracle had been formally charged with murder and I was allowed to visit him, giving what assurances I could. Of course, I couldn't possibly take off to Italy at a time like this, I told him. I wouldn't rest until his good name was cleared. That sort of blather.

I missed the boat to Naples and, later that day, slipped off to see the ascetic banker, Mr Midsomer Knight.

'Mr Box, have you been retained by Scotland Yard in this matter?' he positively hissed. 'Really, I cannot see what the deuce business it is of yours.'

Mr Midsomer Knight looked at me coldly as I sat across from him in his frightful, over-furnished Norwood home. I spread my hands before me in a gesture of supplication. 'It is only that I believe Mr Miracle to be entirely innocent of any crime and I wish to help in any way I can in bringing the true perpetrator of this horrid deed to justice.'

Knight gave a small nod so I continued.

'Can you tell me how your wife came to attend Mr Miracle's drawing class?'

Knight thought for a moment. 'I took some convincing, Mr Box, I don't mind telling you.' He placed his hands on the knob of his stick, leaning forward like a minister at his lectern. 'I believe a woman's place is at her husband's side. However, amongst a lady's accomplishments a little music, a little French a little . . . *drawing* are pleasant.'

'You seem to imagine your wife was in training to become a provincial governess.'

'I sought merely to protect her,' he bristled. 'Her . . . disfigure-ment, you understand. She could not have stood the mocking voices, the averted glances . . .'

'But finally you gave into a little, what shall we call it, female emancipation?'

Knight regarded me coldly. 'She was most insistent. I was sur-prised, I admit. She had never shown any facility in drawing. But, I thought that, after all, the change would do her good.' He closed his eyes. 'How foolish I was. But there is . . . there *was* . . . a streak of obstinacy in her that I made it my business to stamp out. It was a consequence of the unhealthy amount of freedom she was granted by her first husband.'

I cocked my head. 'Her *first* husband?'

'A free-thinker. It was quite a blessing for her that he passed away.'

I sighed heavily. 'As far as I can see, Mr Knight, there is noth-ing to suggest that your wife didn't simply leave Miracle's studio a short time after *you* left *her*.'

'And went where?'

'Wherever you prevented her from going in the past.'

Knight's pallid features coloured. 'What the devil are you sug-gesting?'

I waved a placating hand. 'Merely thinking aloud. Now, would it be possible – I understand how delicate must be your feelings just now – could you tell me how your wife came by her injuries?'

'The police tell me that . . . *rats* had –'

'No, no. Her old injuries.'

The banker's face was impassive. 'Fire.'

'In her younger days?'

'Yes. I believe she was seven- or eight-and-twenty at the time.'

'You did not know her then?'

'Gracious, no. We were married two or three years later. In fact, our anniversary is fast approaching.'

He fumbled in his waistcoat for a moment and produced a

small parcel of tissue paper. Spreading it out on the table before him, he revealed a pair of modestly bejewelled earrings.

'These were to have been my gift. I suppose I will be able to claim back the expense.'

He sniffed lightly and replaced them in his pocket.

I persevered. 'How did you meet?'

'When her previous husband died abroad, my firm sent me to advise her on financial affairs. We became . . . attached. One day, I asked her to marry me, and she agreed. It was a very suitable arrangement.'

I wondered whether he made bank-loans sound as appealing.

I returned home and was astonished to find Delilah waiting in a brougham outside. 'Hevening, sir. Compliments of Mr Reynolds, sir. 'E's 'eard abart Mr Miracle's spot ho' bovver, sir, and wonders hif 'e can be hof hany 'elp.'

'Most kind of him. How lovely to see you restored to health, Delilah. You did give us a turn the other day, you know.'

She clambered from the vehicle as I opened the door of Number Nine. 'Nah. Hit's well known that hi'm himmortal, sir,' she chuckled throatily. 'Unless you cut horf me 'ead and stick ha pike through me 'eart hi'll be 'ere for ha few years yet.'

We stepped inside then, a moment later, I pulled up sharply as Delilah's great thick arm suddenly barred my way. I had the door of the drawing room half open. Something was awry.

'What is it?' I whispered, eyes flashing from side to side.

Delilah stooped to pick up a cardboard tube that was lying on the cork-matting of the hallway floor. One end of it was curiously ragged, as though chewed open.

She stepped in front of me and then beckoned as we made our way silently into the room.

I stopped dead. Lying in a heap, surrounded by letters, was the body of a uniformed postman – stopped dead in a more literal fashion.

'Cor! Look hat 'is bloody face!' gasped Delilah. The skin of his face was hideously inflamed and swollen and almost as black as his boots. 'You reckon the bobby next door let 'im hin?'

I nodded. 'Must have. I was expecting something. Yes. That must be it.'

Clutched in the postman's hands – which were screwed up like rusted keys – was a squarish, brown-paper parcel. 'Get back!' I said, dropping to one knee to examine the body. 'Ah!'

There were two puncture wounds in the right wrist, the skin around them a vile, blistered mess.

'He's been bitten by something,' I whispered.

Delilah looked down at the dead man. 'Come hin this tube, you reckon?' Folding her arms, Delilah looked uneasily around the darkened room. 'Whatever hit was,' she breathed, 'his probably still hin 'ere.'

'Indubitably.'

I glanced down at the Turkey carpet. In the gloom, every shape took on a twisted serpentine form.

'Stay exactly where you are, Delilah,' I murmured. 'I'm going to cross the room and open the curtains. Then we'll get a clearer look at this thing –'

'Stay still, sir! For the love hof God, stay still!' Delilah gasped in genuine horror.

I needed no urging for I could feel a soft, appallingly ticklish movement on my trouser leg. Rooted to the spot, I managed to swivel my gaze around to get a glimpse of the creature, but in the shadows I could make out little more than a spiny shape perhaps a foot in length. It was moving inexorably up my calf.

'What shall hi do?' hissed Delilah.

I rolled my eyes. 'Get the blasted thing off me!'

Shuddering involuntarily, I struggled not to cry out as the creature undulated again and, with its horrible, creeping motion, reached my thigh.

'Light!' I whispered.

Nodding, Delilah crossed clumsily to the window and carefully raised the blinds. Milky light flooded the room.

Delilah's cry of disgust did little to assuage my fears.

I risked a look down. Clamped (there is no other word for it) to my leg was the most disgusting animal I have ever laid eyes upon. Yellowy-black in colour it was somewhere between a scorpion and a centipede, its thick carapace glinting dully like amber beads on a string. Its head – upon which were mounted the vicious pair of pincers that had undoubtedly done for the postman – was moving slowly from side to side in a ghastly, skin-crawling oscillation.

'What his it?' cried Delilah.

'Don't know! Don't care!' I managed to gurgle from between compressed lips. 'We have one advantage on our side though.'

'What's that?'

I peered for a longer moment at the insect-like abomination. Every part of me thrilled with horror at its touch. It was all I could do to stop myself from grabbing the thing and wrenching it from me.

'I think it's blind,' I hissed. 'Must avoid . . . agitating it.'

Delilah nodded slowly. 'Where's your cane? Hi could knock hit off.'

'No!' I swallowed hard, trying not to let my agitation show. 'It'll bite before you could get to it, you dolt!' The creature moved again, its swaying legs pattering hideously against the fabric of my suit.

'Come over here,' I said carefully. Delilah obeyed. 'Now . . . stand behind me . . .'

Beads of salty sweat were puddling in my eyebrows.

Delilah assumed the position, as it were, standing about ten inches behind me.

'Now what?' she said in a high, dry voice.

'Now you must take down my trousers.'

'Heh?'

I tried to steady my breathing. The creature slid further up my leg until it was practically nestling in my groin. 'Don't argue, woman,' I said at last. 'Reach around and unbutton my braces. One . . . at . . . a . . . time.'

She did as she was bidden. Her right hand reached out and slid around my waist, under the waistband of my trousers and found the first button. Her thick, ruddy hands were shaking as she tried to manoeuvre the loop of the braces from around the button.

Without a sound, she brought her left hand to bear on the problem and, after much agonizing fumbling, managed to release first one loop then the next. My trousers sagged slightly.

'Must keep them up!' I croaked. 'If they fall too soon, those fangs will be sunk in me in seconds!'

'Righto,' breathed Delilah. 'Moving to the hother side now. Can you –?'

I could. I moved my own hand down with agonizing slowness and grasped the waistband to keep the trousers taut.

Delilah was already at work on the left-hand braces. The loop slid gently from one, the other was proving more difficult.

'This one's ha bugger,' she muttered. 'Bleeding Tailoring Department and their fiddly ways. Have to go carefully hor else –'

My heart-rate accelerated sickeningly as the second button popped from its stitching with a loud snap and my trousers drooped distinctly.

The insect's head shifted and cocked almost as though it were listening. Its feelers paused in their feeling.

Delilah had moved her attention to the back buttons but I could see from the creature's activity that we had no time for such details.

'It's going to strike!' I screamed. 'Quickly, Delilah. On my word, pull them down and swamp the bloody thing!'

I seemed to draw back from my own flesh as I watched the monster's gleaming head rise, its razor-like pincers juddering and dripping . . .

'Now, Delilah, now!' I cried.

With amazing speed, Delilah whipped down my trousers and wrapped them around the insect as she dragged them to my feet. Wasting not one moment, she stamped her boot heel down hard and repeatedly on the dreadful lump in the material. I winced, despite myself.

A moment later, I had my revolver from my coat and loosed off a round between my own feet. Only as the smoke was rising from the ghastly sticky ooze did I feel able to drag the remains of my trousers over my shoes and hurl them into the corner.

A second attempt on my life! It seemed that someone was absolutely determined to prevent me getting to the heart of this baffling matter. But who?

I set Delilah to work packing my trunk and collapsed into an armchair with a glass of brandy, contemplating mortality. As the invaluable Domestic clumped about upstairs, I sifted through the less lethal portions of my correspondence. I opened the parcel and found inside, as expected, an old book, its pages brittle with age and a square of paper that read *BAIT! Appointment with Quibble – Seven-thirty. 387 Via San Fontanella. M*

Friend Miracle had not let me down. Despite being banged up he seemed still able to pull any amount of strings. He had fixed up an appointment for me with the elusive Professor Quibble and now I had something to entice the Professor into imparting secrets. I turned the book over and the soft binding flashed in the firelight.

Also in the unfortunate postman's pile was a delicately scented note from the divine Miss Bella Pok. I held it to my face and grinned like a love-struck schoolboy. It ran:

Good-bye, devilish Mr Box. Until we meet again.

I placed the note carefully amongst my shirts. The thought of returning to one such as Bella was enough to sustain me through any danger. For now, I had to try to wrap up this Miracle business as expeditiously as possible. I could not afford to miss my appointment in Naples with Quibble. I was unlikely to get a second chance.

X

WHAT KITTY BACKLASH HAD TO TELL

N hour later, Inspector Flush's fat face beamed cheerfully at me from the other side of his desk.

We were in the brown office he called home. There was a little spirit burner in the corner and a quantity of tinned food that led me to believe the inspector kept unsociable hours. Then I noticed a whitish band of flesh on his finger where once a ring must have been. Perhaps Mrs Flush had recently quit the scene.

I had called at the Yard, fully expecting to be fobbed off by some flunky in a helmet, only to find the man himself still at his post, though without a collar and nursing what I think was a mug of brandy.

'Don't you see,' I said. 'It's just as feasible to imagine poor Mrs Knight leaving the Mechanical Institute and being murdered elsewhere as it is Christopher Miracle knocking off the wretched woman in a lavatory!'

Flush made a helpless gesture. 'Mr Miracle is unable to provide us with a witness for his activities between half-past nine and ten o'clock. He could have strangled her and left her in the convenience until later.'

'And carried on an entire class without turning a hair?'

'Some killers are exceptionally cool.'

I gave an exasperated groan. 'But where's the motive, man!'

Flush gave a satisfied smile and produced a long, cream-coloured envelope from his coat. He held it before me like a lure.

'What's this?' I asked.

'It's a copy of Mrs Knight's will. Amongst numerous small bequests is the sum of five hundred pounds to her dedicated art-master, Mr Christopher Miracle.'

'What? Well, what of it? Miracle's filthy rich.'

'Many have killed for less, sir.'

I took the envelope from him and examined the contents. 'Hmm. By that argument, it could look blacker against the husband.'

'The husband?'

'Yes. She leaves him the sum of two thousand pounds, an annuity from her previous husband which ... it seems ... he was unable to control during her life-time.'

'Mr Knight was seen to drive away from the Mechanical Institute.'

'Then he could have employed someone to do it for him.'

'Mr Box –'

'You've met the man, Flush. Even if money wasn't the motive, it's obvious he disapproved of his wife having any kind of social life. When she began to grow more confident and independent he found he couldn't tolerate it and strangled her!'

Flush gave me a hard look. 'You're running away with yourself, sir. What about the glove?'

I waved my hand impatiently. 'Easy enough to steal a lady's glove! And where did this blood come from? The coroner says she was strangled, I believe.'

Flush seemed to consider this for a moment. 'Well, well. I'll bear your theories in mind, sir. Now, if you don't mind, I have rather a lot to be getting on with. I'm afraid this isn't the only case I have on hand.'

I was shown out into a dreary corridor. I thrust my hands into my pockets and walked disconsolately towards the exit, glancing half-heartedly at the walls, scarcely taking in the bills tacked to cork boards, the ugly illustrations of wanted felons, the sooty smears that marked the walls above the cracked gas-lamps. I was utterly stumped as to my next move. It was imperative I get to Naples forthwith, yet how could I leave Miracle in such peril? Would I have to put myself further into Joshua Reynolds's debt by asking him to use his influence? My musings were suddenly interrupted.

'Oh Lor!' came a hoarse shriek. 'Don't 'urt me! Don't 'urt me, please!'

I turned to the left to see a constable 'escorting' a woman from the premises. She appeared to be little more than a heap of dirty electric blue skirts, a grisly-looking drudge, hair all askew.

'You can't just sling me art!'

'You just watch me,' said the policeman.

'But what about me friend?'

The policeman pushed open the door and warm air rolled inside. 'Cor, you're sweating gin, woman! I told you. We got more important things to do than go chasing after your imaginary pals. Now, gertcha!'

He slung the creature through the doorway. As the door swung back, I just caught her croaking call. ''E done 'er in, I know that! That miracle man!'

My ears pricked up and I walked swiftly to the door, which the constable held open for me.

'Evening, sir.'

I gave him a nod and then walked out into the night.

The woman was stumbling to her feet on the steps of the station.

'Forgive me, my dear,' I said, offering my arm. 'Would you like some help?'

She shot me a suspicious glance, then grabbed at my sleeve and hauled herself up.

'We haven't been introduced.' I smiled. 'Lucifer Box.'

'Kitty,' she said, swallowing nervously. 'Kitty Backlash.'

'I couldn't help overhearing you. Something about a miracle?'

She nodded feverishly. 'It's that Mr Miracle. I read the story in the papers. 'E done 'er in!'

'Mrs Knight?'

'No! Mrs Frenzy!'

'Who?'

What was this? *Two* murders poor Miracle was fingered for?

Kitty Backlash blew air noisily from between her lips, making an unpleasantly blubbery sound. 'Couldn't stand us a drink, could you, sir? It's a ruddy long and strange tale I 'ave to tell and I've been tramping 'alfway across town today.'

'Of course. Come on.'

We found a suitably bright and rowdy pub only a street away. I lined up two glasses of gin for my guest, just enough to show I could be generous but also to ensure I got her story while she was still sober.

'Now, Miss Backlash,' I said, sitting down next to her in a corner seat. 'Pray continue.'

She sank a draught of gin and rubbed at her face with a shaking hand.

'It's 'ard to think straight, sir. Honest it is. But I'll start at the start, if you takes me meaning.'

I watched her closely, her ugly face reflecting back even uglier in the shining mirrors of the pub.

'My friend, then, is called Abigail Frenzy. She's a parlour-maid, or was. Worked for a foreign gent over Barnes way. Anyway, one day she says to me, Kitty, I've come into some good fortune. I says, ain't you a maid no more? And she laughs – I've got it easy now. A fiver just for sitting about and scribbling all day.'

I sat up at this. 'What did she mean by that?'

Kitty Backlash scratched at her chin. 'Well, I'll tell you, sir. Seems her employer comes up to her one day, months back and says how would she like to earn proper money? Now Abigail's no slut and I'm sure she thought the gentleman had improper notions, even though she ain't no spring chick, her face must've been a picture, but he says, no, it's nothing like that. Fact is, there's a lady he's sweet on but her 'usband's a terrible brute and he can never get near 'er. Only time she's left on 'er own is when she goes to an art lesson down in Chelsea.'

I leant forward, all attention. 'What is the name of your friend's employer?'

'Don't recall the name. *Foreign*. Great big chap. Eye-talian.'

'Is he, by George?' A little shiver ran through me.

Kitty Backlash drained her second glass of gin. 'Well, anyways,

I'll give you a fiver a week, he says, if you'll only sw
this lady for an hour or two. She says, well, is she n
otherwise people is going to notice and he smiles anc
worry because the poor soul's all hidden behind a veil
of terrible burns she got when she was a gel.'

'And what did your friend Abigail say to this curious
'At first she was having none of it, but then she got to
what a lot of money it was for so little a thing. It's always
lucre, sir, and that's a fact.'

'I have heard it said. Go on.'

'Well, sir, she went ahead with it. Her master 'ad it all w
out. The lady in question would be dropped off by 'er 'usband
always wore the same violet dress and veil. Soon as she was ins
she went to the lavs – pardon me for speaking so, sir – and ou
the other lav would come my friend Abigail in another dress j
like 'ers. One in, one out.'

'Like figures on a weather-house,' I said quietly.

'Yes, sir! Just like the pair on them little houses. Abigail'd go in
and 'ave 'er lesson and the lady'd sneak away for an hour or two
with her lover.'

'Miss Backlash,' I said. 'I cannot tell you how pleased I am to
have met you. Now, tell me slowly, what happened next.'

The crone took a big breath and held out her empty glass.
'Difficult to talk, so parched I'm gasping!'

'All the grog you want, just go on with your fascinating story.'

'Couple of weeks back, she came to see me and poured out the
'ole tale. Fact is, she was nervous. She thought Mr Miracle was
getting suspicious, on account of her being no good at drawing.
Then, just this week – poof! – she vanished.'

'Did you not go to the house where she worked?'

'Yes, sir! But the foreign gent's leaving, they're shutting up the
place and wouldn't give me the time of day. I hung about the
studio 'oping to see Mr Miracle. Thought maybe he knew where
Abigail'd got to. Then I 'eard he'd been arrested for murder and I

idn't know what to do and I went to the coppers but they don't
ant to listen either – oh, sir!'

'All right,' I soothed. 'All right. Landlord! Another two gins
here! Tell me, Kitty, did your friend have any . . . distinguishing
marks on her person?'

There's nothing quite like a visit to a police mortuary to take the
spring out of one's step.

The white tiles of the long, low structure glistened wetly in the
gas-light as Inspector Flush led me inside. The room housed three
or four long tables, their surfaces mottled with unpleasant stains
like a butcher's chopping block. Only one, the furthest from the
open door, was occupied.

'Now look here, Mr Box,' said the policeman in a grumbling
baritone. 'We can't go exhibiting the dear departed to all and
sundry just 'cos of some theory or other. Until we lay our hands on
who did in Mrs Knight –'

'The woman over there, Inspector,' I said quietly, 'is not Mrs
Midsomer Knight.'

That did the trick.

''Er 'usband identified her,' he protested.

'Identified a bloated corpse with its face eaten – or cut – away.'

Flush scratched his ear and shook his head. 'A 'usband would
know 'is own missus.'

'Perhaps not. I didn't enquire as to details, of course, but I got
the distinct impression that *relations* had in all probability never
occurred between the Knights.'

Flush did not look pleased. 'Did you now? Been doing a little
sleuthing have you?'

I slammed my hand on to the stained slab and immediately
regretted it. My hands are delicate and shouldn't be trifled with.
'Damn it, Flush! This is important! If I'm right you have a different murdered woman in here.'

'And who might that be?'

'A Miss Abigail Frenzy.'

'Who?'

'I'll explain everything if you'll just let me see the body,' I said exasperatedly.

Flush sighed. 'Very well. But if this is some kind of prank I'll have your bloody vitals, Mr Box.'

'Lights and lungs, my dear chap, if you want them. Shall we get on?'

'I hope you ain't squeamish.'

Now I have always wondered how one gets into undertaking as a profession. Who, other than chaps who get some sort of morbid thrill from it, would want to do such a thing? Like choirmasters and their desire to improve young boys, one always suspects a sinister motive.

So it was that a goggle-eyed, deeply suspicious fellow with a thatch of ginger hair was the one who pulled back the sheet from the faceless corpse with all the gusto of a stage conjuror.

I gave him a look that told him not to enjoy himself too much and he skulked away to join a very green-looking Flush.

The body was that of a woman of about forty-five. Her torso was stained purple (by the wet dress I realized at once) and her rather fine hair matted and weed-clogged. Vermin – or a blunt blade – had indeed been busy on her face for it was little more than a gory hole. This entire case seemed to be a study in wet reds and blacks.

I stooped to examine the neck, which was livid with the bruises of the strangler's hands then turned the corpse's head slightly. It made a horrible stiff clicking sound like a bag of coral being smashed against a wall.

'You have a lens?' I barked at the goggle-eyed assistant.

He produced one. I took it and stooped to examine the ears of the corpse. 'You see?'

Flush took the lens and peered through it. 'See what?'

'The lobes are not pierced for rings.'

'So?'

'*Unlike* those of Mrs Knight,' I cried triumphantly.

'How the devil –'

'I took the liberty of having a little chat with her charming husband. He had recently purchased a pair of earrings as an anniversary present.'

Flush blushed. I pressed on.

'Whoever killed this woman was careful to destroy her face so that we would think it to be the body of Mrs Knight.'

'What? Wait,' pleaded Flush. 'What is all this? Who is this Abigail Frenzy?'

I tapped the lens against my chin. 'The point is, if this is the substitute, then where is Mrs Knight?'

I drew the sheet back over the horror on the morgue slab.

'Perhaps she is still alive!' I announced, almost to myself. 'Flush, if you will come with me to the Swan With Two Necks around the corner I will introduce you to a very interesting lady by name of Kitty Backlash. After that, I trust you will release Mr Christopher Miracle without delay!'

The upshot was that Mr Knight was sent for and Miss Kitty Backlash interviewed. Rather pleased at my virtuoso display, I waited in Flush's office for Delilah to arrive in the brougham. Kitty had given me the address of her missing friend's foreign employer. Now all I had to do was nip down there and collar him before he disappeared. Exactly who he was, I could not be absolutely certain, but suspicions were forming. Which 'great big Eye-talian' with a connection to Miracle had I recently encountered who was just preparing to shut up his house and leave for the Continent? After apprehending the Duce I felt confident I could leave this curious case in Joshua Reynolds's capable little hands while I pursued the business of the missing professors.

Brooding on this, I thumbed through Mrs Knight's particulars once more. Here was the account of the trip to Chelsea by the grim husband. Here was the last will and testament showing the annuity from the *first* husband.

'A free-thinker,' Mr Knight had said.

I glanced thoughtfully at the reams of print.

Then I saw it.

I read the words over four times before I sank back into the chair, my blood running cold.

In faded black ink was the name of Mrs Knight's first husband. The other man in the photograph of the Cambridge Four!

Maxwell Morraine.

XI

THE LIBRARY OF EMMANUEL QUIBBLE

LL the nice girls love a sailor. That they also like secret servicemen is fortunate as yours truly is no Jack tar. Some days later, while my fellow passengers took in the broad curve of Naples harbour on the prow of SS *Mandragora*, I was lying in my cabin two decks below, head wrapped in a wet towel, becoming intimate with the porcelain of the lavatory bowl.

There was a knock at the slatted wooden door and some flunky entered.

'Mr Box, sir?'

'Mmmhhmm?'

'We're here, sir. Naples, sir. Arrived safely and come to tell you, as instructed.'

'Hhhuunnhhh!'

'You just take your time, sir. I'll arrange transportation.'

The door closed behind him.

Like some valetudinarian, I was carried from my cabin and hurried into a carriage scarcely noticing my surroundings at all as my stomach continued to lurch and my head to spin in defiance of having reached terra firma. I planted

a 'kerchief to my mouth – the stink of the dockside hitting me at once – and was carried the short distance to my hotel.

A sulphurous yellow building loomed before me and I caught snatched glimpses of the great hot sun and the sapphire of the sky before being ushered into the lobby. For a long moment I stood, swaying on my feet in the sudden darkness, while the concierge attended to the details but soon I was being helped into the cool lift and ferried up, up to the sanctuary of my room.

The page unlocked the door and I stumbled past him, collapsing gratefully on to the bed. As I slipped into blissful sleep, I saw him lowering the blinds over the windows and the great blocks of blinding yellow light were shut out.

Sleep came and more sleep.

I dreamt of burst-open coffins and straw men staggering from within them, of a coach-chase through the landscape paintings on Miracle's walls and of a monstrous regiment of veiled women, unwinding the stained bandages which encircled their heads in some horrid Salome-like bacchanalia.

Blinking awake what seemed like months later I found the room around me cool and dark. One of the veiled women seemed to have followed me through from my dreams, her shroud-like garments fluttering in the breeze, until I sat up on the bed and made sense of the curtains.

Feeling hugely better and absolutely ravenous, I raised the blinds and gazed out on the harbour below. Warm air as fragrant as incense washed over me. The weather − foul for most of the crossing − had cleared, revealing the most glorious blue sky and a strong, healthy sun. The wide road before my hotel was crowded with carriages and strolling couples, white parasols flaring painfully in the light. Close by loomed the ugly Castell dell'Ovo and from its rocky foundations skinny brown fisher-boys, as slippery as eels, were diving into the foam.

Dominating all, naturally enough, was the great volcano of Vesuvius, a fantastic hazy blue shape, its lower slopes verdantly fertile, its summit betraying only the faintest wisp of smoke, like a signal from the Vatican chimney.

Shading my eyes against the glare and breathing deeply, I flipped my watch from my waistcoat pocket and smiled in genuine contentment. I had a noon appointment with Cretaceous Unmann, giving me just enough time to bathe and change. I unpacked and set out my hairbrushes and cologne on the dresser. For sentimental reasons I had brought with me the spelter lancer that Bella had drawn on that memorable day. It would serve to remind me of that lovely personage until this curious case was over and I could return to her side.

I always think best in the bath. With the steam drifting about my ears, I mulled over recent events. As you may have guessed, dear reader, the Duce Tiepolo had indeed been the employer of Miss Kitty Backlash and behind the whole substitution scheme.

But Inspector Flush's men had found Tiepolo's house shuttered and empty. The whole business might have been entirely unconnected to this affair of the professors were it not for the fact that Mrs Knight had once been married to Maxwell Morraine. But how the devil was I to unravel this tangled skein?

A couple of hours later, resplendent in a new dove-grey suit, I descended and launched myself upon old Napoli.

The fresh sea air and the sun on my face were like a tonic after the foetid stink of London and I took my time strolling through the teeming city, passing the great swooping crescent of Bianchi's church before settling down at a table at the Café Gambrinus, a gorgeous beacon of extravagance to which I had become extremely attached on my previous visit. Ah, but what a callow youth I'd been in those days! I recalled the dazzling mirrored interior, fancy cakes and bitter black coffee, Guy de Maupassant arguing over his bill and, of course, the foiling of an attempted assassination of the Prince of Wales by means of a poisoned meringue that had been one of my first triumphs.

The café overlooked the opera house and a square that thrilled with bustling life. A grinning *gelati*-seller was peddling water-ices a few feet from me, his mouth packed with broken brown teeth. Filthy urchins, laughing hysterically and as bothersome as mosquitoes were pestering visitors almost to the point of distraction. The aria in rehearsal at the Opera House soared over all, a wonderful baritone that somehow blended perfectly with the smell of fresh rolls and coffee.

I took out the old book that Miracle had sent me as a lure for Professor Quibble and had just ordered a *pressé* from a fat waiter in a crisp white apron when Unmann arrived. He greeted me, stumbling over a chair and giving me a handshake as weak as a baby's. Unmann was what you might call a Natural Bland.

'Mr Box, I am so glad to see you! Joshua Reynolds wired to say you were on your way. Hot on the trail of Poop's killer, I trust?'

'Perhaps. Have you traced that notepaper?'

'Yes. "K to V.C." was written on the rather good stationery of the Vesuvio Hotel.'

'But you have a residence in the city – what was Poop doing in there?'

Unmann shrugged. 'No idea. Keeping an eye on someone, perhaps?' He rubbed his hands together excitedly. 'But you must let me be your guide here, Mr Box! I can use every scintilla of my local knowledge . . .'

'Your contacts will be essential, Unmann,' I said, sipping my *pressé*. 'I'm interested in the activities of a woman and her husband who lived here back in the seventies.'

'I see.' He took out a pocket book and pencil. 'Their names?'

'Mr and Mrs Maxwell Morraine.'

He wrote the names down with great care. 'Does this have a bearing on the death of Poop?'

'I'm not sure yet. I think, though, that whoever did for him may well be on my trail.'

'Good Lord!'

'There have been two attempts on my life,' I said with studied casualness. I gave him a quick sketch of the chase by coach that had terminated in the cemetery and the incident of the venomous centipede. I omitted the attack in the steam-rooms by Pugg.

'At first I thought them unrelated to this business but I'm not so sure now. They were not merely vulgar attacks and I'm certain they will try again, this time with even greater cunning. You too must be prepared for the gravest danger.' I set my jaw firmly.

'Great Scott,' breathed Unmann.

The poor sap swallowed such stoic babble whole. I hoped it would keep the tick out of my way. He was, of course, the kind of dependable idiot upon whom the Diplomatic is founded but, *really*, was this the best they could do these days? If the king had any inkling of the state of things he'd probably pop *another* button off his waistcoat.

'Also, I need to know if someone called the Duce Tiepolo has recently re-entered the country.'

Unmann paused in his scribbling. 'Illicitly?'

'I should think so. The new regime chucked him out. He has some curious connection to the business in hand.'

I snapped my fingers and ordered Unmann a cup of coffee. When it came he drank it in one swift gulp.

'Finally,' I continued, 'I want whatever information you can dig up about the firm of Thomas Bowler, undertaker of London and Naples.'

Unmann nodded, scratching hurriedly in his pocket-book.

'Will you stay for lunch?' I offered, stomach rumbling.

'Can't, I'm afraid,' he jabbered. 'Office in a frightful mess. Got all old Jocelyn's papers to sort through. Quite big shoes to fill. Now I'll get on to these names just as soon as I can, Mr Box. I'll cable the Santa Lucia if there's any news. Got to dash –' He glanced down at Poop's book. 'Holiday reading, eh? Might I ask –?'

'You may not. *Most* secret.' I flashed him my wide smile. 'Good day to you.'

With a nod, Unmann was gone. At length, I ordered scrambled eggs and spiced sausage and turned my attention to the book. It was some kind of novel from what I could glean. And it must be precious indeed if it were to whet the appetite of the famous Sir Emmanuel Quibble.

The venerable scholar had always been, according to my researches, an exceptionally gifted man. He had shown extraordinary facility for music and the arts before turning his mind towards scientific matters at the ripe old age of seven after conducting a remarkable experiment with a song thrush and a vacuum tube. Tragically, only a few years later, he had been thrown from a gelding, sustaining a spinal injury that kept him confined, forever after, to a wheeled-chair. Ill-health had turned into a kind of mania and now he was said to positively thrive on his allergic reaction to the nineteenth (no, I keep forgetting, the *twentieth*) century. In recent years the old fellow had withdrawn entirely from the world, moving to Italy and taking solace in his unrivalled library of arcane literature. Now I was being granted the rare privilege of entry to this inner sanctum. What would I find there?

I sat for a while with eyes closed, listening to the muffled aria that thrilled through the sunshine. How I loved Italy! The heat assuaged by salty air, bright with dragon-flies humming over starched white tablecloths. I caught sight of a woman a few tables from me. She had her back to me and I took the opportunity to drink in the details of her exquisite carriage.

She wore a splendid canary-yellow creation with a high, transparent collar, tight against her throat and her hair was hidden beneath the brim of a huge oval hat. Of course, there are few things in life more deceptive than a person's back view. How many times have you yourself spotted someone at the theatre or on the underground whose magnificent bearing and gorgeous, swan-like neck have lured you into a state of unconditional lust? Only to discover, as they bend to read, to adjust a shoe or step off the staircase, that they have a face like a Transylvanian fish-wife.

I ordered tea with lemon and sat with my chin on my hand, surveying the lovely, graceful woman before me who would, any moment now, turn and reveal herself to be a gorgon.

The woman seemed to be listening to the aria as well. Her head was cocked attentively. I imagined she was smiling. At last she shifted in her seat and the sunshine illumined her face.

My teacup clattered on to its saucer.

The woman was Bella Pok.

I rose and, raising my hat, stepped into her line of sight. Shading her eyes, she smiled sweetly at me as though we had simply run into one another at the Café Royal.

'Lucifer!' she cried. 'I'm so delighted. I had anticipated traipsing all over Naples to find you and yet here you are, large as life.'

She gestured to a chair and I sank into it. 'I don't suppose this is a coincidence?'

'Not a bit,' she said with a grin. 'You really can't expect a girl to return to her drab little existence after becoming involved in Mr Miracle's adventure! Whatever's going on, I yearn to be part of it. Please say you'll have me!'

Which is the sort of invitation one longs to hear from such as Mademoiselle Pok.

I shook my head, however. 'There is nothing going on. As I told you, I have business here in Naples which I hope to combine with a little sketching. You know it is vital for we daubers to refresh ourselves now and then.'

She looked hard at me.

'Don't be so disappointing,' she said.

I sighed. 'I'm afraid I must escort you back to your hotel, Miss Pok,' I said, 'and then put you on the first boat back to England.'

'You certainly shan't put *me* anywhere.'

'Bella –'

'I want to be at your side, Lucifer!'

'On no account!' I snapped.

'But if there's nothing to fear, then why ever not? Am I such an embarrassment?'

'Of course not.'

'Well then.'

She sighed and sat back in her chair, the brim of her hat eclipsing the dazzling disc of the sun. 'Whatever can I do to persuade you?'

Well, she didn't have to do much in the end. Fact is, I was fearfully besotted with her and her boldness in following me to Naples had only endeared her more to me. Over a kir or three, she cajoled and argued until all I could think of was the glow of her lovely face and the wide, inviting mouth I so longed to kiss.

'Very well,' I said at last. 'If you mean to stay then you are

welcome. But this is no holiday for me. You must excuse me if I
have to . . . dash off at the most inopportune moments.'

'Of course.'

'May I see you to your hotel?'

She was staying, appropriately enough, at the Vesuvio. We made
an appointment to meet there the next day and I walked back to
the Santa Lucia, *whistling* if you don't mind.

Well, she would certainly help take my mind off the business in
hand. The danger was that she would do so too effectively. I had
work to do in Naples. This was not a honeymoon.

After dressing for dinner I hailed a cab and barked out
Quibble's address in my ever-so-good Italian. I am, naturally, a
master of languages. I have, in addition to robust Eye-tie, a little
French, a little German and some particularly filthy Latin. I am
also quite good at American.

Stooping to conquer with a '*Pronto!*', I was ferried away up the
steep slopes of the old city towards Capodimonte.

The weather had deteriorated into a stinker of an evening.
Sweaty mist hung in great miasmic wreaths around the jumble of
crumbling stucco, my carriage cutting a coffin-shaped swathe
through it as we climbed ever higher. The humidity was so thick
that the traffic seemed scarcely to move at all. I could hear the soft
clop of horseshoes on the cobbles, muffled by the atmosphere as
though for a funeral.

As we ascended the mountain, the mist cleared slightly to reveal
verdant countryside thick with dark olive groves until, at last, the
carriage drew to a halt. Six or seven lonely cottages clustered
around the edifice of a mansion like mournful piglets around a
long-dead sow.

It must have been a grim place at the best of times, but on an
oppressive evening like this one, I felt positively mournful as I
bid the driver wait and made my way up the weed-throttled
gravel to the gates. Thick creepers were enmeshed in every part
of the ironwork, as though a mob trying to get in had been

turned, by some spell, into a jungle of rain-rotted vegetation.

I pulled at the bell and ran a finger under my stiff collar.

Presently, the gates juddered open, squealing as they were hauled over ground thick with a sediment of dead leaves.

'Good evening,' I said to the ancient butler who emerged around the edge of the gate.

'Good evening, sir. Mr Box, is it? Sir Emmanuel is expecting you, sir.'

'You're English?'

'Naturally, sir. As are the entire staff. My name is Stint. Might I advise you to loosen your garments, sir?'

'Beg pardon?'

'It is a trifle warm within, sir,' he wheezed.

He was like a column of smoke in livery. Pale eyes, pale face, wispy white hair and whiskers. To my very great surprise he appeared to be shirt-less beneath his threadbare uniform.

Stint kicked the front door to open it, so swollen was the woodwork. Once inside, he ushered me down a stifling corridor, the once-bright blooms of its wallpaper faded into bleak greys. Piled high in heaps all along the walls, their cloth bindings waxy with age, were hundreds of books.

'It's very . . . um . . . dark, Stint,' I said at last, removing my coat.

'No lamps, sir.' He shook his white head mournfully. 'Sir Emmanuel does not care for the light, you see. I have been trying to persuade him as to the virtues of the electricity. But that, as they say, will be the day.'

The room I now entered was fat with books. They lined the walls, covered the floor, hung around in tottering heaps in the shadowed corners. The combined mass of ruddy old leather and faded gilt should have lent the room a jolly air, but the fire blazing in the hearth made the place like a hot-house.

The firelight illuminated the figure of Emmanuel Quibble, swathed in black like some behemothal spider. The impression was reinforced by a number of mahogany reading-stands that

projected from his chair on telescopic appendages thus allowing him to consult as many as eight or nine volumes at any one time.

He wheeled himself forward with one china-blue hand. The other, inevitably, clutched a book over his blanket-covered lap. He was probably sixty-odd yet contrived to look twice that. What little hair he had was of an almost translucent blond, as though old straw had been carelessly applied to his scalp with gum. Forever in the habit of licking his lips, an angry red halo had developed around them and his eyes were nigh on invisible behind a pair of ancient, filthy, thickly lensed pince-nez.

Chuckling at the sight of me, he held out his hand and I gingerly gripped the perished-apple knuckles.

'Sir Emmanuel,' I cooed. 'It is indeed an honour.'

'Of course it is! Lucifer Box, eh? Can't say I've heard of you. You're some sort of painter, I gather. I do not normally grant interviews but I was told you had something that might interest me,' he said, adjusting his spectacles. 'Well, pray be seated. Do not mind those volumes. Move them along. There is a very pretty space there by Bleasdale's *Tales of Surgical Misadventure*. There now!'

I squeezed myself into a chair by the roaring fire.

'Are you cold?' he asked, suddenly.

I was already perspiring horribly. 'Quite comfortable, thank you.'

Quibble shook his head mournfully. 'It is like a tomb in here. I can never get warm. The servants complain that I stifle them but how can they object to a fire in December!'

'It is July, sir,' I said carefully.

'Is it?' He began a high cackling sound, exposing tiny peg-like teeth. 'Perhaps I am too cold-blooded. My doctors tell me I have a thin hide.'

I smiled indulgently. 'I wonder you don't have yourself dust-jacketed.'

'What's that?' He cupped a withered hand around his ear.

'You ought to equip yourself with a dust-jacket, Sir Emmanuel,' I shouted. 'Like one of your famous collection.'

He liked that and cackled some more. 'Capital idea! I know just the men for the job. Grindrod and Spicer of Camden Town. Let me see. Hmm.' He extended his stick-like arms before him and looked them up and down as though contemplating the measurement of a suit. 'Yes, blue card with calf-skin end-boards. I think I should go very well just above your head, Mr Box, between *Patterson's Pathology of the Goitre* and *Rabelaisianism*. Can I tempt you with a Madeira? No? Then perhaps we shall eat.'

He rang a little glass bell. I lifted my Gladstone and took out the book that Miracle had sent me. Quibble eyed it hungrily.

'What is it? Let me see!'

I lifted the volume and held it up to the firelight. The title glinted like gold in a stream.

Quibble let out a little cry and wheeled himself towards me with feverish speed.

'It isn't? Can it be? *Daniel Liquorice!*'

'It is.'

I placed the book in his shaking hands. 'I believe it is somewhat scarce,' I said blithely.

'Scarce?' Quibble almost shook with pleasure. 'It is practically unique. *Daniel Liquorice!* In my hands!'

With great care he opened the book and raised it close to his bespectacled face. '"Being an account of the journey of an itinerant gentleman in His Majesty's East Indies",' he read. 'Heggessey Todd's lost masterpiece! Where did you find it, Mr Box? Where?'

He wriggled in his chair like a wormy baby, his tongue flashing around his raw mouth in a little circle.

'I have my sources,' I said, tantalizingly. 'Perhaps we can come to terms over dinner.'

'Yes, yes! Naturally. You must be fed!'

He rang the bell again with renewed urgency. A servant came to the door. Quibble barked orders at him then turned again to me.

'Mr Box, would you mind?'

He waved a skinny hand at his wheeled-chair. I rose and began to push him through into the dining room.

Paintings of what appeared to be Quibble's ancestors were just visible behind yet more staggered heaps of books, varnished eyes staring out in mute appeal, as though their owners were drowning in yellowed paper.

I pushed the wizened man to the head of the table where he sat cradling *Daniel Liquorice* as though it were a child. 'Name your price, my dear sir. I have dreamed of owning this book since –'

'It's not money I want, Sir Emmanuel,' I murmured. 'But information.'

'Information?'

I walked to the opposite end of the table where I found my chair being pulled out by another servant. Dressed, like Stint, in rather mouldering livery, a patina of dust covered his dulled silver buttons and epaulettes. He was a tall young lad with a pebble-smooth face and close-cropped hair. His eyes were very blue under dark brows as bold as strokes of charcoal.

He turned to the soup tureen and placed the lid gently at my side, fixing me with a look I can only describe as impudent. He smiled.

'Evening, sir,' he said, ladling beetroot soup into the dish before me. The voice was throaty from tobacco. Another relic from Blighty, it seemed.

'Good evening,' I said.

He bent low, suddenly, till his face was right by mine. He smelled of honey. 'Charles Jackpot, sir.'

Then, bless me if he didn't wink. 'But you can call me Charlie.'

XII

A LONDON DERRIÈRE

SAID nothing and turned my attention to the beetroot soup.

The nosh was dusty but passable. The soup was followed by a kind of salmon pastry and, after my new acquaintance, Mr Jackpot, had cleared this away, by an absolutely magnificent goose. Quibble clearly remained insulated against Italian notions of cuisine.

Eschewing the grimy napkin, I sucked the grease from my fingers as the servant cradled the dishes in his arms. He didn't speak, merely fixing me with the same impudent gaze. In the glow of the fire he had the face of a Renaissance saint. It was most unnerving.

Clearing my throat, I wiped the dust from Quibble's best crystal and poured myself a generous glass of plonk. I watched Charlie Jackpot as he loped back, with what I can only call a swagger, towards the kitchens.

Quibble turned a page in the book. 'Now, sir. May we get to business? I cannot rest easy until I know this volume to be mine. Time and tide, you know. They wait for no man.'

He craned his neck and peered back into the other room, as though it pained him to be separated from his library for more than a few moments.

'If you should like to know precisely how long they *do* wait, I have a volume on the subject. I believe it is over there between *On the Dangers of Bicycling* and *Coprolites of the Permian*.' Quibble licked his lips till his spittle glistened on their flaking surface.

I felt inside my coat and produced the photograph I had taken from Professor Sash's study. I slid it down the table towards the invalid and watched Quibble carefully as he lifted the photograph and held it about an inch from his spectacles. He coughed throatily. It was a sound like brown paper crackling in an oven.

'Where . . . where did you get this?'

'It was among the . . . er . . . personal effects of Professor Frederick Sash.'

Quibble's head snapped up. 'Effects? He's not dead, is he? Sash isn't dead?'

I nodded. 'And his body stolen. Along with another of the gentlemen in that photograph. Eli Verdigris.'

'Verdigris too? *How?*'

'That remains a mystery. I am investigating the matter, sir, and believe you can be of material assistance.'

Quibble heaved a heavy sigh. 'I hear nothing out here you see. Sometimes I think it was folly to leave the old country but I could get nothing done. The constant distractions! My great burden is work – so much that I am called upon to do!' His tongue flashed around the wet hole of his puckered mouth in great agitation.

'What of the other man in the photograph, Maxwell Morraine?'

'*Morraine?*'

'Yes. I'm sure you know he died out here some years ago.'

The old man suddenly fixed me with a malevolent stare. 'Who are you? What do you mean by bringing this volume here as though I were some horse-trader? What is the real reason for your visit, hm?'

He waved the photograph at me, his shrivelled mouth turning down into a snarl. 'You want to bring all *that* up again!' he yelled. 'Well, it won't wash, d'you hear me? Let the dead rest in peace!'

'All what, sir?'

'Get out, sir! Out! Stint!'

He grabbed at the glass bell and rang it until I feared it would shatter.

I shot to my feet. 'Forgive me, Sir Emmanuel, but I am convinced you are in grave danger –'

'*Stint!*'

The doors sprang open and the pale servant was framed there. 'Sir?'

Quibble writhed in his chair, shaking his bulbous head till

cowlicks of sparse hair tumbled from behind his ears and his book-tentacles rattled. 'Show this *person* out! You are never to admit him into my house again.'

'Sir Emmanuel, please –' I began.

Stint was at my elbow. 'If you wouldn't mind, sir?'

'I believe that a long-buried secret is threatening your life, sir, and that of a very noble friend of mine. Please, help me to find –'

'*Out!*'

I was escorted through the gloomy corridors and shown out into the muggy night.

Well, that hadn't gone very well at all, had it?

Old Stint shook his head mournfully. 'I do beg your pardon, sir. I've never seen the master so upset.'

'Stint,' I said earnestly. 'I have serious reason to believe Sir Emmanuel to be in danger of losing his life. Watch him carefully and contact me should you notice anything suspicious. Do you understand?'

He nodded.

'I am staying at the Hotel Santa Lucia. *Anything* suspicious, mind. And tell your master that the book is a gift. A gesture of my good faith.'

I pushed open the protesting gate and made my way back on to the drive. Grateful for the comparative cool, I stretched and took a deep breath before setting off for the carriage.

As I moved off, however, there came the sound of a match being struck and then a tiny point of amber light glowed in the shadows as someone inhaled greedily on a cigarette.

Sidling up to the gates once more I was somehow unsurprised to find the servant Jackpot loitering there. He smiled and the cigarette in his lips poked upwards, the curling smoke causing him to narrow his very blue eyes.

'Hullo,' he muttered.

I touched my fingers to the brim of my hat and began to move off back towards the road.

Suddenly the boy pushed his face to the railings and, after briefly looking about, spoke in an urgent whisper.

'If you wanna see something of importance, Mr Box, meet me in town. Tomorrow. Midnight.'

'Meet *you*? Why ever should I do that?'

'Via Santa Maria di Costantinopoli. The house with the crimson light. You won't regret it.'

Now it was my turn to smile. 'Won't I? And what could you possibly have that would interest me?'

His answer shocked me for a moment or two. For, stepping back a little from the railings, he suddenly thrust two fingers up at me.

Before I had time to react, he curled two fingers of his other hand into a semicircle and banged them against his palm. The penny dropped. Here was a 'V' and now a 'C'.

I nodded.

The servant flicked his cigarette into the shadows. 'Midnight tomorrow.'

And with that he was gone.

Next day, as arranged, I called on Miss Bella Pok at her hotel. The sunshine had completely deserted us and there was a squally feel to the weather, combined with a high, keening wind echoing banshee-like over the land. After breakfast, at Bella's insistence, we took a two-wheeler along the coastal road until we reached the outlying plains of the great volcano, its peak scarcely visible in the yellowy fog. She had a yen, you see, to travel on the famous funicular railway that had been constructed with great ingenuity (and no little bravery) right up the slopes of the grumbling peak, terminating just short of the cone itself.

'I'm sure there are more interesting ways of passing the time,' I said, smiling my wide smile.

Bella touched a gloved hand to my arm. 'But aren't you fascinated by it, Lucifer? The boiling energy beneath our very feet? The fiery lava just waiting to erupt?'

Well, I was, of course. But just then it wasn't Vesuvius's fiery lava that was on my mind.

There was a station on the lower slopes that resembled nothing so much as a small desert fort, its flat roof thick with grey volcanic dust. I bought the tickets and we watched as the wind whipped balls of dust and old newspaper to worry at the feet of us travellers. A big clock struck two and we got aboard the cramped train carriage, watching the bleary sunlight glinting off the cable wires that stretched ahead up the slopes of the volcano.

The carriage – a curious thing built in a stepped arrangement like a mobile block of steps – was half-empty. Bella sat down on one of the steps, staring with animated curiosity out of the filthy windows. Next to us was an old woman with a bag of knitting and a couple of American boys in offensively loud checked suits and wide-awake hats, already loudly proclaiming the mountain's incredible majesty, though all we could see so far was greasy ash. As we crawled up the sheer slope, great filthy clouds of sulphur billowed over the roof of the train, condensing on the windows like poisonous teardrops.

I suddenly noticed a young man sitting on the step above me. I received a quick impression of neat black suit and long auburn hair. His eyes were huge and brown, his nose slightly snubbed as though he had gently pressed it to a window-pane. He lifted his hat and smiled dazzlingly.

'You are impressed?' he asked.

I didn't know if he meant by the volcano or himself.

'Very,' I said.

Bella glanced up and the stranger smiled.

'Please forgive me, you are Signor Box, yes?'

I nodded.

'My name is Victor,' he said, holding out his gloved hand. I gripped it firmly and introduced Bella.

He took Bella's hand and kissed it gently. 'Our mutual friend, Signor Unmann,' Victor continued, 'expresses his regrets and begs that you accepted me as your guide in his stead.'

'Ah,' I said, losing all hope of useful information from my supposed man in the field.

'You know the mountain well?' asked Bella.

The young man took a deep breath of the frankly noxious air. 'For me, Vesuvius is like a drug. I cannot help but travel up these slopes whenever I have the chance – even though I live here in Napoli.'

'Yes,' I coughed. 'Intoxicating. Known Mr Unmann long have you?'

'Oh we are old . . . how do you say? *Chums*. Yes. Old chums. Now tell me, after we have been up and down the great Vesuvius – like the Grand Old Duke, yes? – what would you like to see? Naples is such a thrilling city.'

Bella began at once to itemise every last church in the place and I was slightly relieved when the guard called out '*Destinazione!*' and our carriage creaked and wheezed its way into the upper station.

Victor got nimbly to his feet and ushered us out of the train into a cloud of ash-filled steam. I wasn't sure I wanted this little Eye-tie crowding my afternoon with Bella and made plans to get shot of him just as soon as we returned to the Funicular station.

We set foot on black volcanic soil. Bella looked down at her feet and lifted her boots.

'Are you all right, my dear?' I asked.

She grinned. 'Just checking that they hadn't begun to spontaneously combust.'

Only three hundred yards from where we stood, the immense caldera of the volcano glowed an intense orange, plumes of white smoke belching from the sizzling rock. The heat was so intense I could feel the tiny hairs on my hands shrinking. I wished I'd worn gloves. Exposure to the Neopolitan sunshine was already threatening to tan me like a navvy.

I turned my face away from the oven-like heat. Victor stood his ground and shook his head in wonderment. 'What a magnificent thing she is!'

'Been quiet for a while has it?' I asked.

He grinned. 'A sleeping giant.'

'But not likely to turn over in her sleep any time soon?'

'You never can tell,' chirped Victor gaily. 'Come, let us go closer.'

He led the way forward. It was easy to spot the fairly fresh lava flows that lay in petrified streams all about us and I shielded my eyes against the glare from the boiling ground.

Victor closed his eyes. Smoke curled over and about his slim frame like ghostly vipers and we stood for a few silent moments amongst the blackened landscape. Bella clambered onto a great square boulder of volcanic rock and pointed down at the verdant plain. 'What is that?'

Far below us lay a collection of whitish buildings, scattered like child's blocks in the greenery.

'That is Pompeii,' said the youth. 'Look there if you wish to see what fearful power the Earth truly has within her.'

We lingered on top of the volcano for some little time with our new acquaintance chatting amiably throughout. Bella seemed quite taken with him but I felt curiously out of sorts. Perhaps it was the impending appointment with the mysterious servant Jackpot. At any rate, I was grateful to get back into the funicular and begin the descent.

Bella noticed how preoccupied I'd become.

'You seem troubled, Lucifer,' she said, crossing to where I stood by the misted window.

I patted her hand. 'Forgive me, my dear. Not quite comfortable in my own skin today, if you see what I mean.'

She nodded, smiled. 'It seems a shame. It's such a bonny skin.'

Our eyes locked for a moment, blue to green. We had the whole evening yet. Was this an invitation . . . ?

All thoughts of a jolly tumble with the divine Miss Pok were temporarily banished, however. As the funicular pulled into the station, I happened to glance through the milling crowds at the exit. At once a huge, barrel-chested figure caught my gaze, dressed in a heavy black coat and hat, his indigo-coloured spectacles lending his face a skull-like air.

'My God!' I breathed. 'Tiepolo!'

I raced to the exit door of the carriage and banged the heel of my hand against the woodwork as the vehicle clanked with painful tardiness into the station.

'What is it?' cried Bella concernedly.

I craned my neck to see the Duce Tiepolo's bear-like figure receding into the crowd.

'Forgive me, Bella,' I yelled, wrenching open the door. I turned and addressed the young man, Victor. 'Sir, would you be kind enough to escort this lady back to the Vesuvio Hotel? Can't explain now!'

I was just aware of Bella's vaguely baffled expression and young Victor raising his hat as I tore from the funicular and out into the station. Barging through the crowd of tourists, I clattered down towards the plain, just in time to see Tiepolo slip into the back of an expensive-looking motorcar which chugged away in a cloud of yellow dust.

I returned to my hotel and changed into evening dress for my appointment with Jackpot, dashing off a note of apology to Bella. I found a pleasant café by the quayside where I downed a few kirs. The Duce Tiepolo was here in Naples! And to risk recapture he must have a very good reason. But what connection did he have to Mrs Knight, her first husband, Morraine, and, by extension, to the professors? That old Quibble was in danger I was now certain but why, if Naples were the locus of this mystery, had he not already been done away with? Perhaps he was the *source* of the danger! Yet his reaction to the deaths of his old colleagues had been genuine enough. Quibble was no dissembler. 'You want to bring all that up again,' he had raged. All what? There had been no word from Unmann regarding the import/export business of the curious undertakers but here, at last, was a lead of sorts. This young man Charlie Jackpot appeared to know something. I clapped my topper to my head and set off for the ancient heart of the city.

The steady chirrup of insects kept me company as I walked the gas-lit avenues of Decumano Maggiore, its cobbles worn into ruts by the traffic of the centuries.

The premises on Via Santa Maria di Costantinopoli were distinguishable from their low and unhealthy-looking neighbours only by the ruby-red light above the lintel. The gas-flame behind the cheaply stained shade shuddered like a rheumy, winking eye.

I made my way softly down the steps to the door. It bore no knocker, nor number of any kind. I had raised my hand when it groaned open, seemingly of its own accord. Shudder not, reader, this is not a spook story! Whatever agency lay behind the door was most assuredly human.

Actually, I must immediately qualify that remark as what lay behind the door appeared to be a monkey. In the light of the sallow gas-jets I could make out poorly papered walls weeping with damp and the stooped figure of whom I spoke: a curious man with very long arms, dressed in green velvet plush. His hair, scraped from a centre parting *en brosse*, stank of oil.

He cocked his pallid face to one side by way of an interrogative. What should I say? Was his master at home?

I took off my top hat with as much nonchalance as I could muster and decided to be bold. 'I understand that a young man of my acquaintance is expecting me. We're old pals and I haven't spoken to him for some time. I wonder –'

The little creature seemed uninterested in my story, however. He moved to the back of the dismal hallway, nodding absently, and drew aside a disreputable-looking curtain.

The monkey-man smiled grimly, his mouth like a wound. '*Si, si. Uno ragazzo.*'

I was spared any more of his charming conversation, however, by the sudden appearance of Mr Jackpot himself from behind the drawn curtain. He was wearing a slovenly jacket and trousers, both too big for him, the pantaloons held to his hips by a thick brown belt and a good two inches shy of his stripe-socked shins. In stark contrast, his collarless shirt seemed clean and there was a white rosebud in his lapel.

'Hullo,' he said.

I gave a little bow.

Jackpot smiled lop-sidedly, his large lips sending dimpled echoes over his cheek. 'Won't you come in, sir?'

He gestured into the darkness. I followed without a word. The tiny doorman melted away into the gloom – for all I knew, he had gone back into the wallpaper from which he had sprung.

I was ushered into a small, square chamber, underlit and over-heated. Perhaps Jackpot had become accustomed to his master's tastes. The décor seemed all of a piece with the grisly entranceway; there was a brass-framed bed containing a stained mattress, and a jug and wash-bowl on a spindly table. On a Turkey rug sat a drab *chaise-longue* of surpassing vileness. A miserable fire sputtered in the grate, damp sea-coal popping and spitting against faded Dutch tiles.

'How nice,' I said at last.

The boy closed the door behind me and took my hat, coat and gloves like the good and faithful servant he was.

I lit a cigarette to disguise the smell and tossed one to Jackpot who ignited his from the fire. Moving to the sofa, I flapped aside the tails of my coat, prior to sitting. I stopped with my rear end halfway to the upholstery. 'May I?'

'Of course, sir,' said Charlie. He hovered by the door a moment, wiping his hands over the greasy fabric of his jacket. Then: 'Might I join you, sir?'

I was already lounging back as if I owned the place. I waved a hand and bid him do so.

As he sat down next to me, I pushed him sideways with my leg and, grabbing at his cropped hair, pulled back his head until he yelled in pain. His fag dropped to the dirty floor.

I smiled. 'I believe you have something to tell me.'

Charlie scowled and fixed me with a penetrating and vaguely unnerving stare. I tugged his head back still further but he had stopped yelling. 'That won't get you anywhere,' he murmured in a low voice.

'Then perhaps this will,' I cried, grabbing my pearl-handled revolver from beneath my shirt. I pressed the cold barrel to the youth's temple and glared at him. 'Now. What precisely do the initials VC mean to you?'

But still he seemed unmoved. I watched as his Adam's apple bobbed slowly up and down.

Charlie Jackpot just smiled.

Irritated by my failure to intimidate him, I moved the revolver slowly down his smooth face and pushed the barrel between his lips. Charlie's very blue eyes regarded me levelly over the glinting gunmetal.

I withdrew the pistol from his mouth with ill-grace.

'There now,' said Charlie with a smirk. 'Isn't this nicer?'

Mr Jackpot turned his huge eyes on me in a kind of mute enquiry. A moment later he put his hand on my thigh.

Well, what was I to do? For the well-bred gentleman there was surely only one recourse. I fucked him.

XIII

L.B. TO V.C.

CHARLIE Jackpot had that annoying knack of looking ravishing even in sleep. He lay stretched over the burst stuffing of the chaise, starkers except for his striped socks. Whatever these had once possessed by way of elastic had long since perished and they hung slackly over his white shins like discarded caterpillar pupae.

For myself, I sat on a creaking chair, also in the buff, relishing the gorgeous glow of the fire as I contemplated this most recent act of naughtiness. You are shocked, are you not? Or, perhaps, reading this in some distant and unimaginably utopian future like that funny little man Mr Wells would have us believe in, you are not shocked at all! Fact is, Lucky Lucifer here has still more secrets. My arsenal is formidable – a sentence which comes across more interestingly in a French accent.

As you know, there is no service I

am unprepared to render for King and country, and I am not averse to a pretty face and a pretty rump, whether they be man's or woman's (I draw the line at beasts, unlike at least one member of the Cabinet). It is the prerogative of the secret agent to be (and to have!) whatever he fancies, don't you agree? This is not a privilege extended to the population at large, as I found when I was discovered in a house off the Bow Road – the incident that brought me to the attention of Joshua Reynolds. The old dear helped extricate me from that spot of bother but saw it as a very useful way of getting me on to his payroll. In the yellow-backed novels it is known as *blackmail*.

You must remember that London was in a bit of a panic, with the recent exigencies of Mr O.F.O'F.W. Wilde so fresh in the memory, and J.R. had me by the unmentionables. The compensation was that my divers assassinations took me all over the globe where the love that dared not speak its name was positively encouraged to bellow from the rooftops. Such as in old Napoli, it seemed.

Still, it was a dangerous game and I was in no great hurry to do two years' hard labour just for a frolic with some dolly renter.

Charlie opened a sleepy eye (exhausted, poor thing) and smiled his simian smile. Reaching over to my discarded coat, I retrieved my cigarette case and lit a fag for myself and then for him, padding naked over the cheap carpet to the *chaise* and delicately inserting the cigarette between his kiss-crushed lips. Charlie sucked in the smoke as though his life depended on it and let it rise over his mouth like the curly tips of a ghostly moustache.

'Ta,' he said softly.

'How much do I owe you?'

'Owe me?'

'For services rendered.'

The boy dragged on the cigarette. 'My pleasure.'

I bowed my head. 'Then, tomorrow, you must at least allow me to buy you a bun.'

Charlie draped himself across my lap with his knees up. Gazing into my face he idly scratched his balls. I could feel his hot feet against my thigh. ''Spect you're wondering why I was so forward with you,' he said at last.

'Forward?'

'You know. This evening at the old fella's place.'

I blew smoke into his face.

'Young men often throw themselves at me. I've come to regard it as something of a burden.'

'I'd seen you before.' He grinned.

'Really? At Ascot? Windsor? I was in Mentone last summer, perhaps we met there?'

He scowled again, rather pleasingly, and wiped at his nose. 'Do you know where you are?'

'Yes. A filthy knocking shop for undiscerning tourists.'

Charlie got to his feet and perched on the edge of the table, crossing one foot over the other. 'No, no. There's a little more to it than meets the eye.'

I grunted sceptically. In my experience there's very rarely more to these places than meets the eye.

'This one's different,' he said quickly. 'Better even than that big yellow house in Islington.'

That was where he'd first spotted me! A Hallowe'en Masque held by a very pretty couple called Flora and Walter Paste. I had come as the Prince of Darkness (of course) and come *across* a fetching Succubus in very tight fleshings. It had been a night of grand indiscretion. Lawks. No wonder Jackpot been so damned impudent at Quibble's.

'It's supposed to be strictly members only but I know a trick or two. Get your togs on.'

'I am not in the habit of obeying orders.'

'All right. But it's the only way you're gonna find out about the VC.'

I pulled up my braces. 'Very well. Shall we get on?'

Charlie dressed quickly with the abandon of one who cares little for his appearance. Curbing my natural instinct to spend at least an hour getting back into my clothes I graciously allowed Charlie to help me with my collar studs and cuffs. I shrugged on my cut-away and, moments later, looking only a little the worse for wear, followed him back out into the corridor.

Several identical doors studded the shoddy walls, plaster hanging like rotten cloth in the spaces in between. The place reeked of damp. There was no sign of the ape-like doorman.

Charlie walked on ahead, ignoring these doors, all of which undoubtedly led to similar bleakly furnished rooms.

As we advanced I became aware that we seemed to be moving almost imperceptibly but inexorably *downwards*. Also, the corridor's decoration stabilized so that smooth expanses of crimson wall began to emerge, as though we were travelling along an artery and had left behind some morbid and diseased junction.

I flipped my watch from my waistcoat. Nearly two o'clock in the morning. From ahead of us came a curious subdued hubbub. Music. Chatter. What I can only call *carousing*.

We had come to the end of our journey. Before us stood a massive set of ebony doors. They looked very old indeed, banded in iron and carved into grotesque, leering faces.

Charlie gave me a strange smile and then hammered on the doors, like some scruffy Black Rod. The doors shuddered open. I caught a vague impression of a hulking doorman with whom Charlie exchanged either words or a kiss. Then I was ushered through.

Beyond the doors was a vision of Hell.

Don't fret. It is Lucifer's domain, after all.

The chamber we had entered was very large and lit by dim gaslight. A series of swooping arches stretched away into the darkness and I realized, dimly, that we must be in some kind of adapted tunnel system running right under the roadway above. The walls were expensively rendered in a brilliant display of the *art nouveau*, black and gold tendrils curling like some monstrous plant from floor to ceiling.

Tapestries and great swathes of scarlet cloth billowed overhead like the skirts of a giantess. Upon them was wrought, in (well, exquisite is not quite the word) well-observed detail, classical pornography of the most astonishing variety. Priapic old lechers pursued virgins with a passion around a witches' sabbat, dominated by a frightening goat-headed Devil. Girlish youths and Rubens-esque ladies formed a frame around scenes of Caligulan excess, where satyrs had their way with women deprived of their togas, and centaurs carried off drunken revellers.

The embroidered shenanigans, however, were as nothing to what was being enacted beneath them.

Flashes of colour rose up out of the gloom; male and female faces fixed in orgasmic relish, oil-slicked hair bobbing over a sea of unbuttoned britches, silken knickerbockers flung up from the mêlée like flags of surrender. The stench of absinthe and tobacco was overwhelming.

I glanced at Charlie Jackpot but his expression was unreadable in the murk. Of course my overwhelming emotion was one of horror. Not at the extraordinary outrages being committed in the name of love all about me, of course, but at the dreadful, unarguable fact that such a place existed and it would take me four days throwing up over the side of a steamer to get to it! What price my poor Pomegranate Rooms now?

Charlie pushed his way through the fleshy miasma, kicking aside copulating couples, until he found us a kind of ottoman. The pair he dislodged from this with the toe of his boot rolled off on to the floor with hardly a murmur, locked together like the jaws of a ferret.

I leaned back against the cushioned velvet. Charlie disappeared for a moment and then returned with a battered silver tray, bottles and glasses crammed upon it up to its tarnished edge. Pouring me some kind of hideous brandy, he gulped down most of a pint of porter and wiped his lips with the back of his hand.

'You work in shifts, then?' I pondered.

'How's that?'

'I was just wondering how you find time to look after Sir Emmanuel. It must be exhausting to wash dishes and then come on to this place.'

He giggled. 'I like my work.'

I drank the brandy as swiftly as I could so it didn't have time to touch the inside of my mouth.

Charlie leaned closer until his lips brushed my ear. 'I'll tell you it all, Mr Box. But you have to promise to get me out of here. Set me up.'

'I can make no assurances,' I said, my attention distracted momentarily by the sight of a Negro youth in a guardsman's uniform merrily tossing himself off over the patrons to our left. 'Not unless you have something of real import to impart.'

'That I do. See, I hear things,' murmured Charlie, darkly. 'They don't know that I work up at the house as well as here.'

'Who are *they*?'

There was a swish of skirts close by. I was conscious of a scent of mimosa and suddenly someone was standing right at my elbow.

'*Buonasera*, Charlie.'

The low voice belonged to a girl of middling height, exceptionally slim, wearing only an ivory corset and mustard-coloured stockings. Her long auburn hair was piled high and interlaced with flowers, crowning a face of surpassing loveliness; almond-shaped eyes heavily lined in kohl.

'Venus!' cried Charlie delightedly. He pulled the girl on to his lap and kissed her fiercely, running his hand up and down her stockinged leg. She adjusted herself in his embrace and cast a furtive glance to me.

'Who ees this?' she asked in the same seductive whisper. Her accent was as thick as tomato sauce.

Charlie grinned. 'This is Mr Box. Mr Box, meet Venus.'

I gave a little bow. Venus proffered a painted hand. I kissed the middle knuckles, taking care to let the tip of my tongue linger a moment. It seemed the form in these environs.

Venus's gaudily rouged lips puckered and she looked down, all abashed, the little minx. I had the queerest feeling that we'd met before.

'You like-a ma place, Signor Box?' she said with a half-smile.

My eyes widened. '*Your* place, my dear? Well, you do surprise me. Yes. Yes, it's quite something. What do you call it?'

It was Charlie who answered, fixing me with a meaningful stare and taking a plug of his porter. 'This? This is the Vesuvius Club.'

Well, of course I *noticed*. Vesuvius Club. V.C.! Not the Verdigris Collective, not the Verdi Cabal, not the Victoria Cross and not the bloody Venomous Centipede. The Vesuvius Club! K to V.C. Poor old Poop must have known of this place!

'Is-a something wrong, Signor Box?' cooed Venus.

I shook my head to clear it. 'Not a bit, my dear. It's just that Mr Jackpot and myself have some . . . business to conclude . . .'

Venus put one hand on her hip and smiled. 'I never stand in thee way of custom, eh? Perhaps you would be more comfortable in ma private quarters?'

I glanced at Charlie and he nodded.

'How kind,' I cooed. 'Will you lead the way?'

The delightful girl batted her kohl-rimmed eyes and swept off into the crowd. Charlie drained the last of his pint and followed with me bringing up the rear. Wary of stepping into a bear-trap (as this much honey might turn out to be), I walked with hands clasped behind me to feel the reassuring presence of the pearl-handled revolver strapped to the small of my back.

Venus led us through the roaring mêlée and through a side door into a cooler, darkened room that smelled of rose-petals. She lit the lamps, revealing a scarlet boudoir of impressive proportions, divided by silk curtains and scattered about with fat oriental cushions. A dressing mirror dominated the far wall.

'Please make-a yourselves at home,' said Venus, sitting down on the dresser and crossing her legs. Her mustard stockings flashed in the half-light.

'Most obliging of you, miss,' I said.

Venus cocked her head again. 'Charlie and I . . . we are old friends . . . yes? And any friend of his . . .'

Charlie grinned at her and, picking up a bottle of cham, wrenched out the cork. He poured three glasses. Venus drained hers in one go, span her champagne glass between her delicate fingers and fixed me with a slightly intimidating stare. What had those fiery eyes seen in their few years? She made me feel positively callow.

'I hope-a to see much more of *you*,' she said. With that, she swept past us both, paused to kiss Charlie briefly on the cheek and then was gone.

'Christ, ain't she something!' cried Charlie. He lifted the champagne bottle to his lips and guzzled down more plonk.

'That she is. Are you two –?'

'Some chance!' laughed Charlie. 'Even if I were that way inclined. No. She's got a fella, the real boss. She runs this place for him.'

Charlie threw himself down on to a cushion.

'But you want to know about a man called Poop.'

I sat up. 'Go on.'

'Well, he came in here a while ago, asking questions. Thought he was a punter. He stood me a drink but he weren't interested in getting, you know, *friendly*. He just give me some moolah to keep me eyes open. Said he was on to some kind of racket.'

I frowned. 'Racket?'

Charlie nodded. 'Treasure. Seems that he'd had some kind of nark sniffing around but he'd gone missing. Wondered if I'd be interested in taking up where the nark left off –'

The boy stopped dead.

'What is it?' I cried.

'Dunno. Can you smell something?'

Charlie coughed. His hand flew to his throat and he coughed again, more raggedly. Then it was my turn. The air had somehow turned too stifling to breathe, like being in an overheated steam bath.

I turned and saw the thread of some strange, purplish smoke drifting towards us. Feeling suddenly sick, tears sprang to my eyes and I too began to cough uncontrollably.

I tried to reach out to Charlie but suddenly found my limbs weighed down as though they were statuary. Scarcely able to move, I half-stumbled, half-fell to the floor. Through a mist of stinging tears, I could just make out Charlie's broad back. He tumbled to the floor, scrabbling at the air as though it were attacking him. With a titanic effort I hauled myself on to one knee and peered blearily about the room. What devilry was this? A Venus fly trap – and us the flies! Clutching at the oriental cushions, I staggered to my feet and tried to head towards the door.

Every step seemed to take an eternity. It was as though I had a diver's lead shoes upon my feet. Coughing constantly I put my hands to my face and slapped myself in an attempt to clear my befuddled brain. My mind seemed to be swirling and tumbling and swimming madly, as though I'd drunk a quart of absinthe.

Reeling around, I found I had lost the door. It was as though I'd been transported to some other room, so strange and alien did Venus's boudoir appear. The dressing table stretched crazily before me on stilt-like legs. Great heaven! The furniture appeared to be moving! The drawers of the dresser gaped open like hungry maws, snapping at my legs as I lurched and stumbled across the floor.

The oil-lamp loomed largest of all. It was then, with my eyes almost popping from my bursting head that I saw that the lamp was the source of my terror. For, gushing from the shade like a spectre or genie was a billowing quantity of some noxious gas, mauve in colour, settling heavily on the floorboards and sending me into near-convulsions.

I reached for the lamp but the closer I got the more dreadful were its effects. My fingers seemed to bend and stretch like the talons of a terrible bird as I groped at empty air, the image of the lamp blurring and multiplying before my exhausted eyes. I looked wildly about for Charlie but could make out nothing in the greasy smoke.

With one last attempt at clear thought I grabbed hold of the lamp's iron base and picked it up. Perhaps I intended to smother the damned thing or hurl it into a dark corner but, in truth, I do not know. My senses whirled, a great blanket of mauve darkness enveloped me and I was falling, falling, falling into an abyss . . .

XIV

THE PALE MAN

IN the distance, a clock struck four. I stirred and found myself lying prone on cold stone. Shifting a little, I cracked open stinging eyes, peered blearily about, coughed and opened my mothball-stale mouth. I tried to sit up but sank back at once on to the chilly floor, skull throbbing as though it were fixed about with a tight iron band.

Where the hell was I?

I raised my head again, widening my eyes in a last-ditch attempt at wakefulness. I was in some kind of cell, windowless and cramped. Slimy straw lay all about me and there was a pervasive odour of ammonia.

Head splitting, I somehow managed to stumble to my feet and then sank back against the wet bricks. Looking down at myself, I saw that I was in full evening dress, my shirt-front torn and the lapels of my coat plastered with mud.

I could recall nothing at all. Never mind where was I! *Who* was I?

I hammered my fist against my forehead and screwed up my eyes. Something about a box. A box with a centipede in it. No. That wasn't right. Perhaps it was a book. A book in a box. Daniel Liquorice! Was that my name? No. A Jack in a box? Jack Box? Jackpot? That was someone else entirely, I felt sure. *My name is Box.* Ah! *Lucifer Box. Yes. Yes.* I placed the flat of my hands against the chilly wall and willed myself to remain calm. *Lucifer Box. Of Downing Street, London.* I shook my head over and over. I must concentrate. *Where was I? Italy. Italy, of course. Naples! But why? Why?* I snapped open my eyes and struggled to focus on the cell door. It looked depressingly solid.

Bending down, I peered through the rusted keyhole. I could just make out a suggestion of a gloomy corridor beyond.

I sank down against the wall then leant forward as I became aware of something poking into my back. I had a dim remembrance of a similar feeling, connected to a yellow villa in Islington but this was not quite the same. Exploring under the tail of my ruined shirt my fingers closed upon the warm, reassuring presence of my revolver, still strapped in the hollow above my buttocks that nature almost seemed to have provided for the express purpose.

I took it out, opened the chamber and span it.

'That won't help you,' came a whispered voice from the darkness.

I started and whirled round, brandishing the pistol.

Nothing.

'Who's there?' I demanded.

A hissing chuckle sounded close by. I crept towards the far wall. Just about visible was a tiny, barred window, evidently connecting to the cell next door. I pressed my face to it, making out a crouched figure in the gloom beyond. He turned his face towards me but little detail was visible in the filthy mass of hair and beard.

'Oh . . .' I cried. 'Hullo.'

'Good evening. Or is it morning? I no longer know.'

'My name is Box.'

'And mine's the Count of Monte Cristo! Hee-hee!'

I pulled back from the window slightly, alarmed at the fellow's crazed laughter. He fixed me with a wild eye and shuffled across the floor of his cell. 'As I say, that weapon of yours won't do you any good. They don't feel pain. They don't feel anything!'

'Who don't?'

'They came for me, you see. I was getting too close. Too close to the truth. Mr Poop – he was on to them.'

My ears pricked up. 'Poop! What do you know of Poop?'

The strange old man coughed noisily. 'Looting they was! Stripping the excavations bare and flogging the stuff to keep this wretched place going!'

'Excavations?'

'They've forgotten me now. Hee-hee! Thrown away the key. Maybe you'll rot here too!'

As if in response, a key rattled in the lock and my door was thrown open. A strange figure was framed there; very tall, clad in black and wearing what appeared to be some kind of brass helmet. I rubbed at my eyes. Was this still part of my strange purple dream? Had the notion of a lead-shoed diver sprung to life before me?

My neighbour in the next cell jumped to his feet and pressed his grimy face to the bars.

'Look out! They've come for you! Don't resist! They don't feel anything! Hee-hee!'

The extraordinary helmeted figure stumped across the cell towards me and opened his great arms as though offering an embrace.

I thrust the revolver into my pocket and backed away. Pale as death, the man's jaw hung slackly open, a strand of drool dangling from his lips. His eyes, staring blankly ahead, were a horrible yellowy grey like the yolks of over-boiled eggs.

My gaze was drawn, however, to the strange brass thing that covered the top part of his face. On the closer inspection I was now afforded, I could see it was like a Norman helmet, though the upper part was made of glass and glowing a weird, sickly purple. Great brass screws were inset at the temples, effectively clamping the helmet to his head.

Stepping quickly to one side, I raced towards the door, bargaining that the brute's sluggish gait would count against him.

'No good!' croaked my neighbour through the barred window. 'He'll get you!'

At once the creature changed direction and cut me off, his eyes rolling in his head, arms outstretched in deadly intent.

I resorted to my pistol but he swung at me, knocking the weapon flying. As I moved to retrieve it, his sweaty hands jerked forward and clamped about my throat.

I staggered backwards, gasping at the terrible pressure.

'Hee-hee!' cried my neighbour. 'Now you're done for!'

The fiend's bloated white face was right by mine and I could see directly into the glass section of his strange headgear. Inside seemed to float a purplish miasma.

I dug my nails into the flesh of his throttling hands but he did not even react, forcing me backwards as I beat and pounded at his face. My head felt as though it would explode at any second. Desperately, I thrust my thumbs into his eyes and pushed with all my strength. The soft flesh gave sickeningly but still I pressed on, digging into the very sockets and forcing my thumbs upwards.

No scream did he make, nor sign that he felt even a scintilla of pain.

'Told you! Told you so! They feel nothing! The devils!' cackled my fellow prisoner.

I hammered my fists against my attacker's chest but his great weight forced me to my knees. I groped wildly about in the straw. The revolver!

Rolling us both over with a supreme effort, I grasped at the pearl handle of the gun, aimed desperately and loosed off a bullet into the brute's chest.

He was knocked back as though plucked by a giant hand, staggered and slumped against the wall. I groped at my throat and rubbed my crushed wind-pipe, struggling to draw ragged, whooping breaths.

Suddenly the helmeted monster was on his feet again, seemingly oblivious to the wound in his chest. He surged forward, his great hands flexing, intent on rejoining battle at once. Though dazed and exhausted, I scrabbled to my feet and made a dash for the door. The fellow threw himself forward and grabbed at my ankles, succeeding in getting both hands around one of them and bringing me down on the floor. I swivelled on my rump and planted my boot in the middle of his face, kicking savagely until I felt his nose crack and bright blood fountain on to my trouser leg.

I tried to take aim again but the lumbering giant gripped my other ankle and shook me about like a rag-doll. The pistol went off but was sent clattering against the wall.

With a cry I shuffled forward and managed to get my fingers under the edge of the helmet. I tugged violently, desperately.

Swarming forward with one last effort and gripping the helmet for dear life, I kicked the fellow in the throat sending him vaulting backwards. I was left clutching the brass helmet in both hands.

And now he began to scream. A dreadful tortured gurgle it was as his suddenly bare head was exposed to the world. There were huge gory gouges in his temples where the attaching screws had been ripped out and he raised his hands to them, gasping in pain and shock.

'Lor! You done for him! How did you manage that?' hissed my hairy cellmate in amazement.

I glanced down at the helmet. The strange, gaseous substance still swirled within the glass enclosure but I could now see that thin, delicate pipes led from it into the screws that been affixed to my attacker's temples. A tarry liquid began to leak from inside and its dark mauve colour was at once familiar. And then I remembered. I felt my overtaxed brain making connections like points changing on a railway. It was the same stuff that had nearly done for me and Charlie.

Charlie! Of course! The boy had been on the point of telling me something of vital import. When . . .

I looked down at the strange helmet again. Piped directly into its poor owner's blood-stream the mauve stuff had rendered him little more than a zombie!

Putting the helmet carefully aside, I scrabbled for my revolver and levelled it at the prone figure.

The man had begun to weep from his gory eyes, great heavy tears mixing with the drool and blood plastered over his dead-white face. He tried to raise himself up on one hand but sank back to the floor with a great cry. I suddenly realized there wasn't much time.

Scuttling across to him on my knees, I managed to raise the fellow's head up, cradling it in the crook of my arm. It was like the Death of bloody Nelson.

'Tell me,' I whispered. 'Who did this to you?'

The mauve fluid was trickling out of the wounds in his temples. Great rasping gulps began to sound from the fellow's blood-caked mouth and then, with a dreadful, rattling gurgle, he pitched back into my arms, quite dead.

I got to my feet. The fellow had been sent to collect me or to kill me. Either way, it was wise to get moving.

'Wait! Wait!' cried my neighbour. 'What about me?'

I paused on the threshold. 'You're no use to me in this babbling state.'

I slipped through the open door and out in to the darkened corridor.

As I passed the adjacent cell, the old fellow thrust towards me desperately. 'Please! I'll tell you. Just let me out!'

I took a chance and shot the lock off. He raced out into the corridor but I covered him warily. He seemed just the type to leap for my throat.

'All right,' I muttered, backing away from the stink he gave off. 'Where are we?'

He pushed his long grey hair from his eyes. 'Why, the Vesuvius Club, of course!'

'Still? Good. That's good. Now tell me more about Poop and these looted treasures.'

I gestured with the pistol and we began to creep off up the corridor, keeping our voices low.

'I knew Mr Poop. Did a lot of work for him. I know my way about this city, you see.'

'You're an informant?'

The old man cackled. 'I keeps my ear to the ground.'

'Go on.'

'Well, Signor Poop was on to some sort of racket in stolen stuff.

Old statues and that sort of thing, hocked off to the best Chelsea drawing rooms and nobs' offices. He reckoned that's how Venus's fella got the V Club up and running. They was smuggling stuff out of Naples in coffins, pretending it was bodies, then smuggling the moolah back in. We was getting close to nabbing them when . . . well . . .'

I nodded slowly. 'You got your ear a little too close to the ground, eh?'

This must be the fellow Charlie had mentioned. I scratched my chin. Where was Charlie now? It was vital that I find him and pump him (for information, you understand).

We emerged suddenly into a curtained area and there, sitting on a stool with his back towards us was the curious ape-like chap who had greeted me when I first arrived. I gestured to my bearded friend that he should make for the front door and scarper. He nodded and gave me a little bow then I cleared my throat noisily and the monkey-man turned on his stool.

Out of the corner of my eye I saw Poop's informant steal towards the exit and, silently, slip through it to freedom.

My head still ached appallingly from the mauve gas but I thrust my hands into my trouser pockets and looked about with a casual air. 'Hello again! Got a little lost in all these damned corridors. Had a little adventure, but found my way back. Not to worry.'

With a merry wave, I strode off down the long corridor. When finally I stood once more before the great doors I paused to make myself presentable. Magnified by the gasping gas-jets, my shadow leapt hugely over the walls. Once again, the sweet sounds of debauchery bled from under them.

Raising my fist, I hammered twice on the black surface.

Almost immediately, the doors rasped open and a flickering red light washed over me. I stepped inside but felt my way barred at once by a great bear-like shape.

Membership was clearly an exclusive affair.

Charlie, of course, had previously gained us ingress and I suddenly realized that it might be a little more difficult alone.

'Yes?' came a thick voice from the dimness.

I was damned if I was going to say 'May I come in, please?' so instead I ordered 'Stand aside' with all the boldness I could muster.

There was movement in the darkness which I realized must be the fellow shaking his fat head. 'Can't do that, sir. You have to give the signal.'

I nodded and shrugged as though cursing my own stupidity. 'The signal! Of course!'

I rubbed my hands together and laughed lightly. What signal?

The impressive shape shifted on its feet. I patted my pockets as though the solution might be found in there. Why hadn't I observed more closely when Charlie had stood in this position? Had he given a password of some kind? No, the doorman would have said so. It was a *signal* he was after.

The shape began to move towards me with some menace. I knew I would be put out on the wrong side of the door within seconds. A signal? Something to do with the Vesuvius Club. Something simple and recognizable.

Then a notion popped into my head. I took a chance and thrust my fingers up before his nose in a 'V' shape.

He stopped his inexorable progress. I curved my hand and formed a 'C' that I slapped against my palm as I had seen Charlie do. The creature stepped aside. 'Have a very good evening, sir,' he growled.

'Thank you. I intend to.' I breathed with relief, moving swiftly past him and into the heaving chamber beyond.

The room was still what you might call a *pornucopia*.

My ragged appearance excited no comment and I proceeded to a couch, occupied solely by a mournful-looking youth with terrible acne. I sat down as far from him as possible and stuck out my long legs before me. He began at once to cast shy glances at my loveliness but I studiously ignored the hideous bugger, content instead to watch the activities of two splendidly naked ladies who were cavorting on the floor with their bums in the air.

A rough-looking waiter sauntered past with a tray of drinks and I grabbed him by his skinny wrist. He thrust a shot glass into my hand and moved off into the crowd. I turned back and discovered I was still under the scrutiny of the grisly youth perched at the other end of the sofa. I raised my glass and toasted him. His cheeks, angry with blemishes, burned redder still.

'I am Ricardo,' he mumbled.

'And I'm . . .' I threw him a pitying look. 'I'm afraid you're terribly ugly.'

His whole frame sank with shame.

'*Buonasera*, Venus!'

I turned at the cry. It had come from a thickset fellow far to my left who was wiping beer from the wet stalactites of his moustache.

Venus! She had fetched up more respectably this time in a dress of dazzling crimson, one hand on her shapely hip, in the approved style, the other clutching a long amber cigarette-holder. She was exchanging gossip and laughter with her clientele, her kohl-rimmed eyes shining with mirth. Charlie had said she was the paramour of the villain who owned this place. Had she been complicit in lighting the lamp with its strange mauve poison or was she merely an unwilling pawn?

Either way, I had to hide. Without a second thought, I reached across the sofa, grabbed the spotted Dick by his tweedy lapels and pulled him to me.

'On the other hand,' I said, moving him round to screen me, 'I've always had a penchant for ugly boys.'

Master Ricardo set to with a vengeance, his pinkish lips slapping against my mouth in a squid-like action that was most disagreeable. To my astonishment, an albino in a beret then toddled towards us as though the kiss had been some general call to arms. He began fiddling with my fly-button as my eyes goggled above the pitted curve of acne-boy's cheek. As soon as Venus had moved away, I repelled all boarders with a disgusted cry, pushing young Ricardo to the filthy floor and kicking the albino in the solar plexus.

He flopped like a bag of wet washing and I stooped at once as though to help him, all the time keeping an eye on Venus as she made her halting progress through the chamber, wreathed in the bluish smoke of her cheroot.

At the end of the long, mirrored bar was a door inset with a frosted pane. Venus glided towards the door and then, glancing swiftly around, passed through into the darkness beyond.

I rolled the albino into a corner and then swiftly followed Venus, threading through knotted limbs conjoined in shameless excess. Turning the handle, I opened the door and slipped silently through.

The sudden quiet startled me. Torches sputtered in gold stanchions, revealing the curve of a broad corridor disappearing into gloom. I smiled to myself. Now this really was a secret tunnel!

I could hear the tat-tat of Venus's elegant heels on the stone floor ahead. Pulling off my boots as quietly as I could and, clutching them to my chest, I followed her.

Padding along, I kept myself snug to the wall until I came to a branch in the tunnel. It continued to my left. To my right I could make out the top of a spiral stairwell. Only the first three of the worn stone steps were visible as they descended into darkness.

Unsure as to which route Venus had taken, my attention was momentarily caught by a heavy tapestry that was fixed to the brickwork. In the flickering torchlight, its threads leapt out in golds, reds and purples. It was clearly very old and seemed to show the broad sweep of a harbour, dominated by the great hulk of a black mountain. I moved closer. The weave was disintegrating but I could just make out that a pillar of smoke was escaping from the embroidered summit. Vesuvius!

XV

INTO THE CRIMSON CHAMBER

HERE were footsteps in the tunnel. Caught in the open corridor, I rapidly rifled through my options. Only one. Lifting the edge of the tapestry, I tucked myself in behind it, and pressed myself flat against the wall which had a distinct curve I had not previously noted. I listened attentively as several pairs of feet passed by and began to descend the spiral stair, accompanied by a rustling sound.

As I stood with my back to the wall, I noticed a point of bright yellow light emerging just above my left shoulder. As soon as I was sure the passers-by had gone I turned around and put my eye to the hole in the crumbling mortar.

What I saw was a strange, circular room that, like everywhere else in that place, was the colour of flame. This time, however, the decoration actually imitated the pit of Hell or, more probably, the crater of a boiling volcano. Painted fire licked the round room,

twisting into orange shapes like barley-sugar canes and merging into patterns of deep crimson lava.

The room was dominated by a massive round table with four ornately carved chairs set about it. In them had been placed straw figures, exactly like the one I had found in Professor Verdigris's coffin.

The air seemed heavy with oily incense. Its foggy weight hung under the ceiling, swirling like a nest of serpents as it was disturbed by draughts from the crumbling walls.

As I watched, a yellow door opened and an extraordinary procession came in: three figures, resplendent in red velvet robes, decorated all over in blazes of gold and silver sunbursts. All three wore what looked like masks from the Venice Carnival, exquisitely rendered in similar hues, the cruel, snarling features picked out in white. Not for the first time in that bizarre place, I wished I'd had my sketchbook. Though this was, perhaps, a rare occasion where the

Duce Tiepolo's photographic apparatus might have been handier! Without it, who would believe such a sight? My thoughts dwelled on the Duce for a moment. Could he be the paramour of Venus? The organizing brain behind this whole enterprise?

One of the robed figures, slight in build, took up a gavel that lay at his right hand and rapped it on the table.

'I, Vesuvius, summon thee,' he said.

The next figure, altogether more imposing, bowed his head saying, 'I, Stromboli, answer.' This could be Tiepolo. His build was similar.

The third, tall and thin, bowed too. 'Etna answers thee,' he squeaked.

My eye widened as I pressed closer to the spy-hole.

Now I've been around a bit, as you can imagine, and I knew at once that this was more than a knocking shop's AGM. Few go about their business in motley and even fewer adopt names stranger than 'Mister Chairman' as their monikers.

No, this was rummer than a baba.

More torches had been lit and now I could see that there were maps and what appeared to be charts pinned to the walls. I looked more closely at the four chairs. Bizarrely, the straw figures had been shackled to their seats, as though to prevent their escape.

Vesuvius set aside the gavel and spread his hands wide, looking for all the world like a sinister masked version of the Messiah from Da Vinci's *Last Supper*. A queer, piercing note began to rise in his throat. After a moment the sound was taken up by his two fellow volcanoes who moved swiftly to apparently pre-appointed positions around the circular chamber.

I narrowed my eye in an effort to see more. Now I realized that the place was littered with curious paraphernalia, scattered about like grave goods in a plundered tomb. There were great brass bowls filled with what looked like spice standing on piles of glittering rock. Red candles were held in tightly bound bundles atop a mahogany rail that ran right around the room.

Still the shrill note continued. As I watched, they picked up the brass bowls and carried them over to the centre of the table. Stromboli's robed chest rose and fell visibly as he began to scoop out handfuls of mauve-coloured powder – a colour that was beginning to make me uneasy.

Vesuvius turned his masked head and, just for a moment, I had the curious sensation that his fixed features were moving, glowering. The painted mask gave him a strange pagan appearance and behind the diamond-shaped slits, his eyes were merely black hollows.

Stromboli handed him a brass goblet, into which the mauve powders were rapidly poured, then placed two of the black rocks into his outstretched hands. I saw now that they were chunks of raw flint.

'O Vulcan!' bellowed Stromboli. 'Son of Jupiter and Juno! Forger of Creation! Labourer beneath the slopes of great Etna. Smith of the Gods!'

'Vulcan!' cried the assembly.

I strained to hear.

The intonation rose ever higher. 'Builder of the brass houses,' thundered Stromboli. 'Shoer of the golden shoes with which the gods trod on wind or water.'

Something about wind?

'Ye who shod the mighty steeds of Jove's chariot! We honour thee!'

What was that? Cobblers?

'Vulcan! We honour thee!'

Stromboli brought his hands together with a great crack as he smashed the flints against themselves. At once, they sparked and in the blink of an eye, the ruddy powder that lay piled high in the goblet caught and flared up with a glorious purple flame. Yet the smoke did not seem to choke the assembly as it had with Charlie and me. Rather they seem to relish it, swaying gently as though in the grip of some powerful drug.

The hem of his velvet robes rustling over the flagged floor, Stromboli strode towards the wall.

'Now! In honour of the mighty volcano of Vesuvius, we offer our sacrifice!'

With great precision he took hold of one of the torch-sconces and pulled it toward him.

At once unseen gears began to clatter into life. Then, to my astonishment, the great round table began to hinge open like the lid of some titanic coffee-pot revealing, beneath it, the top of a stone-faced well. A waft of dank air came flooding towards me. It reminded me of the bottom-of-the-vase stink of Tom Bowler's office. Then, with the sound of further machinery, the whole roof began to open, as though some baleful eye was set there. What I first took for a puppet began to droop downwards. In the guttering torch-light I could see bare feet and legs, then, with a crunch of gears, a whole body flopped into view, suspended by its arms above the hole in the floor.

It was Charlie Jackpot!

He had been beaten, manacled at the wrists and hung from chains, clad only in a pair of grisly grey undergarments.

'Oh Christ!' he groaned. 'What do you want with me? Let me go!'

Stromboli was standing with hands on hips, surveying his nefarious handiwork. With a great clank like the moving hand of a town-hall clock, Charlie fell another few inches.

'Please!' he begged. 'Don't hurt me!'

'Our gift to Neptune!' For the first time, the pomposity of the ceremony was broken as Stromboli burst into throaty laughter.

Clunk!

Charlie's chained form descended a foot further towards the well. The boy cried out but the figures remained unmoved.

'So much for traitors,' hissed Vesuvius.

Then, with a snap of his fingers, he turned on his heel and marched out with Stromboli, Etna scurrying behind them. The yellow door slammed shut.

Footfalls on the spiral stair told me that these strange apostles of the volcano, were passing right by my hiding place. I waited until their steps had receded and then, taking a chance, I slipped out from behind the tapestry and dashed down the spiral stair towards the door of the round chamber.

With a quick look around, I pulled it open and nipped inside.

The air was still thick and unhealthy. Above me, Charlie, eyes closed, was groaning softly to himself. The strange system of cogs and pulleys that suspended him juddered again and his bound body descended another inch.

'Hello, Charlie,' I said, leaning against the edge of the well.

His eyes flicked open and he stared wildly down at me.

'Oh thank God! Mr Box!'

I, in turn, looked down into the dark water below. It was moving – either a sewer or an underground river of some sort. Either way it would be enough to dunk Charlie to death like a human madeleine cake.

'Glad to see you hale and hearty. Now where were we? You were, I believe, about to tell me something rather important.'

'Mr Box! Please. You got to get me out of here!'

I shrugged casually, jumped up on to the lip of the well and grabbed at one of the boy's shoulders but only succeeded in setting him swaying to and fro in a fashion that endangered us both. The mechanism dropped again; it seemed to have increased its speed. Charlie groaned pitiably.

'Can you move your hands at all?' I cried.

'No,' he gasped.

With a great creaking shudder, he dropped a whole foot into the well and gave a little yell.

I shook my head. 'If I can't stop this infernal device of theirs then you'll drown for sure.'

'Thanks a million.'

Again, Charlie's chained form dropped alarmingly. Now his head, hair stiff with sweat and grime, was level with the lip of the hole. Rushing to the wall, I scrabbled about amongst the maps and charts that littered the wooden rail. One, its colours gleaming darkly in the torch-light, was some kind of tough paper stretched between two cream-coloured tubes of metal. Snapping the thing together I moved quickly to the lip of the well and thrust it up towards the mechanism. On cue, the great cogs turned again and Charlie disappeared into the hole. Only his manacled arms projected now.

I strained on tip-toe but finally managed to shove the tube into the gears. At once the cogs seized, although it was obvious I hadn't bought Charlie much time. The oily teeth of the machine were already squeezing and crushing the thin metal of the map-tube.

Throwing myself over the stones of the well I pulled Charlie's arms towards me with one hand and tore the knife from my watch-chain with the other.

Feverishly, I pierced the lock of the manacles with the thin blade and rattled it about inside.

'Quickly, sir!' squealed Charlie, his voice a hollow echo. 'Oh, quickly!'

The lock snapped open. I slipped the blade between my teeth and, forcing the metal cuffs apart, I dragged Charlie from the hole just as the map tube was ground into pieces and the cogs resumed their inexorable round.

Little pieces of the destroyed chart fluttered like dead leaves all about us. Panting for breath, I found myself on the floor with my arms around Charlie as the now-empty manacles continued their descent into the depths.

'Well, Mr Box,' grinned Charlie. 'It seems you can't keep your hands off me after all.'

'You are very impudent, young man,' I replied. 'It will get you a long way. Now, let's get out of here.'

Just at that moment the yellow door was flung open, crashing back against the painted brick. Our hearts, I feel sure, stopped at the same moment.

Stromboli stormed in. The mask still disguised his eyes but it seemed a fair guess that he was staring down at Charlie and me as we lay in an undignified heap on the floor.

'What's this?' he thundered in Italian. 'The club has increased its membership somewhat unexpectedly, ah?' His masked head inclined a fraction as he looked at me.

I'm pretty nifty at thinking on my feet, even when I'm actually sitting down with a renter in my embrace, but this fellow's sudden appearance had me more than a little stumped.

With as much dignity as I could muster, I extricated myself from Charlie and got up.

'Do forgive the intrusion,' I said, twiddling with my cuff-link. In one swift terribly well-rehearsed movement I had my revolver out and levelled squarely at Stromboli. 'But please don't move.'

The tall man held up his hands but seemed quite calm. 'What is your business here, signor? Are you a . . . customer?'

'This boy,' I said, indicating Charlie, 'is . . . my valet. I received word that he was being held here against his will.'

'So you came here to bring him home?'

'Correct. My laundry, you see, is in a frightful state.'

Stromboli shrugged. 'Well, my dear sir. We need detain you no longer. There has evidently been some . . . misunderstanding. Your valet has been employed in this establishment and it appears that one of our gentlemen's . . . er . . . games . . .' He pointed to the chains hanging from the ceiling. 'Took on a logic of its own. If you were to let this little matter blow over, I'm sure no more need be said.' He indicated my revolver with a casual swing of his arm. 'There is really no need for these . . . histrionics.'

I glanced quickly about. Could we really get out of here without the alarm being raised? I was armed, of course, but these people were evidently fanatics and knew that Charlie had betrayed them. What punishment had they meant for me, I wondered?

'Well, this is all most irregular, sir,' I said, reaching down and hauling Charlie to his feet. 'I am not in the habit of rescuing my servants from dens of unnatural vice and then letting the matter pass.'

My indignity was, in all probability, a mite unconvincing.

'Given my pressing need for fresh linen, however, I am prepared to go no further with this. But I should like to know who I have the honour of addressing.'

The tall man laughed lightly and dropped his hands a fraction. With a jerk of the revolver, I indicated he should get them up again, sharpish.

Instead, three black-coated and very well-armed thugs emerged from behind their master.

Stromboli's arm shot out towards me. 'Kill him!' he yelled.

Oh lor.

One of the thugs dropped at once to his knee, assumed the position and prepared to fire his pistol. I shot him through the forehead and took a grim satisfaction from watching his brains slide across the wall like clay-slip.

Charlie rolled over and hid himself behind the lip of the well. Stromboli and another thug took cover behind the great raised table as I fired again. My report was answered with two shots of the thugs' own. We were effectively pinned down, cut off from the only door.

'Bloody hell!' whispered Charlie. 'This is a fix, Mr Box. What're we going to do?'

I levelled my revolver on the stone facing of the well and tried to get Stromboli's masked head in my sights. Frustratingly, it bobbed up and down like a shooting gallery target.

'You are trapped, my friend,' he called. 'We had been saving you for our next . . . *rehearsal*. But now I fear we must put a swift end to this sport.'

I was breathing hard. There seemed no way out. Bullets sang off the stonework that was our only cover. I held up my arm to shield myself from the splinters of masonry. There was a cry to my left and I saw that Charlie had been hit by the debris. He crumpled to the floor at my side.

'Take them!' roared Stromboli. 'Take them even if you have to die in the attempt! Forward, you scum!'

Obediently, the remaining thugs dashed forward. I looked around desperately. Only one bullet remained in my pearl-handled life-saver. No options presented themselves.

Except one.

I glanced down at the well.

Peeking over my stone barricade, I fired my last bullet. One black-coat was hit in the eye but the other was undeterred. Grabbing Charlie by the arm, and rolling over the lip of the well with a great unwilling cry, Lucifer descended into the pit and into the stinking darkness.

XVI

A DESPERATE FLIGHT

TRIED to grab at the chains that Charlie had hung from but we fell into nothingness: a sickening, awful lurch that felt like the hangman's drop. I was conscious only of my arms holding on to Charlie for grim death and my stomach flipping and my head spinning as we were precipitated downwards. If this was The Fall then I understood why my namesake came out so ill-tempered.

All of a sudden we were in water; warm, brackish, filthy water that seemed all around us, though I was hardly aware of a splash.

I swallowed a pint and then felt myself rushing towards the surface. Charlie was like a dead weight in my arms. Our heads broke the surface and I shook mine, blinking furiously as I tried to get my bearings in that horrible blackness.

Treading water, I managed to tuck Charlie's head in the crook of my elbow and wipe the slime from my stinging eyes. We were in some sort of tunnel, as expected, though whether this was a sewer or the course of an ancient river was impossible to tell. That there was a form of current was unmistakable, however.

I glanced upwards quickly. Above us, I saw the surviving thug's white face looking down at us as through the wrong way down a telescope. Would Stromboli order his man to jump after us? I gave in to the current. Charlie, oblivious it seemed to everything, was swept along with me.

In seconds we were moving swiftly away, borne like corks upon the effluent. As yet, no one seemed rash enough to follow us down.

After a little time, I became aware that the tunnel broadened out and I craned my neck from the water's embrace.

We had reached a confluence where three tunnels met and merged. A great iron grille barred further progress. The current took us up to this barrier and I clung on to the slime-strewn metal with one hand while cradling the unconscious Charlie in the other.

I peered through the grille. The river sluiced through it and plunged down into further darkness. It was a man-made waterfall of some kind, though not the type that Blondin would ever have chosen to cross.

Charlie opened his eyes. He stared at me for a few moments, then his bruised face broke into a grin. He seemed entirely unaware of his circumstances.

'Hullo,' he breathed.

I nodded. 'How're you feeling?'

He glanced down and his eyes widened as he found he was almost totally immersed in black water. His face suddenly creased in pain. 'Been better, Mr Box. Where the hell are we, if you don't mind me asking?'

I manoeuvred him towards the grille and unhooked my arm from beneath his jaw.

'Hang on to that,' I ordered. 'Need a rest.'

He managed to push his fingers through the holes of the wet metalwork and clung on, though I could see the pain in his stretched arms was returning with a vengeance.

I struggled out of my lovely tail-coat. It was nothing but a saturated encumbrance now and I pushed it away into the frothing water. Its immaculate tailoring ballooned briefly on the surface and then disappeared.

'There doesn't appear to be any exit this way,' I said at last. 'So we'll probably have to swim back against the current. Are you up to it?'

He didn't look it but he said yes.

I shook the grille with my hand but it was solid despite the corrosion on its surface.

'Where's the light coming from?' said Charlie.

'Where indeed?' I said, hauling myself up the grille and peering through the murk. A glow-worm phosphorescence was visible somewhere past it to the right of the waterfall.

'There's another tunnel through there,' I muttered.

Charlie shook his head. 'No. I meant *that* light.'

He raised his arm from the water and pointed back the way we had come.

Bobbing in the darkness were the unmistakable outlines of men in the water, the searing white light of flares hissing in their upraised hands.

I looked around wildly. The livid new light threw huge jagged shadows against the grille before us. I looked it up and down, thinking frantically, then pushed myself off from the tunnel side, took a huge breath and plunged down into the river. It was utterly disorientating.

Thrusting forward, I immediately felt for the grille in front of me. It was impossible to see a thing in the murky brine so I ran my hands over the surface of the submerged metal, groping for any change in the structure. Somewhere at the back of my mind I could picture one such sewer construction; a vast gated thing perhaps glimpsed as a child on a school-visit to one of Joseph Bazalgette's shit-sifting palaces.

For a few seconds, I groped blindly in the disgusting water, feeling nothing but the same repeated pattern of slimy iron bars. Then, yes! At last! My hands met space and I was dragged forward by the tug of an undoubtedly faster current. There had to be room for first Charlie and then me to push ourselves through.

I kicked off from the grille and raced to the surface. Shaking the water from my hair I briefly glimpsed a flotilla of flares bearing down on Charlie then, without a second thought, I grabbed him, pushed his head under the water, took another breath, and followed.

Bubbles rushed along the lines of our soaked bodies as we reached the hole in the grille and I forced us through.

All at once we were tumbling down, down, half-emerging into the air, then immersed again in the falling water, finally crashing into the tunnel on the other side and freedom.

Well, freedom of a kind. It wouldn't take those thugs long to discover what we had done and plunge through after us.

Charlie was taking in huge gulps of the foetid air.

'All right?' I quizzed. He nodded exhaustedly.

I swam ahead a little. There was now a clearer view of the strange light source. Not far from where we were floating there was a small hole in the tunnel wall. Half a dozen or so rotten bricks had tumbled through revealing a chamber beyond. I swam quickly towards the breach, gained it and managed to scramble up to get a better look. Before I slid down into the water again I saw, strung over the salt-corrupted walls like Christmas decorations, the unmistakable glow of electric light!

Relief flooded through me. Weak as he was, I knew that Charlie would rally at the sight of dry land and the chance of a rapid escape from our pursuers.

When I swam back to him, however, I could see that our recent exertions had taken their toll. His head was lolling back in the water and his eyes were showing white.

'Charlie!' I hissed. 'Wake up! There's a way out ahead. Just hold on a little longer.'

He fell forward and attempted to focus on me. He smiled stupidly and closed his eyes.

With a heavy sigh, I began to drag him onwards. The water in this new tunnel was much more shallow and I could feel the sediment-covered bottom squelching beneath my shoes as I threaded my arm under Charlie's and staggered towards the hole in the wall.

Meanwhile, a series of cries and oaths told me that our pursuers had worked out our method of escape through the grille.

When we reached the breach in the tunnel, I pushed Charlie through it and into the room beyond. Normally, the feel of strong buttocks in wet trousers might have made my thoughts wander but I shoved Charlie on without a second glance. As soon as he had fallen forward into a crumpled heap, I leaped up and pulled myself through.

I lay dazed for a long moment. Then, as my eyes adjusted to the light, I saw that we were surrounded by packing cases and ladders, black against the garish flare of the electric light. Charlie stirred and opened an eye experimentally.

'Some sort of warehouse,' I said, getting up and testing the windows. One creaked open on a hinged pane and moments later, we had clambered out on to the street. Perhaps it was not surprising that even in Naples we had some trouble finding a cab, given our state. Eventually, we gave up and managed to drag ourselves back down towards the harbour and finally into the reassuring warmth of the Hotel Santa Lucia.

The next day dawned blazing hot. Through the half-drawn blinds, I could see Naples sparkling almost painfully in the searing sun, as if in celebration that my life had been spared (one gets these fancies now and then). Perhaps I would go for a constitutional? A walk by the sea on this glorious morning would clear my head and lift my spirits! I drew the blinds shut and, shambling back to bed, lit a cigarette. Sod that.

Charlie Jackpot, whose tired face and dark-ringed eyes still somehow conspired to make him a corker, lay sprawled on the bed next to me. In the mess of sheets his form showed pale and flawless as a marble tomb effigy.

I slapped at his buttocks and he grudgingly emerged from sleep.

'Good morning, Charles.'

He grunted and burrowed further into the sheets.

'Let us return to our previous conversation,' I said brightly. 'The one so rudely interrupted by the noxious oil-lamp. What's going on in the Vesuvius Club?'

Charlie rubbed at his hair and groaned. 'Not now. I'm half-dead.'

'And thanks to me, only half.' I examined my bare knee. It was barked and bloodied. 'As I recall, you were trying to interest me in a little bargain.'

He raised himself up on one elbow and yawned. 'That's right.'

'You want a leg-up, yes? A way out of your sordid little existence?'

Charlie hugged himself and shivered. 'I just want to get a start in life, Mr Box. In return for what I know. Don't seem too unfair from where I'm lying.'

I nodded. A notion was forming in my early morning brain. 'Mr Jackpot, I currently find myself in the position of requiring a valet.'

The lad's face fell. 'What?'

'Don't answer me back like that, you little villain. Just listen –'

'Not *service*!' he moaned. 'That's what I want to get away from. I meant get *set up*! You know. Like a gentleman.'

'Dear me, we are ambitious, aren't we? What do you fancy? A villa in Broadstairs and two hundred a year?'

He frowned sulkily.

'If you don't wish to be pitched into the street I suggest you shut your pretty little mouth and pay attention.' I drew deeply on my cigarette. 'Your duties will be fairly light. Valeting, as I say. Cleaning. A little cooking. Running my baths. Saving Britain from mortal peril. That sort of thing.'

Charlie looked nonplussed. 'What . . . what happened to your old valet?'

'Shot,' I said blithely. 'You see Charles, I'm in a rather special-ized line of work. If you're genuinely interested, my *firm* will take you on.'

'Who do you work for?'

'His Majesty's Government.' I reached across him to stub out my cigarette on the marble table. 'I'm a spy, Charlie. An agent. An assassin. A sharp instrument of the powers that be. And I need an assistant. What do you say? It's not a bad life and you will have King Edward's undying gratitude.'

He frowned. 'I dunno.'

'"Don't seem too unfair from where I'm lying",' I threw back at him. 'There'll be a nominal wage. Just think! You'll be a pepper-corn renter!'

Charlie patted his bruised eye tenderly. 'What do you mean *nominal?*'

I snorted. 'You're on approval, my boy. There can be no question of a decent salary until I am quite satisfied as to the depravity of your character.'

'Bloody hell!'

'Cheer up,' I murmured. 'I'm sure we'll rub along together very well.'

There came a knock at the door. Cursing, I jumped from the bed, slipped into a dressing gown and padded to the door.

A uniformed telegraph boy bowed to me. He was a stringy thing wearing the insolent slouch of the adolescent like a badge of pride.

'Signor Box?'

I nodded and he placed the wire into my hand. I scrabbled at the envelope. *Sir Emmanuel vanished*, I read. *Come at once. Thos Stint (Butler)*.

The boy cocked his head. 'You answer, signor?'

'No. No answer.' I closed the door.

Charlie had risen and was struggling into his frightful grey knickers and striped socks. 'What is it?'

'Your former master has disappeared, Charles. We must make our way there forthwith. You can continue your interrupted tale as we go.'

I dressed in a whirlwind, reloaded my pistol and, as I followed Charlie to the door, passed the pile of clothes I had discarded from the previous night's adventures. I pulled up sharp. Something shiny was projecting from the damp-mottled cloth of my destroyed waistcoat.

Stooping, I pulled it out. It was a fragment of chart that I must have salvaged from the round room. It showed some kind of cross-section, coloured in various lurid inks. It was impossible to make out much detail and I realized at once that I must consult some literature on the subject.

'Two birds with one stone,' I muttered to myself with a smile.

'Eh?' said Charlie.

'Nothing. Come on.'

We raced down the quayside and found a cab. The driver, an old fellow with eyebrows like white sea-urchins, propelled us northwards with gratifying expedition.

Rocked from side to side as we sat in the dingy carriage, Charlie continued his story.

'Well, I kept me eyes and ears open, like Mr Poop'd said to do. I didn't pick up anything for ages –'

'Not like you.'

'Then one night I overheard a bit of talk. It concerned some old geezers back in Blighty and one over here. Well, my ears pricked up because the one over 'ere was his nibs – Sir Emmanuel. My bleedin' employer. Hello, I thinks, what're they up to?'

'And did you find out?'

'Not exactly. But I 'eard them saying there was a woman to be brought across too. Party called Knight.'

I gave a satisfied grunt. 'K to V.C. Go on.'

'Well, I told all this to Mr Poop but then he never come back.'

I looked out of the window and frowned. 'No, he wouldn't have. They were on to him, Charlie. They smashed his brains in with one of their quaint antiquities. Anything else? It seems to me your precious information is rather thin.'

Charlie shrugged. 'Listen, I've risked everything to throw my lot in with you. I tried to hear more but I weren't allowed in. Venus's fella –'

'You've seen him?'

'Just the back of 'im.'

'Big fellow? Broad back?'

Charlie shook his head. 'No. Not at all. Slight, really. He had a hat and cloak on but he looked pretty slight to me.'

'Oh I see. Well, you were saying?'

'Don't know if I should tell you, seeing as how you set so little store by my "precious information".'

I sighed. '*Please* go on.'

Charlie gave a small smile. 'All I know is, Venus's fella has something to do with the House of the Lightning Tree, the biggest den in Naples.'

'Den?'

'Opium, Mr Box.'

I was pondering this when I was jerked forward as the cab drew to a halt. 'Ah! We're here!'

We were outside the crumbling manor house. I jumped from the cab and positively wrenched the bell from its housing as I summoned the butler.

The old retainer came stumbling out and pulled open the gates. He glared at Charlie.

'Where the devil 've you been, young man?'

'Never mind that now,' I interrupted him. 'What's happened? We came as soon as –'

The servant was shaking his head mournfully. 'He's gone, sir. Vanished!'

'Anything unusual in his behaviour?'

Stint ushered us towards the door, casting venomous glances at Charlie. 'No, sir. Not at thing. I brought him the post as usual at a quarter to nine. I returned at ten to bring him his morning coffee but found the library locked. When there was no reply to my knocking I had the door broken open.'

We had stopped at the library door and saw the lock was shattered. Stint pushed it open. 'The library was empty.'

I looked over at the wheeled-chair – the imprint of the ex-occupant's arse plain in its faded orange cushion – and then at his desk. Nothing leapt out as being particular although the atmosphere of the room was unusually stifling even allowing for the weather and Quibble's infernal over-heating. Moreover the windows were open . . .

'The question being then, how does a crippled man escape via the French windows?'

'It is unthinkable, sir. That the windows were open at all is most singular given Sir Emmanuel's horror of cold.'

I nodded absently. 'The post you brought. Of what did it consist?'

Stint pointed towards the desk. 'There they are, sir.'

I looked down. Spread out on the blotter were a quantity of envelopes. I reached towards them and then, thinking better of it, took out my handkerchief and, covering my hand, spread them out in a fan.

'Nine, all told,' I mused. 'But only four have been opened.' Bending down, I peered at the opened letters. 'Invitations all, it seems. Hello! What's this?'

Almost obscured by the blotter was a tenth envelope, a tell-tale mauve in colour and edged in black. I picked up the letter knife and worried it from its hiding place.

'Addressed to Sir Emmanuel,' I said, flipping it over.

Stint moved closer to the desk. 'But no enclosure, sir?'

I shook my head. 'Where did you find your master?'

'He was over there by that bookshelf. Between *Decline of the Procreative Urge* by H. H. Nunstead and Pothan's *On the Efficacy of Tarmacadam.*'

I looked up at him.

'Hard not pick up the master's habits, sir,' he said with a sniff.

I crossed to the bookshelf and took the place occupied by the late scientist. I glanced over at the cold, empty grate of the fire.

'There was, of course, a fire burning?'

'Of course, sir.'

'Over here! Mr Box!'

I turned at Charlie's cry and moved swiftly to where he stood, swinging one of the French windows open and shut. He stepped outside and pointed to the exterior lock. A swift examination told me all I needed to know.

Striding to the fireplace I again folded my handkerchief over my hand and began to root about in the blackened embers.

'Ah!' I cried, my fingers fastening upon a small fragment of charred mauve paper. '*Here* is that enclosure, Stint. Or what remains of it.'

I held the scrap of paper close to my face. A strong odour at once assailed me. It was pungent and familiar.

'D'you smell that, Charlie?' I cried, waving it under the boy's nose. 'I'd say ... I'd say this paper has been impregnated. Impregnated with a chemical with which you and I have had some little acquaintance!'

'Good grief!' gasped Stint. 'You mean you are addicted to some *drug*?'

'Eh? No, no!' I stood up straight. 'This is what I believe happened here this morning. The letter in the mauve envelope was a lure, containing some bogus message and instructions that it was to be burnt upon receipt. Your master did as he was told and was then overcome by the noxious substance in which the letter had been soaked.'

Stint bit his lip anxiously. 'And then he threw open the windows in an effort to clear the fumes?'

'Nay, for the windows have been forced open from the outside as Mr Jackpot here discovered! Whoever sent this letter lay out there in wait. When they saw that their plans were working they broke open the windows and grabbed Sir Emmanuel. They then left the windows ajar to allow the toxin to escape.'

'But who, sir? Who would do such a thing?'

The odour of that vile chemical contained in the mauve letter was unmistakable. The purplish dust on Verdigris's desk! The charred paper in Sash's grate! All three must have received a mauve envelope. Whatever had been written therein must also have contained instructions to burn its deadly enclosure.

Now I knew how – just not by whom.

It was time to test just what Stint had absorbed. I took the scrap from my waistcoat pocket. 'What do you make of that, Stint?'

The butler peered at it.

I thrust my hands into my pockets. 'A cross-section of some kind. I wonder if you could point us to a volume or two on the structures of modern machines?'

Stint shook his head. 'Oh no, sir.'

'No? Why not?'

'It's not a machine, sir. It is a volcano,' he said.

XVII

THE LAIR OF MR LEE

'IS it, by George!'

I looked over his shoulder and indicated a double line that had been inked into the shape on the chart. 'And this?'

'I believe it is known as a vent, sir. A fissure in the rock through which the magma flows to the surface.'

Charlie took the fragment from him. A series of arrows had been drawn by hand inside the lines. 'Then why are these arrows pointing towards the *inside* of the volcano?'

'I really cannot say,' sniffed the butler.

We advanced towards the book shelves. 'Tell me, Stint. Do you think, by any chance, we could track down the particular volcano?'

A smile fluttered over his pale lips. 'Every chance, I should think, sir. I'm sure Sir Emmanuel would be very happy to know his collection is being put to good use. I believe we shall need the steps, sir, if you'd be so kind.'

Charlie pulled the revolving library

steps from their shadowy niche. Before I could protest, he had mounted the steps and began pushing his way along the shelves. The steps' wheels squealed appallingly.

'Hmmph,' said Stint, disapprovingly. 'Now then,' he said and pointed upwards. 'Third shelf. What do you see?'

In the feeble light Charlie passed treatise after dreary treatise. There were atlases, text-books . . .

'*Manlove's Tectonic Activity*,' Charlie read. '*Vulcanism in the Pacific Rim . . . The Lava Bomb . . .*'

'We're getting warmer, you might say.'

Charlie had stopped with one hand on the shelf, preparing to push himself off again when a hefty book in a cloth-bound cover seemed to catch his attention. '*Magnetic Viscosity*?' he called hopefully.

'That's the one,' said Stint.

'Maxwell Morraine,' I cried.

Stint looked over at me. 'Yes, sir? What of him?'

'It never occurred to me to ask *you*, Stint. What do *you* know of your late master's colleague, Morraine? He threw me out of the house at the very mention of his name.'

Stint shrugged. He seemed suddenly weary. Charlie came down the steps and stood by him, handing him the book. Stint began to flick through it as he spoke. 'You are far too young to remember, sir, but it was quite a tragedy. Professor Morraine went . . . funny.'

'Funny?'

'In the head, sir. They do say it was on account of his wife running off with some gent but Sir Emmanuel told me Mr Morraine had always been a little touched. Even when they were students together.'

'Yes. I had heard they attended the same college. And they came out here, didn't they, to work?'

Stint nodded vigorously, then paused, comparing the fragment of chart with an illustration within the great book. 'Sir Emmanuel's father had this house and he always loved the Italian countryside. Seemed like a natural place to pursue their researches. All Greek or Italian to you and me, I suppose, sir, but Professor Morraine had theories about the massive potential energy contained within the lava, within the very stuff of the earth's core! But it all came to naught. Then there was the fire and poor Mrs Morraine . . . well. Aha! I have found the volcano, sir.'

He held the book aloft, the piece of chart pressed against the relevant page. To no one's great surprise, it was a cross-section of Mount Vesuvius.

Emmanuel Quibble's extraordinary library was proving to be invaluable. Following the positive identification of the geological chart, we began digging for a clue as to the identity of the strange chemical used on the old man.

Charlie sat down and put his feet up on the desk, pulled off his boots and began to pick at his toes, earning fierce stares from Stint.

'Make yourself useful,' I ordered, tossing him a copy of *Arsenical Poisoning and its Causes*.

'I am. Being useful, I mean. I'm thinking.'

'Ha! I am on His Majesty's service. You are on mine.'

He put his hands behind his head. Is it possible to swagger whilst sitting down?

'Seems to me there is a connection between this purple stuff and what I told you about Venus's fella.'

'What about him?'

'The House of the Lightning Tree. Remember?'

His face dimpled into a cock-eyed smile.

'Opium?' I cried.

And within a very few minutes, thanks to Stint's cross-referencing, we had it. 'A distillation of the seeds of the manganese poppy,' I read, tracing a finger over the delicate colour-plate showing the flower.

'Never heard of it.'

'I don't doubt it. Grows only in certain parts of the Himalayas. Now, get your boots on, Charlie, you're going back out.'

'I am?'

'Yes. Arrange some transport for our visit to this den. We'll reconvene in the lobby of the Santa Lucia at ten.'

'Righto, chief.' Charlie got up and struggled into his boots, holding the door frame for support.

'Oh, and Charlie?'

'Yes?'

'Do mind out for yourself. I fear you are becoming indispensable.'

The boy smiled and I felt a curious twinge as he closed the door after him. I thought at first it must be some undigested fancy from the Café Gambrinus but I finally recognized it as an almost alien emotion. *Fondness*.

I took my leave of Stint and returned to the hotel. Quibble, Verdigris, Bella, Reynolds, Charlie – my head was spinning. After a long bath I soon felt more like myself. I felt myself so much, in fact, that I ended up having one off the wrist, imagining the wondrous Bella wrapped in my fevered embrace.

We dined together that evening and Miss Pok looked more glorious than ever, I thought, glowing like a moonbeam in the gilded shadows of the restaurant. I apologized again for the unseemly hastiness of my departure from the funicular.

'There's really no need,' she said lightly. 'You did warn me you might have to . . . pop off a little hastily now and then.'

'Did that Italian chap see you back all right?'

'Oh yes. He was quite charming.'

She smiled and raised her glass. 'To you, Lucifer.'

I responded, clinking my crystal against hers. 'No, to us.'

'You have not though, been entirely frank with me,' she said after sipping her wine.

'No?'

'No. Unless you felt a pressing need to sketch the crowd, it did look very much like you were *chasing* someone.'

'Ah,' I said. 'Umm . . .'

She held up her hand. 'Don't say anything. I know you would tell me if you were able. There are matters of great import on hand, are there not?'

I nodded slowly.

'And this business with Mr Miracle is somehow part of it.'

'Indeed.'

She nodded. 'Then one day, perhaps, you will tell me about it.'

I liked the sound of that. It promised a *future*. Together.

We said goodnight at her hotel room door and, for the first time, I was allowed a kiss on her smooth cheek.

Ah, me!

Anticipating a night's work, I returned to my own room and changed into a Norfolk jacket, nautical sweater and light but sensible tweed trousers. On the stroke of ten, I slipped down to the lobby and found Charlie waiting for me.

I looked about for a four-wheeler but Charlie pulled at my sleeve. 'No carriages. They'll hear us coming a mile off.'

To my amazement, he pulled aside a quantity of canvas that lay in a bundle in the street. Beneath it, at an angle to the wall, was a tandem bicycle.

'Is that the best you could do?' I cried.

'Needs must,' he grinned. 'I nicked it.'

I have never been a, shall we say, *fan de cycle*, and was not in the best of moods for mounting one. However, Charlie was right – it would be a far less conspicuous way of approaching Naples' premier opium den than a cab. I grudgingly acquiesced and dragged the machine from its hiding place. Together we managed to mount it. After a few wobbly moments, we mastered the thing and began peddling feverishly up the slopes to Capodimonte, following Charlie's directions. I was grateful, at last, for all those bone-shaker lessons my governess forced me to take.

At length, we turned into some kind of rookery, a shambolic collection of semi-ruined villas adjacent to a vast olive grove. The rotten plasterwork of the structures was visible even in the starlight; the eaves of the buildings practically merged into one another like a line of guardsmen toppling on the parade ground.

I hopped off the bicycle and held it steady so that Charlie too could dismount. Then we began to push it quietly along the road. Before us was a large and disreputable-looking building with a blackened, twisted olive tree dominating its façade.

'That looks like it,' whispered Charlie.

I nodded – even in this town of curiosities, what else could it be? – and indicated that we should lay down the bicycle on the parched earth.

I felt glad of my reloaded revolver as we advanced into that filthy hole.

Torches burned in sconces on the fronts of some of the dwellings and it was possible to see figures huddled in the shadowed gloom.

That they meant us ill was obvious and I raised the gun and cocked it in as blant a fashion as I could.

'Stay close by me, Charlie,' I hissed.

The shadows fell back a little but we hurried briskly along past walls of blotched green plaster.

Charlie hammered repeatedly on the door of the big house.

I slipped into a shadowed niche, watching as the figures that surrounded us grew bolder. I distinctly saw a great bear of a man with a kerchief knotted around his head grinning at me in the flickering torch-light. In his hand he carried a thick cudgel and he was slapping it repeatedly into his palm.

'Let's cut along, eh, Charlie?' I said quietly.

Suddenly, the door creaked open and an indisputably Chinese face loomed out of the darkness.

'What you want?' squawked the newcomer, his scantily bearded face appearing as a strip of red flesh in the torch-light.

I surged forward through the door and pushed him backwards. Charlie bounded inside, darted past him and slammed the door shut behind us.

'What you do? What you do? You cannot come in here!' barked the little man. He was round as a pudding and clad in a filthy muslin robe.

I levelled the revolver at him. 'I think this will do as my passport,' I hissed in his face.

'No need for this!' cried the Chinaman in a hoarse whisper. 'Why you come like this? We all friends here. You want pipe?'

'No. Yes. Let's get inside,' I urged.

We followed the Chinaman through a warren of rubbish-strewn corridors, emerging eventually into a large chamber that might once have been a sitting room. The walls were festooned with cobwebs and damp-blossoms. What was visible of the floor showed naked and broken floor-boards leading to some noisome cellar beneath.

The prevailing impression, however, was of a terrible fug, a poisonous atmosphere rich in the unmistakable scent of the poppy. Opium smoke hung in wreaths over the heads of the multitude that crammed the room, their slack jaws and rolling eyes speaking of days and weeks lost to the pipe. Like so many sacks, the addicts lay strewn over the floor, gurgling happily as they sucked, the shining black beads of opium glowing like fireflies.

Don't get me wrong. I'm no prude and like a pipe as much as the next man. But all things in moderation, as Genghis Khan used to say.

Our Chinese host was threading his way through the heaps of human detritus, lantern in hand. 'My name Mr Lee. You fine gentlemen. I have office. We talk there.'

The 'office' was at least clean. Two chairs and a table comprised the only furniture. I sat in one and Charlie sat down heavily on the other. Lee set the lantern on the table and giggled most unpleasantly.

'I have extra fine poppy for you, English. Very cheap –'

'No thank you. I have very expensive tastes. I want some of the purple poppy.'

Lee's blinked then laughed. 'I not understand. House of Lightning Tree have many pipes. But no purple poppy. Come. Relax.'

I stood up, seized him by his filthy robe and pushed him up against the wall. 'My friend and I are in something of a rush, do you see? We need to know to whom you supply the *purple* poppy?'

His fat face flushed in alarm and he shot an appealing look over my shoulder at Charlie.

'You crazy! You crazy! Please!'

Charlie got to his feet. 'I can't help you,' he said to Lee. 'This fella's a painter. He'll as like bite your ear off unless you tell him what he wants to know.'

Lee gave a gulp and his chins wobbled. 'I know nothing.'

I slammed him against the rotten plaster. 'Tell me, you glorified tobacconist.'

'There no such thing as purple poppy!' he squealed.

I nudged the barrel of the pistol into the folds of fat around his wet mouth. 'Believe me, I will take a professional interest in seeing the red of your blood running against the yellow of your skin.'

Lee looked at us desperately, wringing his chubby hands. 'I tell you! I tell you!'

Shaking with terror, Lee sank back against the rotten plaster. His pin-prick eyes closed momentarily. 'Purple poppy come over especial from Shanghai. Most rare. Most precious. It is much dangerous. It has many faces. Up, down, forget some, even kill you. Must be very, very careful. Needs expert. No good for you nice gentlemen!'

'I see,' I said quietly. 'And you've been supplying this filthy stuff to someone, haven't you? To what end?'

'I cannot tell you . . .'

I pressed the pistol further into his face. Sweat was streaming over his oily skin. 'Please! Please! I know only my instructions! I deliver purple poppy and I hear no more.'

I stepped away from the perspiring fat man while still keeping him covered with the pistol. 'Deliver it where, exactly?'

Lee smiled his fat smile. 'I can give you address, but it is impossible for me to leave these premises, my business, you understand –'

I levelled my revolver at his nethers. 'You will take us there, Lee. Or the Neapolitan castrati will be acquiring a new member.'

The darkness was thickening as I commandeered a dog-cart and set off with Charlie and the reluctant Chinee into the sleeping streets. We must have made a pretty sight, lashing away at the skinny steeds but then Naples is accustomed to strange sights; half-mad city that it is.

Lee spoke little but contented himself with pointing and urging as we clattered through the narrow alleys, ducking wet washing that was strung between the houses and shops.

We clattered out of the city and along the coastal road.

'Now look where we're heading,' observed Charlie with a grunt. It was no great surprise to see the great volcano looming before us, its fiery crown smoking like a beacon. After an hour or so, we rolled on into an area of broad parkland. A strange collection of buildings formed a squared 'C' shape around the perimeter. In the ruined isolation of the C's centre stood a blackened villa, its windows fogged with soot.

'This place,' said Lee. 'Place where I bring poppy.'

I jumped from the cart and swung my pistol round to cover Lee. 'Come on, out!'

The Chinaman shook his head. 'Please. Do not make me. I not want to go in there.'

'What's the matter?' cried Charlie, clambering out and lighting a lantern. 'We'll look after you.'

Lee did not appear to be reassured and shook his head violently, eyes glittering like jet. 'Not that. I never see anybody when I come. But . . . house haunted.'

'Pah!' I ejaculated.

'No, no!' protested Lee. 'Is the truth, sirs! Please let poor Lee go home now.'

I shook my head. 'I fear not, old man. Don't worry your top-knot, though. Any spooks will get a blast of this.' I cocked the revolver and the three of us began to make our way stealthily across the grass.

A dim light shone in the lower floor of a neighbouring house. We slipped into the shadows so as to remain invisible. I looked about. A pair of old, blistered black doors were visible at the base of the building. The coal cellar.

'Where did you bring the poppies, Lee? To this cellar?'

Lee shook his nervous head. 'No, no. Through front. Come, come.'

We moved silently forward to the blackened edifice of the villa and crept over the gravel to the porch. The front door seemed intact but all the windows that were visible had been boarded up. I reasoned it was wiser not to advertise our presence so, in a very few moments, I had pulled down some of the splintering wood and exposed a smoke-blackened window-pane. I took off my muffler and, wrapping it around my fist, smashed the glass. It gave with only a faint tinkling.

The three of us clambered inside, our feet sinking slightly into a carpet of glass and debris, Lee whimpering and squealing like a nervous child.

The atmosphere was at once oppressive with decay. The lantern showed fire-damaged furniture, their varnished surfaces blistered and cracked.

I turned to Charlie. 'Seems quiet enough.'

'As the grave.'

Lee wailed softly. I grabbed him by his robe. 'Where did you leave the opium?'

The Chinaman was looking about in terror. 'Here in hallway. Not want to stay longer than need to.'

The dusty floor of the entranceway had clearly been disturbed. Charlie held up his lamp revealing a series of trails, as though sleds had cut swathes through the dust.

I tapped him on the shoulder. 'You explore the house, Charlie,' I whispered, lighting my own lantern. 'Mr Lee and I will take the cellar.'

'Righto.'

I watched him heading for the mouldering staircase then began swinging the lantern about in search of the entrance to the coal cellar. I found what I was looking for in a recessed corner beneath the stairs.

'Please, sir,' whimpered Lee. 'Let us go now. This place bad.'

I felt for a door handle. It was big and carved into a hexagonal shape. To my very great surprise, it turned easily and the door creaked softly open.

Gingerly we stepped down on to a poorly lit wooden stair. The smell of damp assailed me at once but my attention was riveted on the curious sight before me.

The coal cellar appeared to have been adapted into some kind of laboratory. The remains of tubes, flasks and retorts littered benches and there were fragments of geological charts pinned to the wall. Fragments, merely, as the place now resembled the flue of some great chimney. The broken walls were soot-streaked and wet. Glass lay twisted into fantastic shapes on the remains of benches and cupboards. In the corner was a broad, fat-legged table and on it burned a single candle.

There was someone else in this house.

Just as the thought crossed my mind, I heard a terrible moaning.

For a moment I took it to be Lee but the fat creature was jibbering with fear right by me, his eyes clamped shut. I glanced over my shoulder and back the way we had come. The sound was coming from up the stairs, an awful, wretched groan, followed by a burst of ragged sobbing.

'Charlie!' I cried. 'Is that you?'

At once the noise ceased. I felt the hairs on the back of my neck rise.

'Charlie?'

I jammed the pistol in Lee's back and quickly we mounted the cellar steps, pushed open the door and stepped back into the hallway.

I held the lantern high above my head but could see no one.

Then the moaning began again, as though a soul were in torment. It seemed to be coming from upstairs. I swung the lantern in that direction and, just for an instant, caught a glimpse of something white on the landing above. It seemed to flutter into the shadows like a great bird. I started. Lee absolutely yelled in shock.

'Shut up, you fat fool!' I spat then, and, urging him forward with the revolver, made for the staircase.

The creak of our feet on the rotten stair seemed to halt the sobbing once more. We pressed on, ascending swiftly.

I called out for Charlie, then swung the lantern round as I caught sight of the whitish shape again, still above us on the staircase. It was a figure, dressed in some sort of billowing white gown. Or shroud, I thought dully.

I strode towards the phantom shape, determined not to be rattled.

'Who's there?' I demanded. 'Show yourself!'

With Lee almost hysterical at my side, I reached the top of the staircase and was confronted by a door. Gingerly, I reached out a hand and took hold of the knob.

I swallowed, nervous in spite of myself, and began to turn it.

A hand reached out of the shadows and clasped my arm. I pulled back in undisguised alarm, thrusting the lamp aloft and shining a light down on the frightened face of Charlie Jackpot.

'Bloody hell, Mr Box! Did you see it? Did you see it?'

I nodded, a little too quickly. 'I saw it!'

'The face!' he whispered. 'Did you see its face?'

All at once, the door in front of us flew open and the figure in white seemed to swarm upon us.

I yelled in stark terror and batted at the thing with both hands. Lee took to his heels and pounded down the rotten stairway. Charlie threw himself behind me and we sank back against the wall as the spectre went hurtling down the stairs after the Chinaman, screaming and sobbing as though it were a denizen of Hell itself.

'Christ Almighty!' I gasped, after we had picked ourselves up off the landing. 'What was it?'

Charlie shook his head. 'It went . . . it went towards the cellar.'

I stood up and opened the lantern to its fullest extent.

Slowly and silently, we descended the stairs and approached the door to the cellar.

There was no sign of Lee.

I opened the door, taking care that it should not creak, and then took a few tentative steps downwards.

I lifted the lamp. Behind me, Charlie gasped and clapped a hand to his mouth.

Sitting in a fire-charred chair was the ruin of a woman. Dressed in a stained and tattered white robe, her hair hung about her shoulders in great, knotted clumps. It was her face, though, which drew all our attention. The eyes looked out from a skull-like visage from which the flesh seemed to have been boiled away. Great blistered lumps of skin hung like candle-wax from the jaw and cheek-bones.

'Good God,' whispered Charlie.

The woman looked at me wildly, those dreadful eyes glistening in the lantern-light. Then she began to moan once more, her whole body shuddering as though a disinterred mummy had been brought to some foul simulacrum of life.

And all at once I knew her.

'Mrs Knight?' I cried. 'Mrs Midsomer Knight?'

'Yes,' said the voice of Lee behind us. 'Most regrettable that you will never have chance to meet her properly.'

He was brandishing a Colt in his pudgy hand.

'Please to stay still. I can certainly kill one of you before you have chance to overpower me.' The Chinee turned his narrow black eyes upon me and smiled. 'Drop gun.'

With a sigh, I dropped my revolver to the tiled floor.

Lee levelled his own gun at me, a horrible snarling grin flickering over his lips as he bent down to retrieve mine. He thrust it inside his robes. 'You have done well, Mr Box. But it is time to stop toying with you. You dangle like child's puppet. So sorry.'

He advanced on the wretched woman before us. He plucked a hypodermic syringe from somewhere in his robes, and with practised efficiency plunged it into her forearm. With a groan, she slumped forward. 'Now, please to escort lady from cellar.'

He gestured with the Colt and Charlie and I manhandled Mrs Knight up the stairs and back into the hallway. Thanks to the nameless drug – no doubt the purple poppy in one of its many guises – she was the very opposite of a ghost. She weighed a ton.

Lee ushered us through the house, into a large, gloomy room dominated by a pair of disreputable-looking French windows. Its floor was an inch-thick in dust but clearly visible in its centre were four coffins, dragged in from the hallway.

Three of the coffins were sealed, the fourth open. Lee smiled. 'One bird fly. She not have enough of purple poppy. Now she sleep better. Please to put her in.'

Reluctantly, Charlie and I lowered the woman into the empty coffin, its satin lining rustling in a peculiarly horrible fashion.

'Let us check on others,' said Lee with a smile. 'Please to open coffins.'

Gingerly, Charlie knelt down and lifted the lid from the first of the grisly boxes.

'Raise lantern please, Mr Box,' said Lee with infuriating politeness.

Within the coffin was what appeared to be the corpse of a man, his skin waxen and deathly pale. He was of large build and had a very prominent chin. His eyes were spaced wide apart. Professor Eli Verdigris.

The remaining coffins revealed, as expected, Professors Sash and Quibble. All of them lived on. Lived on in some ghastly, drug-induced coma.

'So all is ready. The party is complete.'

'What the hell is all this for, Lee?' I demanded.

Lee said nothing but indicated that we should move towards the French windows. Charlie pushed at the rotten woodwork until the doors groaned open.

Beyond lay an extraordinary landscape, lit by flaming torches – a vista of shattered stonework, tree-lined avenues and ancient, rutted roadways. I stepped out on to the flagged ground and gasped.

'What is this place?' cried Charlie.

'You not know?' said Lee with a horrid smile.

'I know,' I breathed. 'It is Pompeii!'

The torches illumined the ruins in a fearful relief, the hazy black hump of Vesuvius rearing over the lost city like the back of some dreadful beast.

'And now,' said Lee, hissing with laughter and brandishing both pistols. 'It is time for you to die.'

For an instant, I despaired, letting my hands drop to my sides. But in that moment, Charlie jumped out in front of me and hurled his lantern at the Chinaman. It hit him full in the chest, there was a satisfying splintering of glass and as the startled Lee looked down in surprise, his foul gown burst alight, and he was enveloped in flame.

I darted forward and brought my own lantern crashing down on Lee's head. He staggered and fell forward on to his knees, dropping a pistol and battering desperately at his blazing robe with his free hand.

Despite his panic and his hideous shrieks of pain, Lee raised a shaking hand and aimed a pistol at me. Roaring like an enraged tiger I ran at him full force and planted my fist in his throat. I felt the flesh give sickeningly and he toppled to the flagstones, smacking his cheek against the crumbling masonry.

Charlie was at my side in an instant. He whipped off his jacket and succeeded in putting out the flames.

'Well done, Charlie,' I said, breathlessly. 'Let's get the fat lump inside. Once he's recovered his senses, he can tell us what the hell's going on.'

Charlie looked down at Lee and shook his head, "Fraid not, sir. You don't know your own strength. He's a gonner.'

I turned the Chinaman over. His wind-pipe was crushed and he was quite still.

'Bugger,' I said eloquently.

Exhaling heavily, Charlie sat down on the flagstones and looked at me. 'Now what?'

I peered into the fiery gloom. 'Now, Mr Jackpot, we wait. Sooner or later, someone is going to come and collect those coffins.'

XVIII

NECROPOLIS

FOR what seemed like hours, there was no sign of activity. We passed the time exploring this relic of the ancient world – a frozen, grey world, stopped in a moment by the power of the great volcano. The ruins that littered the gardens of the villa did not seem to form part of the main excavation, and were unattended – a private monument. Charlie came across what appeared to be the entrance to a tunnel but it proved to be merely an ancient well. Neither of us felt further inclined to mess with wells.

I recalled my previous visit to the ruin and how, despite the loathsome press of gawping day-trippers, I had found Pompeii quite magnificent; its frescoed villas, its filthy pictures, its roads still rutted with the tracks of ancient carts. Yet it also wears a melancholy aspect, for here are laid bare past lives, here is the shattered grandeur that was the Roman Empire, here lie the actual folk themselves, or casts of their tortured remains – *the skeletons still within* – so that teeth show horribly in rictus grins from shapeless lumps of plaster.

In the flickering torchlight now, undisturbed by the goggling crowds, it was possible to feel one had actually slipped back in time. I explored the villa while Charlie walked about the grounds. The black and gold murals I found looked fresh and vivid, the ancient scribblings on the walls outside as though the graffitist had only lately quit the scene. When Charlie returned from his recce, I half expected his silhouetted form to resolve itself in toga and sandals.

I gazed over his shoulder at the smoking summit of the volcano.

'Look at her, Charlie,' I whispered. 'Vesuvius looks down upon Pompeii as if to say "I have destroyed you once. How dare you show your face?" One day it'll make good its threat and cover all this up again.'

'Then people could come and stare at us,' chimed in Charlie.

'Not a pleasant thought is it?' I replied. 'I'd hate to have some hairy fool poking a stick at my petrified bum.'

We laughed. Charlie sat down next to me as I stretched out over the flagstones, enjoying my fag. Above us the stars packed the black sky.

'What are you thinking, Mr Box?' said Charlie gently.

I continued to stare at the sky. 'Only that a night such as this should not be spent in the contemplation of mortal danger but of love.'

The boy lay down next to me. In the soft silence I could hear his quick breathing. I suppose I knew that he wanted me to place my hand on his, to turn him towards me and kiss him with all the fever that that sulphurous atmosphere demanded. Instead I flicked my cigarette away and heaved a sigh.

'But business before pleasure,' I said, sitting up. 'Miss Bella Pok will have to wait.'

'Who?' said Charlie sharply.

'A rather singular young lady of my acquaintance. Perhaps when all this is over . . .'

The boy's face fell. Aren't I a rotter?

Before Charlie could say something he might regret I stayed him with an outstretched hand. Just visible in the distant gloom was a curious purplish glow.

Charlie had already moved away and I could see him straining to listen. Soon I became aware of the sound of trudging feet on stone and, a little afterwards, seven or eight unnaturally tall men lumbered into our line of sight. Charlie gasped and I too wondered briefly whether they were some kind of phantasm. The queasy mauve light above their heads told its own story, however; the poor wretches wore the same brass helmets as my attacker from the Vesuvius Club.

They clumped in single file towards the villa and I beckoned Charlie to duck behind the cover of the opened windows. As the strange procession trooped past us and into the villa, we stood stock still, aware solely of the warm breeze in the great dark trees.

With effortful grunting, the helmeted zombies trudged back into the garden, carrying the four coffins between them. We waited as long as we dared and then set off in pursuit.

The unearthly glow from the brass helmets functioned like the Israelites' pillar of fire and so Charlie and I were able to shadow the funereal procession with some deftness. Appropriately enough we were making our way through the city's ancient cemetery, the rather charmingly named Via delle Tombe. Passing through the old town gateway, we soon reached what seemed to be a massive earthworks. The zombified men put down the coffins and stood stock still, as immobile as the tombstones that surrounded them.

Crouching low, I peered across the earthworks. A thin strip of yellowy light was just visible.

'Where's that coming from?' gasped Charlie.

'I do believe,' I said, getting to my feet, 'from under the ground.'

Charlie began to rise also but stopped, half-crouched. 'Sir?'

'Hmm?'

'You hear that?'

I listened. Very, very faintly, I could hear a curious susurration.

'What is it?' said Charlie.

It was indeed a strange sound, somewhere between the wheeze of a bellows and the whir of a motorcar engine. Suddenly one of the helmeted men jerked into life like a wound-up automaton and bent down towards the ground. The strip of light widened as, with a rending squeal, he opened some kind of hatch set into the rubble. With surprising dexterity, the others then began to lower the coffins through the hatch, clambering down after them. We gave it a minute or so after the metal door had finally swung to before we advanced across the excavation.

With the quiet concentration of a professional, I got to work on the hatch and within a few minutes I had levered the thing open. Despite my best efforts, it creaked loudly as I pulled it back on its hinges.

I peered down into the hole beyond. A shaft led steeply

downwards, its sides studded with small electric lights. I could just make out the top of a metal ladder.

'Down?' queried Charlie.

'Down.'

Leading the way, I swung myself over the lip of the shaft and began to clamber down the ladder, the rungs sharp with the blood-like smell of warm iron. We seemed to have been descending for a full five minutes when I paused for breath and reached out a hand for Charlie's ankle on the rung above me in order to stop him clambering on to my head.

He crouched down and tried to peer past me into the gloom. 'Seems to me someone's been doing quite a bit of digging.'

The helmeted automata could have only manhandled the coffins down here with inhuman strength. We recommenced our descent, and after a further minute or so we reached a layer of soft volcanic rock where the shaft abruptly flattened out, stretching ahead in a kind of dreary, dusty grey corridor. Again, electric lights had been strung from the walls, coiled wire looped between them like strange umbilical appendages.

'That sound's much louder now,' commented Charlie as we advanced.

I nodded. 'Perhaps some kind of air-pump.'

After a time, the loose, shale-like rock began to give way to the familiar sight of a Roman pavement. Seemingly we were now in the unexcavated bowels of Pompeii, amongst structures no man had seen for almost two thousand years. No man save those we now sought. The road branched off to the right almost immediately, giving on to a wonderfully preserved archway. The light was brighter here and clearly getting brighter still as the whole structure was suffused in a great ball of luminescence.

Charlie stumbled slightly on the pavement and I looked down to see that the stone floor was concave, a great grooved channel having been excavated in its centre. I glanced around swiftly then noticed the distinctive decoration that covered the walls in a series of serried niches, each containing a yellowy electric bulb.

'That appears to be Neptune,' I cried, pointing at the carving's twisting tail and powerful muscled torso. 'This must have been a bath house.'

Charlie nodded indifferently. 'What is it *now*, though? That's what we have to worry about.'

There seemed to be no one about, so we pressed on. The first chamber we entered, again decorated with the motif of the sea-god, had been only partially excavated from the rock. A series of chair-like niches, not unlike church vestibules, occupied each wall. Here the Pompeiians had evidently changed out of their togas and gone skinny-dipping in the plunge pools. One such pool, now half full of the rain water which streamed in from above, still stood close by.

Charlie gave a sharp gasp and I turned on my heel.

'It's all right,' he breathed, steadying himself. 'Just didn't expect *that*.'

He brought the torch-beam to bear on one of the vestibules where lay sprawled a complete skeleton, its arms flung wide, its jaw grotesquely open. The soft grey rock still swathed half of its carcass like a volcanic robe.

'Come on,' I urged.

We passed through the ancient changing rooms into a much larger chamber, supported by more of the Neptune columns and boasting a grand, domed roof. Within was a frankly fantastic sight.

One might have been forgiven for thinking some *nouveau riche* tradesman had decided to desert his aspidistra-stuffed environs and move into the old Roman fort down the road. Every inch of that great chamber was crammed with a weird combination of domestic contemporary furniture and looted ancient treasures. A headless nymph stood next to a huge armchair. Magnificent glass-ware shared table space with fruit bowls and a Napoleon-hat clock. The whole place was steeped in a curiously pellucid green light, as though the baths were still active.

At the far end of the room stood a huge fountain shaped like a round table with a raised edge to contain the forgotten water-stream. One great crack marred its flawless surface yet it had been altered by newer and stranger additions. Papers and charts were strewn across it, together with a quantity of queer-looking machinery. At the centre of the fountain a three-dimensional cut-away model of the volcano was hooked up to some sort of Wimshurst-device. Wires spilled from the stonework, and huge pipes had been erected against the walls. From these emanated the strange, wheezing whirring we had encountered on the surface.

Charlie stepped gingerly into the room, his mouth agape. He held up a hand towards the great fat pipes, then looked back towards me, smiling delightedly.

'Feel them, Mr Box!' he cried. 'They're warm.'

It was true. Whatever strange machinery had been erected here, it brought light and heat to the dead ruins.

'Quite something, ain't it?' said Charlie.

A footstep. Then the voice, familiar to me yet strangely elusive.

'Isn't it just?' said the voice from the shadows.

Both Charlie and I turned towards the sound.

Framed in the doorway stood a beautiful figure, resplendent in a crimson velvet gown. Her auburn hair was piled up and her dark-eyes lined with kohl as I had first seen them that night in the Vesuvius Club.

'Venus!' cried Charlie.

'Good evening, my dear,' I said mildly.

The gorgeous creature inclined her head slightly. 'Charlie. Signor Box. Such a pleasure to meet you again,' she said gaily, clapping her hands together and advancing into the room. 'Let us have wine! Despite the improvements, it is still chill down here and one feels the damp.' The Italian accent seemed to have gone west.

Venus strode to a fat-legged mahogany table and poured three glasses of wine rather carelessly.

'What's going on, Venus?' said Charlie plaintively. 'That fella of yours has gone too far this time. You've got to throw your lot in with us.'

Venus smiled. 'He's gone too far, has he, Charlie?'

She offered me a glass but I shook my head.

'We've supped, thanks,' I said curtly. 'Now, if you come quietly, I swear I will do what I can for you.'

Venus paused with a crystal goblet of dark wine halfway to her lips and began to chuckle, her laugh filling the ancient room. 'You will do what you can for me?' she roared. 'Where? When?'

'At your trial,' I said evenly.

'My trial?'

'Yours and that of the villain you call your lover.'

'My dear sir, you are quite comical. For what should . . . we . . . stand trial?'

'For the attempted murders of Professors Sash, Verdigris and Quibble.'

'Pooh! They are alive! What have I done but give them a little trip abroad, gratis.'

'And for the abduction of Mrs Midsomer Knight.'

'Safe and well and here also.'

'Well then, for the murder of Jocelyn Poop of His Majesty's Diplomatic.'

'Ah well,' said a new voice. 'I'm afraid I must plead guilty to that one.'

A man walked into the room, also dressed in crimson robes, his face covered by one of the masks I had seen at the Vesuvius Club.

Venus took his hand and kissed it. He removed his mask with the other hand and smiled. 'Good evening, Mr Box,' said Cretaceous Unmann, raising a pistol.

'I'll take that drink now, if I may,' I said quietly.

I sank a goblet of wine in one draft. 'Won't you join me?' I asked Unmann, proffering a glass. 'It's really very fine.'

Unmann shook his head, a sly smile playing over his lips.

'Well then,' I said, 'Perhaps you'd like to tell me what the blazes you're doing burrowing beneath Pompeii and who it is that you're both working for.'

Unmann smiled again and cocked an eyebrow at Venus. 'Shall I explain?'

'No,' she replied. 'Let us allow that honour to pass to the genius behind this whole scheme. A greater mind, even, than his sainted father who the world so cruelly wronged. Please say *buonasera* once more, Mr Box, to the man you know only as Signor Victor. Signor Victor *Morraine!*'

I turned instinctively, expecting to see the slim, striking young man from the funicular railway entering the cavern but there was no sign of anyone. I turned back when I heard a faint rustling sound.

Venus was untying her hair so that it fell in heavy, auburn loops about her neck. With a jerk of her hand, the hair flopped to the floor. A wig! She stared at me, grinning wildly, her dark, dark eyes ablaze with triumph, then hoisted up her crimson skirts, exposing bare, muscular legs and what we doctors call a cock and balls.

'Christ Almighty!' was all I had to say.

'Venus!' gasped Charlie. 'You're a boy!'

XIX

THE ENGINES OF VULCAN

ND so 'she' was. The beautiful Venus was the youth I had been introduced to as Victor. But Victor Morraine! This was almost more extraordinary. The dazzling creature inclined his head and moved towards my manservant, skirts swishing over the cold stone floor. 'Oh, Charlie. If only you had been true to me!'

The boy was staring at him, openmouthed. Venus flopped down in the armchair. Unmann continued to cover Charlie and me with the pistol.

'I suppose it takes all sorts,' I said philosophically. 'Really, Unmann, I can't see what you can gain by helping this . . . *person* with whatever pathetic revenge he's planning.'

Unmann laughed, no longer the silly ass. His composure was quite chilling. 'You can have no conception of the scale of Venus's ambition. But you're right in one respect, Mr Box. It *is* revenge that he seeks.'

I twiddled the stem of the goblet between my fingers. 'Do tell.' In my experience, that's all it takes.

Venus's eyes blazed. 'Yes! I want revenge! Revenge on those treacherous men who earned their reputations from my father's work yet had not the brains to complete it! Revenge against the woman who betrayed him and broke his fragile mind. They shall all suffer.'

I cocked my head to one side and waved a hand around me. 'But this is all very elaborate, isn't it? What exactly do you have in mind for this "suffering"?'

Venus's face set into a hard mask as though he were gazing back through the years. 'My father was a great man – a visionary. He lacked only the discipline to see his work through to its logical conclusion. Fortunately his genius was passed on to me! And I have completed his work.'

I felt suddenly cold. 'Completed? You mean that's what all this is?'

'It is. Heat and light from the immense power of the volcano.'

'Very commendable,' I said levelly. 'I presume you intend to help the world?'

Unmann chuckled. 'Yes – to understand its mistakes.'

I sighed. 'I imagine you intend to hold civilization to ransom or something equally dreary.'

Venus rose and held out his arms wide, so that the velvet hung down from his marble-white flesh like the wings of a monstrous bird. 'We stand in the ruins of a once-teeming city. A city destroyed by the might of the great volcano, by the wrath of the very earth herself! But consider for a moment, Signor Box, the geology of this great country. From north to south, she is encircled by a ring of fire, a network of volcanoes erupting like sores on her beautiful form. Etna, Stromboli, Ischia, Vulcano –'

'Campi Flegri! Cimino! Vulsini!' chimed in Unmann.

'And greatest of all,' cried Venus breathlessly. 'Vesuvius!'

I blinked. Thought a little. Thought a little more. 'What are you saying?'

'An immense explosive device placed within her very bowels . . .' whispered Venus. 'A weapon of such incalculable power that the world will shudder at the very thought of it!'

'And when the bomb goes off . . .' I cried, appalled, 'a chain reaction!'

'A stupendous river of fire will erupt,' crowed Venus. 'Tearing apart the rock, consuming the seas, plunging this kingdom into oblivion for ever!'

'My God!'

'You're out of your bloody mind!' cried Charlie.

'But what do you gain from such an act?' I demanded. 'The destruction of your entire country? Centuries of culture?'

Venus's eyes grew brighter yet. 'I owe this country nothing! It was the arena for my father's dissolution and ruin. I only know that I must show those traitors that Maxwell Morraine was the greatest scientist the world has ever seen! They, and all this sordid land, shall perish in the flames of my vengeance.'

I shot a wild glance at Unmann. 'And you want this too?'

'I want what Venus wants,' said the young man simply.

'And you'd condone the destruction of all Italy, the deaths of millions, just to slake your thirst for retribution?'

'Why not?' He shrugged.

'I must inform you that I cannot permit that.'

Unmann laughed. 'It seems to me, Lucifer Box, that you have very little say in the matter.'

Venus crossed to the great round table and pressed an ivory button on the machinery that had been clamped on to it. There was a loud squawking sound and within seconds four huge, helmeted thugs had slipped silently into the room.

I was rapidly searched and my precious revolver confiscated. I found myself pinioned with my arms behind my back by Venus's creatures, Charlie likewise and, together, we were 'escorted' from the bath house.

My question remained unanswered. I caught one more glimpse of Venus's scowling face and then we were being pushed out into another of the grey corridors.

Charlie seemed to be in something of a state of shock. 'Bloody hell,' he muttered. 'If I'd only known her fella was *her* all the time!'

'Well, you certainly missed out on a rare frolic, Charlie boy, but you mustn't get sentimental. Remember it was he who tried to drown you in the sewer. And God alone knows what he means for us now.'

The helmeted thugs pushed us on until we came to a set of doors, incongruously shiny in the blank grey walls. One of them wrenched back the grille that covered them and I realized that some kind of elementary lift had been constructed. For a horrible moment, I thought they meant to do us in there and then by hurling us into the empty shaft but, no, there were brass doors behind the grille and, at the touch of a button they squealed open.

The tiny cabinet beyond could scarcely contain us, but all four thugs duly squeezed inside, their meaty hands clasped tightly about our arms.

One of them rotated a handle and the lift began to judder downwards; the temperature constantly rising and the sound of clanking, grinding machinery beginning to throb from all around.

Finally, the lift shuddered to a halt. There was a pause and then the doors sprang open into a dismal tunnel. The very air seemed heavy with steam as though we had entered an atmosphere only fit for the Titans to breathe.

A jab in the back told me to get moving. As we walked I saw that one whole side of this tunnel had been panelled with crystal as though to provide a viewing platform and I strained to peer through it. Such was the quantity of steam that had built up, however, the crystal window was totally fogged. What devilry lay beyond?

'Chin up, Charlie,' I called.

'Will do, sir,' he responded with more cheeriness than I expect he was feeling. 'You reckon these gorillas speak English?'

'I'm rather relying on them not to,' I said, casting a quick look and grin at my captors. Their only response was another shove in the small of the back.

'Got any ideas?'

'Well,' I sighed. 'It's a very pretty mess. We are dealing with a lunatic. There's no way to reason with him because he wants nothing but destruction.' I pulled up suddenly. 'Hello, what's this?'

We had approached another lift inset in the blank wall. The doors were open and two more of the helmeted zombies were engaged in curious activity within. The lift cabinet itself appeared to have been halted one floor below so that the two men actually stood on its roof. One was holding the thick, oily chains from which it was suspended whilst his fellow busily sawed away at them.

'What're they up to?' hissed Charlie.

'I don't understand it,' I whispered. 'They seem to be cutting off all escape routes. Including their own. If he keeps sawing like that . . .'

But perhaps these zombified husks had no concept of personal mortality any more. I tried to see more but was shoved onwards. I just glimpsed a series of metal rungs sunk into the lift-shaft, glinting in the sallow electric light and extending towards the surface.

We had reached the end of our frog-marching and stopped outside the door of some kind of cell. One of the thugs jerked his thumb at Charlie and, when he failed to move, the others grabbed him and began to haul him away.

'Charlie!' I cried. 'You fiends! Get your ruddy hands off him!'

I was then bundled unceremoniously into the total blackness of the cell. The clang of the door behind me was like the Last Trump.

I sank to the floor and wiped the streaming sweat from my face. How far below the ground I was I could not tell but the heat was almost unbearable. And all the time came the constant *thrum-thrum* of mighty engines.

I crawled over to the wall and blindly examined the structure of my confinement. There was no hope of escape. The walls were of solid rock and the floor, though softer, was hardly less impenetrable. I could only wait until they came for me and then attempt to flee. If they came at all. Perhaps they meant me to boil alive in here as the great volcano erupted!

I was left alone in the pitch-black cell for perhaps an hour and my head was nodding on my breast in the stuffy darkness when, at last, there came footsteps. The light from the corridor flooded the cell and I shielded my eyes as the door swung open and Venus stood before me, his swarthy face wet with perspiration, his dark eyes shining malevolently.

'Very sorry to have kept you, Signor Box,' he said with palms outstretched. 'But now all is prepared.'

'All *what* is prepared?'

'I wish you to see my little project. I would not have you die in ignorance.'

'Not today, thank you,' I cried cheerfully and turned my back on him.

'It is important to me that you appreciate the sheer scale of my achievement,' insisted the deadly beauty.

'Is it? Well, yes, I can see that from your point of view it probably looks that way but, forgive me, what's in it for me? I mean, surely, after the shilling tour, you're going to bump me off.'

'Not I. I have very little quarrel with you, Mr Box. In fact, I have enjoyed our brief association immensely. I only wish we could have known each other better.'

'There's still time!' I cried, turning to face him. 'What say we find somewhere nice and cool and have a little lie down, hm?'

But Venus evidently didn't take to my kind of flippancy. That smooth hand cracked me nastily across the kisser. 'It is my associate Mr Unmann who will do the deed. I believe he has something particularly unpleasant in mind.'

He threw back his head haughtily, and gestured to the corridor beyond. The guards dragged me from the cell and we retraced our steps up the corridor. Venus paused and leant across to the crystalline window, wiping away the condensed steam that clouded it with one delicate hand. Evidently satisfied, he pulled open an iron door. As I was about to be pushed through, I strained at my captors' hold and jerked my head back.

'What's going on there, *Mr* Morraine? Your lackeys are sabotaging the lifts. Are we all to die in this great revenge of yours?'

Venus merely smiled and I was hurled through the door into what I can only describe as a mechanical cathedral.

It was a vast chamber, hewn from the very rock, perhaps half a mile across and so high that its upper portion was obscured by clouds of steam. Behemothal brass and copper pipes as thick as tree-trunks fanned from a central, organ-like structure resembling tentacles on some giant metal squid. Said pipes had been channeled into the glistening rock-walls, leading, I imagined, deep into the very heart of Vesuvius. Vast pistons slammed into one another, sending up great clouds of super-heated steam and flooding the floor with gobbets of black grease. Above all this wonder had been erected a network of spindly galleries and platforms, all connected by row after row of spiral staircases. Helmeted zombies swarmed everywhere, monitoring switches and levers and cranks, attending to the minutiae of Armageddon.

Seated in four chairs near us, their wrists and ankles securely bound, were Mrs Knight and Professors Sash, Verdigris and Quibble. The effects of the purple poppy seemed to be gradually abating. All four were stirring slightly in their bonds.

'I always need an audience to bring out the best in me,' trilled Venus.

One figure detached itself from the crowd of helmeted workmen and came towards us. It was wearing some kind of protective clothing, fashioned from rubber and a helmet with square glass eye-holes. He removed the mask revealing himself to be none other than Mr Tom Bowler of Belsize Park. Or Stromboli, as I now realised he must be.

'You!' I hissed.

'Me. Hullo, Mr Box. So sorry I couldn't help you with your bereavement. I promise to be very attentive, though, when it comes to your own interment.' He flashed a horrible smile and turned to Venus. 'We are almost ready to begin the ceremony.'

'Wonderful!' enthused Venus. 'But first we must show Mr Box our little toy.'

I stared at Bowler. 'Great God, man!' I shrieked. 'Why are you doing this? What hold does this creature have over you?'

He wiped at the sweat that was pouring into his eyes. 'This is the future, Mr Box! A new world of machines and engines! We shall control the magma flows of this entire planet and once the world witnesses the destruction of Naples, they will give us anything we want!'

Something about Bowler's tone gave me pause. He obviously had plans beyond this day of destruction. The destruction of

Naples was to be a grand demonstration, not a suicidal act of revenge that would consume all Italy. I seized upon this chance. 'There's more to it than the end of Naples!' I yelled above the clanking din. 'You don't know, do you?'

'Silence him!' cried Venus.

'Tell him, Venus! Tell him about the chain reac –'

I felt a rough gag being fastened over my mouth. In the filthy, steaming heat it was a desperate struggle to breathe.

I was dragged back (which is better than being dragged up, like mein host).

Bowler gave me a strange look then shook his head and returned to his diabolical work.

Venus grabbed me by my shirt-front and pulled me towards the centre of that soaring chamber. At the heart of the forest of boiling pipes stood a curious round structure, riveted together in brass panels like the segments of an orange. Steps led to it and Venus dragged me up them until we were looking down on the brass globe. A glass panel occupied its upper surface and Venus forced my head down so that I could see inside.

Within, surrounded by a mass of wiring was what I knew must be the convection bomb. The whole interior of the thing sparkled with power.

And stuffed in like a rag-doll beside it, his eyes wide and terrified, was Charlie Jackpot.

Venus rose to his full height on the steps, held out both his arms wide, then began spinning about, like a giddy child. His peculiar chuckle merged with the pounding *thrum-thrum* of the colossal machines as he gloated in the midst of his infernal creation.

'Behold!' he thundered. 'Behold the Engines of Vulcan!'

He stood in a frock, I stood in mute impotence, the thugs restraining me as those fearful contraptions hammered and shuddered all around. What was I to do? I could feel the veins throbbing sickeningly in my head.

Venus began to grow calmer and then, with a jerk of his head, indicated that I was to be taken away.

'To Signor Unmann,' he cried, flashing me a dreadful grin.

Protesting and stumbling I was hauled from the room. I managed at least to shoot one last pleading glance at Bowler.

After the hellish atmosphere in the bomb-chamber, the grey featureless corridors came as something of a relief. It was to be a temporary respite only, however, as I was hauled into another room, one dominated by a huge iron pipe, in which Cretaceous Unmann awaited my convenience.

Unmann, holding the fearsome mask – that of Etna – regarded me impassively as I was hurled to the rocky floor, and then rattled out an order. I was pulled up on to my bloodied knees and securely bound hand and foot. Finally satisfied that I posed no immediate threat, Unmann indicated that we should be left alone.

'Where is your oh-so elegant poise now, Mr Box?' he taunted.

Filthy and gagged, I was in no position to reply.

I tried to assume an air of nonchalance. Terribly difficult when held captive by lunatics beneath an active volcano, I'm sure you'll agree.

'How you patronized me!' hissed Unmann. 'Took me for a shambling fool. Yet now it is you that kneels before me!'

He paused. Perhaps realizing that a one-sided rant is nowhere near as interesting as a taunt-based dialogue, he crossed the floor towards me and pulled down my gag.

'Much obliged,' I panted. 'Listen, old man. I've no doubt I misjudged you but you did put on such a good display of playing the fool. Now, can't we talk this over like gentlemen?'

If I'd hoped to appeal to our national sense of decency I was sorely disabused.

'Gentlemen?' he spat. 'How trivial you are, Box, when there are matters of the greatest moment on hand.'

He seemed to require prompting. 'Will you not at least tell me,' I said wearily, 'how the blazes you got caught up in all this nonsense?'

Unmann chuckled to himself. 'There's little to tell. But, after all, why not? Venus was abandoned by that Medea of a mother of his and drifted into crime where I was already happily billeted though the Service knew nothing of it. We began our little enterprise by founding the Vesuvius Club. It paid awfully well. At first it catered purely to, shall we say, the more straightforward desires but there is always a ready market for those of our persuasion, eh Mr Box?'

'I'll thank you not to lump me in with you two,' I muttered. 'I find frock-coats more convenient than petticoats.'

Unmann scowled at me. 'Venus is Victor Morraine's true self. The self he retreated into when his life was torn apart. The self who has schemed and plotted all these years to avenge his father's humiliation.'

'Yes, yes,' I cried. 'But why kill Poop?'

Unmann shrugged. 'We have been relieving Pompeii of its treasures in order to finance the glorious technology you see about you.'

I nodded slowly. 'And that poor sap Poop stumbled upon the truth?'

'He barely glimpsed the truth! But that, sadly for him, was enough. I lured him out to the harbour and bashed in his brains.'

I sighed exhaustedly. Unmann seemed to have stalled again. 'And what of your plans for the professors and Mrs Knight?'

'They will witness the end of all Italy as they are consumed in the fire. It will be a quick death. I think Venus is being immoderately merciful. Not a courtesy I will be extending to you, Mr Box.'

Sweat was trickling down my back. Unmann rapped hard on the door and bellowed for the guards.

The door flew open and the thugs entered. They seemed to know what was required, pulling me up by the arms and pushing me towards the great iron pipe.

Unmann slipped his fingers around a small handle and pulled at it. With a metallic screech some species of hatch was revealed. I struggled to take in the details, my eyes awash with sweat – a grilled section was fitted across the pipe and its twin was positioned directly above, so that a small cage was effectively formed, allowing a man to crawl inside and inspect the interior, albeit with some difficulty.

I knew at once that I was to be that man.

'Hey-ho,' cooed Unmann.

I was lifted bodily and thrust into the pipe.

'It will not be comfortable for you, I'm afraid.' Unmann smiled. 'It is somewhat akin to the medieval torture I believe they called "Little Ease". But whereas those unfortunates were kept crookbacked for years your time inside will be brief.'

The grille supported my weight, neatly caging me.

'This pipe acts as an exhaust from the steam-pumps. Every few hours, a vast jet of surplus steam is channelled through here and out on to the surface.'

He let the implications of this sink in.

'I had considered all manner of delightful demises for you. But time is pressing and I really cannot imagine anything much worse than having the flesh boiled from your bones by a stream of superheated steam!'

Nor, for that matter, could I.

'Oh fuck!' was all I could manage. So much for last words.

'Close the hatch,' he said, his face settling back into a mask of impassivity.

One of the guards eased the hatch back into place.

'*Ciao!*' I heard Unmann cry over the rending creak of the iron shutter.

Then all was hot, unbearable darkness.

XX

DEATH BY STEAM

LTHOUGH dear Mr Unmann hadn't furnished me with a precise time, I knew I wouldn't have to wait long, stuffed like a plug of tobacco in an iron pipe, for my end to come. I also knew that it was ludicrous to think of shinning my way upwards. Even if I could get out of the bonds that imprisoned me, it was clearly a very long way to the surface. No, I had one chance and that was to get down the pipe and into the bomb-chamber.

All this flashed through my head as I sat there, my lungs burning in the airless tube, my head throbbing appallingly as I fought down the urge to panic.

I am no escapologist but had taken the very basic step (heaven bless my tutoring at Lady Cecely Midwinter's!) of expanding the sinews of my forearms and ankles as much as possible so that, when relaxed, there was at least a little give in the ropes.

I tested that give now and found that it was inexpressibly comforting.

I would not be saved from being boiled alive like a crab in a kettle by having my hands and feet free, however. My immediate priority was to break through the grille upon which I was perched.

Conscious that Unmann and his thugs might still be in the room I began to press down as silently but as hard as I could on the meshed surface. Cramped by the identical grille above me it was almost impossible to get any kind of momentum going but I struggled on, sweat coursing down my body, occasional jets of steam warning me of the horror to come.

I brought both feet down harder and harder on the grille yet it seemed scarcely to yield an inch. Now caring not a whit that my actions might be overheard, I slammed my whole bodyweight on to the grille, grunting in frustration and pain as the heated metal bit into my flesh.

At last I felt a tiny movement. The grille had drooped at one edge. I felt with soaking fingers and touched bare, sharp metal. Elated, I moved my hands towards the break and began to rub my bonds rapidly over it.

From deep below came an ominous rumble.

I had to escape at once! *The bonds were tearing.* If I didn't, then I was doomed. *They seemed about to give!* If only I could get a chance to talk to Bowler. His mania – *one rope gone* – seemed only for power – *a second bond snapped* – not the wanton destruction of the whole of Italy – *Free!*

I manoeuvred myself round in that tiny space and wrenched at the broken grille with my hands. The deep, disquieting rumble, like a giant clearing its phlegm-choked throat, sounded again.

As I forced the grille back upon itself, it sent out a dreadful shriek of tortured metal. Without a second thought I wriggled like a caterpillar into the shaft beneath it and let go.

Under different circumstances it might have proved exhilarating but my head was pounding sickeningly, my arms and legs ached and bled and I was still in imminent danger of tumbling straight into the bowels of that infernal machine.

As it was, I skittered pell-mell through the great iron pipe until I crashed, feet-first into another grille. I sank back and yelled in pain as my knees cracked on impact. A great trembling began in the pipe and red-hot vapour began to bleed upwards through the grille. The steam! The steam was coming!

Where there was another grille there had to be another inspection hatch. I began to kick frantically at the grille beneath me. If I could only get through it and into the next of these cramped chambers, I might effect an escape through the side of the pipe. It mattered not that I might find myself amongst the enemy, that I might even flop out at Venus's feet, if I didn't get out of there in minutes I was doomed.

I kicked again and again and still the temperature rose. Sweat seemed to gush from my face and arms as I rolled on to my back and rammed my feet against the metal floor for all I was worth.

Then! A gap! I squeezed myself through, the wire tearing at my flesh and immediately pressed my palms to the hatch. With a shove, the latch broke and the door crashed open. I tumbled through into light.

The cooler air hit me like an Arctic front. I dragged myself out of the pipe and slammed shut the hatch just as a colossal blast of steam came soaring upwards.

Falling to the floor, I pressed the door closed with my feet. I watched the pipe tremble and bulge and rattle, and even through the soles of my shoes I felt a terrible heat rise, then all was quiet.

Scarcely able to believe I was alive, I took stock of my situation. I looked up and saw the pipe extended upwards as far as I could see. Below, through clouds of steam and some kind of gantry I was standing on, I could make out the great volcanic chamber and, at its heart, the convection bomb.

I was on one of the catwalks that criss-crossed the upper levels of that vast, rocky chamber. Incredibly, because of the tremendous noise and confusion all around, I had not been observed.

Reduced to a sodden wreck in shirt-sleeves, I crept along the gantry, stealing occasional glances over the railing at the scene below.

Helmeted men were milling everywhere, checking gauges, monitoring the great motors, affixing God knew what to the great brass globe in which poor Charlie lay. I spotted Bowler, hard at work inside some strange brass and mahogany panel shaped like a church pew. And there were the berobed Venus and Unmann, crossing the floor of the chamber arm in arm, like Bertie and Alexandra on a blasted state visit. They approached the imprisoned quartet of Mrs Knight and the professors and there was some talk and mocking laughter, though I could make out nothing specific above the din. With a final flourish, Venus and Unmann put on their grotesque ritual masks and separated, Unmann towards my side of the cavern, Venus up a spiral staircase and into a small hut that projected from the rock walls like a wasps' nest.

I kept well-hidden and watched as Unmann quit the chamber through the iron door. I glanced down at the hapless hostages and then over towards the curious hut. Unarmed, I had little chance of blustering my way into it and ending Venus's deranged plans. But if I could get to Bowler there was just a chance I could convince him of his folly.

And, of course, there was Charlie Jackpot who seemed to require rescuing six times before breakfast.

I sped down the spiral staircase, round and round and round until I emerged, giddy and breathless in the shadowy perimeter of the great cavern. I looked about cautiously then took my chance, sprinting over to the central machine and clambering as silently as possible up on to the dais where the brass globe stood. I spread my hands over the glass panel and peered inside. Charlie caught my eye at once and reached up to bang his fist against the glass. I stayed him with a hushing finger to my mouth then sank down and attempted to hide myself in the lee-side of the object.

I looked quickly about but no one seemed to have detected me. Making an instant examination of the bolts that held the device together, I knew I'd require some kind of tool if I were to release Charlie.

I got to my feet once again, tapped on the glass panel and gestured to Charlie to have patience. Then, I slipped away down the steps and looked about for some method of opening the sphere.

A burly helmeted fellow with a 'kerchief wrapped around his mouth and a rifle around his shoulder was the closest person to me. In a broad brown belt around his ample waist I spotted tools including spanner, screwdrivers and knives.

Noiselessly, I crept up behind him, pulled the spanner from his belt and cracked him over the back of the neck with it. If I had expected him merely to sink to the floor like any reasonable thug I was disappointed. I had forgotten about their immunity to pain. I tried again, even harder but the spanner merely thwacked over his bull-like neck as he turned sluggishly toward me. I really didn't have time for this. I dropped to the floor, pulled a knife from his belt and, sliced away his hamstrings in one graceful roll. He dropped like a stone. Grabbing the belt, I dragged him over towards the sphere and then planted the knife into his chest as though staking a vampire.

That was the end of him. Sometimes one must be direct.

Relieved, I picked up the spanner and turned towards the sphere.

Bowler was waiting for me.

I raised the spanner above my head and the shocked undertaker ducked. At once, I locked my arm around his throat and dragged him back towards the hissing machines.

'You're mad!' he cried. 'I will be missed!'

'I'll smash your bloody head to pulp if you don't listen to me and keep quiet!' I ordered.

Cowed, he held up his hands to the level of his ears and shrugged. 'You're too late anyway, Box. The ceremony will begin in minutes.'

I tossed the spanner to him and poked the end of the guard's knife into his nose. 'Unscrew that thing and get the boy out of there.'

Bowler got to his feet and began to unscrew the glass panel slowly.

'Hurry! Or you'll be seeing the inside of a pine box damned sooner than me.' I jabbed the knife toward him and his actions grew noticeably quicker. 'Now listen to me, Bowler. Venus has lied to you. This bomb will start a chain-reaction that will cause all of Italy's volcanoes to erupt. It will destroy the entire country.'

'Ha!' Bowler unscrewed another nut and tossed it to the floor. 'He would never –'

'Wouldn't he? Now tell me what your evacuation plans are.'

Bowler shrugged. 'At the climax of the ceremony, the process will begin and we will be ferried back to the surface.'

I shook my head. 'In what? Venus's trained zombies have been making short work of the lifts, Bowler. There's no way out for anybody. He wants you all to remain here with him. For his ultimate revenge.'

Bowler took this in and then shook his perspiring head. 'Why should I believe you, Box? Venus is an honourable . . . person, terribly wronged. He will lead us out of the fire and towards glory!'

The panel was off and Bowler lifted it carefully to the floor. Keeping him covered I looked down into the device.

'Charlie!'

Looking tired and ill, the youth began to clamber out of the sphere. 'Put it on my tab, Mr Box. Thanks. What do we do now?'

I swung back towards Bowler. 'Now we're going to pay a little call.'

It took only moments for Charlie to change into the dead guard's clothes and to disguise his face with the sweaty 'kerchief. I tossed him the rifle.

'Lead the way, Mr Bowler. I'm your prisoner.'

I raised my hands and encouraged Charlie to make a good show of threatening me with the rifle. With a deep sigh, Bowler led the way and the three of us advanced through the steaming mess of pipes and machines towards the spiral staircase.

Bowler took out his watch from the pocket of his oil-stained coat. 'This is senseless. The countdown will have begun. You are too late.'

'Shut up and move.'

We ascended rapidly and approached the metal landing on which the observation room stood. A solitary guard stood outside the door. Bowler gestured to me and the guard stepped aside. The undertaker knocked and opened the door. Charlie pushed me through in a show of aggression and suddenly we were inside.

The chamber was rather curiously like a signal-box on some suburban railway line. The window was fogged so that the only light in the dim little room came from the multitude of panels and switches that covered the far wall. Sitting in a swivelling red chair was Venus, resplendent in the scarlet robes he had adopted in the Vesuvius Club for that little 'rehearsal' I had witnessed.

His delicate white hands were busy at the controls and he glanced over at us absently. 'So, Bowler! You have brought us a little present. It seems my dear Cretaceous was not able to finish you off, Signor Box.'

'He very nearly poached me,' I said, taking the rifle from Charlie and advancing on him. 'But I'm a resourceful fellow. As you can see.'

Venus's face fell. 'You are too late. The –'

'Yes, yes, the countdown has started. I know. But you can stop it from here. Very carefully but very quickly.'

'Or what?' hissed Venus. 'You think I fear death? I embrace it! It is my destiny!'

I looked at Bowler. 'You see, man? He's utterly deranged. He has no intention that any of you should leave the volcano.'

Bowler gave a strained laugh. 'You're pathetic! Do you really think that . . .' He tailed off and his gaze became fixed on Venus who had a strange, messianic smile on his fine features. 'Is . . . is this true?'

Venus threw back his head and laughed. 'It will be a glorious end, Signor Bowler. We shall take all of Italy with us!'

Bowler's hand flew to his mouth. 'Oh my God!'

He raced towards the door. Charlie caught him. 'Oi! You're going nowhere, mate.'

Charlie hauled him back into the room. Bowler's chin was trembling. 'But we've got to get out of here!'

'We shall *stay*,' I commanded. 'And stop the countdown. All of Italy is at stake. Mr Morraine, will you oblige?'

For answer, Venus merely folded his arms.

'Then if you will not, I shall!' cried Bowler. 'You cannot be allowed to destroy us all.'

So saying he dashed across the cabin and began to wrench wires from the machinery. With a roar of rage, Venus was upon him, pummelling Bowler's face and chest with surprising force. I wasted no more time and shot at the flashing scarlet form. The first bullet hit Venus in the arm and he staggered back. The second tore through the fabric of his robes and bit into the wall.

Clutching his injured flesh, Venus powered past me and, knocking Charlie to the floor, flung open the door and was gone.

'Quickly!' called Bowler, pulling more of the complicated mass of wiring. 'The device. If he reaches it, he could still set it off!'

I needed no further encouragement.

'Come on, Charlie!' I urged and we raced from the hut. Charlie took the rifle and shot the helmeted guard dead without breaking his stride. I leant over the staircase and could see Venus's slim figure flitting through the steam-shrouded pipes towards the sphere. I grabbed the rifle from Charlie, rested it on the iron banister and loosed off a volley of shots.

Venus emerged from the steam with a large group of his opium-sodden drones. He pointed up at us.

'Kill them!' he howled. 'Kill them!'

With their curious, sluggish movements, the helmeted fiends began to fire back at us. Charlie picked up the rifle from the dead guard and we careered down the spiral staircase at a fearsome pace, dodging bullets and responding in kind.

'We have to stop him getting to the bomb!' I cried as we reached the base of the steps. We ran in a frenzy across the floor of the chamber until we reached the brass sphere. Venus was nowhere to be seen.

'Mr Box!' gasped Charlie. 'Look!'

I noticed in that moment that the glass panel was no longer where Bowler had left it. It was being screwed back into place from *within* the sphere. His slender frame squashed visibly, Venus lay crouched inside, grinning madly.

He raised his hand and smiled. The crazy fool was waving at us.

Then there came a strange ratcheting sound and the sphere rolled forward like a billiard ball, vanishing into the great bronze pipe.

Despite the noise and the heat and approaching thugs it felt suddenly as if a great hush had descended.

'We've failed,' I said quietly.

XXI

ASCENT TO PERIL

CHARLIE grabbed me by the shoulder. 'We're not beaten yet, sir! The fella in the hut knows where that pipe leads. There must be some way to stop the bomb.'

I nodded quickly. 'You're right.'

We clattered back up the spiral staircase, picking off the last few zombies lumbering towards us as we did so, and threw open the door of the observation room. Bowler was still there, poring over reams of documents and plans.

'Betrayed!' he groaned, hammering his fist at his forehead. His hair hung in a great black slap over his pale forehead. 'Betrayed at every turn! To think I could have trusted that monster!'

I pulled him round. 'There's still time to make amends, Bowler. The bomb has been launched. Where is it heading?'

He shook his head mournfully. 'Into the belly of the volcano. There is a weakness in the crust. The bomb will blast it away and the magma will erupt!'

'How do we stop it?'

The undertaker put his head in his hands. 'We cannot. We shall die in the flames. Die at any moment!'

Not what we wanted to hear, naturally.

'There must be a way!' I thundered, grabbing him by the lapels. 'Think, man. You know everything about this blasted scheme!'

'Yes! And we were clever! We allowed for every eventuality.'

Charlie came over and sifted through the blueprints. 'What sort of eventuality? What could go wrong?'

I nodded furiously. 'You're right, Charlie. We will sabotage one of the fail-safes.'

Bowler looked at me as if I were mad and then smiled. 'There . . . there may be something in what you say. There is a junction. I knew it was dangerous but the rock-formation made it unavoidable. It's where the steam shaft crosses the bond pipe. The two chutes join for a moment and then continue on their way.'

'And is there any way of closing off the junction?'

Bowler dashed to the wall where a screen of some kind indicated where the bomb had got to.

'Yes! If I repair some of the damage I managed to inflict, I can control it from here.'

He sucked at his knuckles anxiously. 'The bomb has reached *this* level.' He jabbed his finger at the curious display. 'The junction is some way below.'

'Then there's still time.'

Bowler was practically gnawing his fist. 'But if we close the pipe and trap Venus there, the bomb will still explode. It will be close enough to cause an eruption!'

It was my turn to ponder. I looked quickly at the plans and then at the display. 'And if you shut off the steam-pipe, what then?'

He shrugged. 'The steam-pressure will build.'

'Dangerously?'

'Of course. The system is designed as a safety valve. If the pressure is not released . . .'

'That's it!' I cried delightedly. 'Bowler, close the hatch on the steam pipe.'

'But why?'

'Just do it!'

He dragged Venus's great leather chair to the console and began furiously punching at buttons and pulling levers. Then he dropped beneath the display and began frantically rewiring the machinery. For a few anxious minutes he fiddled and pulled at the complex copper circuitry, swore several oaths and then, with a great cry, sat back. A coloured disc slid into place on the display before us.

'It's done! The steam pressure is building.'

'Now, tell me when Venus and the bomb are almost at the junction. How accurate is this thing?'

'Pretty accurate.' He rubbed his hands and licked his dry lips. 'Level Eight. Achieved. Level Nine . . .'

'He must be boiling alive inside that thing,' said Charlie.

I nodded. 'Just what he'd intended for you. He doesn't give a damn now. He must see this thing through.'

'Achieved,' continued Bowler. 'Level Ten . . . approaching junction . . .'

'Prepare to open the hatch!' I cried.

'Level Ten achieved!'

'Open it!'

The disc slid out of its housing, revealing blank space. 'It's done,' said Bowler simply.

'What is?' queried Charlie.

I held up my hand. 'Wait, wait . . .'

From deep beneath us we heard it. A deep, booming, clattering roar. The floor of the room began to shake with massive violence.

'What . . . exactly have we done?' said Charlie.

'Projected a huge body of steam at the sphere, Charlie! If I'm right then –'

'Then it should be forced right back up!'

'Exactly!'

The three of us stood there in an agony of suspense as the hut and the great chamber itself trembled. I glanced over at Charlie. His face was white and he had sunk his teeth into his lower lip. Bowler was smoothing his hair down in a repeated gesture as though comforting himself. If, *if* we got out of this insane situation, how were we to escape? There would be seven of us all told, including the captives. My thoughts raced back to the lift-shafts and the men who had sabotaged them. Of course! The chains had been severed but the iron rungs set into the wall must survive. It would be a hell of a climb but it was surely our only chance.

I was yanked back to the present when a tremendous, shattering roar came from the chamber beyond. Charlie, Bowler and I raced out of the hut and looked down. The great brass sphere had come tearing back through the bronze pipe, shredding its end in the process and slamming into the walls of the cavern. Its impact

fractured a number of the huge iron pipes and steam began to flood the chamber.

'We did it!' cried Charlie.

'Yes – we've brought the bomb back. To us!'

The undertaker looked worried. 'The bomb won't go off now, the steam pressure is still building. The pipes are ruptured.'

'But there'll be no eruption?'

'Not as Venus planned, no. But the explosion could still damage the magma shell higher up. There's no time to be lost!'

'First we have to free Mrs Knight and the professors.'

'What?' wailed Bowler. 'To hell with them! We have to get out!'

I trained the rifle on the reluctant mortician. 'You have much to make up for, Mr Bowler. I suggest you get down those stairs and help them. Forthwith.'

With a scowl, he ran pell-mell down the stairway, Charlie and I close behind. As we picked our way across the floor, I glanced over to where the sphere lay embedded in the wall, crushed like a spoiled fruit, the glass panel shattered. Hanging half out of it was the body of Venus; his scarlet robes plastered to his body like a shroud, his once-beautiful face set in a crazed rictus grin, the sinews exposed red raw by the heat that had boiled away his flesh. His eyeballs goggled at us in a macabre, steam-palled death-stare.

'Come on!' I urged. I turned my attentions to the captives in their chairs and was at once confronted by the not-too-dissimilar features of the unfortunate Mrs Knight.

'Are you all right?' I enquired. She merely groaned in reply. Charlie was already hacking away her restraints. Despite their weakness, Verdigris and Sash were able to make some sense of the situation and once free pulled themselves up the gantries towards the next level. I helped support Mrs Knight, who had been more recently stupefied and Charlie and Bowler carried the crippled Quibble between them. The old man groaned pitiably as we clattered up the steps towards the next level.

Of a sudden, there came an ear-splitting crack and the floor of the cavern began to shift and undulate. With a horrible, belching roar, molten lava began, inexorably, to force its way through the gap.

We needed no more encouragement to tumble through the door and bolt it behind us, falling gasping into the corridor beyond.

'The lifts!' I yelled. 'Quickly!'

Charlie let out an exhausted sigh, then all seven of us staggered off up the corridor, the way we had been brought what seemed like half a lifetime ago. We reached the lift doors, closed now, and Charlie and Bowler lowered Quibble to the floor. I stabbed at the controls but the blasted things refused to open. Mrs Knight appeared to have fallen into a faint.

'Professor Sash!' I barked. 'Are you fit enough to help open these doors? Verdigris – you too? Charlie, Bowler, give them both a hand. I'll see to our invalids.'

It is not in my nature to slap a woman, especially when she looks like a boiled hog's head, but now was not the time for subtlety. I batted as kindly as I could at the poor soul's ruined cheeks until she became once more sensible of her surroundings.

'We have to climb, Mrs Knight,' I hissed. 'All of us. You too, Professor Quibble. It's our only hope.'

'What?' he gasped from his resting place on the shuddering floor. 'What is all this?'

'We're inside Vesuvius, Professor. I know it's hard to credit but Maxwell Morraine's deranged son has developed his theories into practical form and a great big bloody bomb has set off an eruption. You understand?'

He peered at me myopically and opened his mouth to protest.

'You want me to leave you here?'

Quibble's rat-trap mouth closed firmly.

From deep below us came a fearful rumble. I glanced feverishly about.

'They're moving!' gasped Charlie, his fingernails jammed into the crack between the lift doors. 'Come on! Put your backs into it!'

Slowly, the doors began to screech apart. Around us the electric lights studding the walls had begun to spark and sizzle. All at once, the doors gave and Charlie, Bowler, Verdigris and Sash hauled them apart. Inside there was only empty space.

I gazed up at the shaft, the chains from which the lift had been suspended swung uselessly, stirred by the hot winds from below.

'We have to get on to those rungs,' I cried. 'Charlie, you go first. We'll get Quibble up after you and I'll push the bugger. Got that?'

Charlie nodded and swung himself up on to the first rung as another tremor hit and the shaft visibly rocked.

'Keep going!' I urged. Charlie, hanging by one arm, helped me to launch the shaking Quibble on to the rungs. Behind me came Verdigris and Sash, doing the same for the still-enfeebled Mrs Knight; the penitent Bowler brought up the rear. We climbed and climbed but Quibble's ruined body became heavier and heavier. I pushed as best I could but his withered hands were struggling to support him on the hot iron rungs. My own arms ached fearsomely.

Chest heaving, I struggled on, Quibble's useless legs dangling before me like empty stockings. 'Must . . . get out, Professor,' I gasped. 'Can't rest . . . *Move!*'

The old man was certainly game. Somehow, incredibly, we made progress. I craned my neck to see above.

'Charlie!' I called. 'How far?'

'We're getting there!' he cried.

Suddenly the lift-shaft shook again and there came a bizarre sucking, grumbling sound.

'Don't stop!' I shouted. 'All of you! Keep climbing.'

But I sneaked a peek down the deep shaft and saw that instead of the darkness we had left, there was now a dreadful fiery red.

'My God!' I cried hoarsely. 'The lava! It's rising!'

Far below (thank the Lord Harry), crowned by flame and smoke, a vast plug of molten rock was surging up towards us.

I swung my head up to yell at Charlie to help drag Quibble up but the words died in my mouth. The top of the lift shaft was only ten feet or so above us and looking down, holding my revolver, was Cretaceous Unmann.

'You have a choice, Mr Box,' he called down. 'Jump down into the lava or be picked off by me.'

'What the hell do you mean?' I cried.

He loosed off a shot that sang off the ladder with a screeching clang. I heard Mrs Knight squeal in terror.

'What I say. I offer you a choice of demises.'

'Listen, you mad fool,' I shouted diplomatically. 'If we don't all get to the surface in the next few minutes we're going to fry! Is that what you want?'

'You think I wouldn't do it?' he yelled. 'You think I don't have it in me to shoot you down?'

'I have no doubt you have it in you.' I cast a quick look downwards at the rising tide of lava. The figures of Sash, Verdigris, Mrs Knight and Bowler were silhouetted starkly against a curtain of blood-orange.

'I'm only saying you will die as surely as the rest of us if you don't move right now!'

'But that's what Venus wants! Death! Destruction! Annihilation! Ha, ha, ha!'

Another shot rang out and I heard Bowler scream. I looked down and saw him swaying on the rungs below, blood pouring from his throat. Then the poor fool was gone, spiralling down, down, down into the blistering lava flow.

'Choose, Mr Box!' screeched Unmann, his ripped robes flopping forward over the lip of the shaft.

The whole edifice shuddered again and I felt Professor Quibble begin to topple backwards on to me. I thrust out a hand and pushed him back but the walls were shaking so violently now that it was almost impossible to get any purchase on him.

I looked up and saw Unmann levelling the pistol at me. I was a sitting duck.

Quibble's withered head turned to look down at me and a strange look flitted over his pallid features. I suddenly knew what he was going to do. I pulled myself tight to the rungs in order to present as small a target as possible and flinched as I heard Unmann's shot blast out. At the same instant, Quibble let go of the rungs and fell back into the void, taking the bullet that was meant for me. As he spiralled noiselessly down the shaft, all was confusion. I tried to clamber the last few feet towards the top of the shaft before Unmann had a chance to recover but was suddenly aware that Charlie, with a great bellow of rage had taken hold of the ripped fabric of Unmann's robe that hung streamer-like over the lip of the shaft and pulled on it for all he was worth.

With a great disbelieving gasp, the lethal diplomat toppled forwards.

I caught a glimpse of his startled face as he sailed past me and then he was just a ball of swirling scarlet, plummeting down the shaft after the noble Quibble into the pulsating stream of molten rock.

Just before he hit, though, there was a bright flash and pain seared through my shoulder. I gasped and looked down at where Unmann's parting shot had penetrated my flesh. I swayed on the iron rungs.

In a second, Charlie's strong arms were under mine.

'Hang on, sir. I've got you!'

Waves of nausea began to pulse through me and I felt my senses swim. Charlie grasped at my shirt and heaved me out of the lift shaft. I staggered to my feet as the invaluable valet helped the others out and then we staggered as one unit through the volcanic tunnels towards the Pompeiian bath house.

As we emerged into that strange room, the pellucid lights were flickering and the ancient walls shuddering under the impact of the eruption. I was only dimly aware of all this as Charlie plunged on, dragging me with him, my whole body shot with pain. The others were merely a dim blur behind me.

Somehow he got me to the ladder and, weak as a kitten, I managed to pull myself up and up, every step an agony. Surely there must be an end to this climbing? All at once we were at the hatch and tumbling into the bleary dawn.

Of course, we were not yet safe. The livid sky told us what we already knew. Vesuvius was erupting and, whilst it was not the cataclysm Venus had hoped for, it was still not wise to hang about.

I chanced a look back as Charlie lugged me out through the Pompeiian ruins the way we had come. Above us, the great black hump of the mountain was belching smoke and a thin river of livid red was dribbling from the cone like Gorgon's blood.

And then the five of us were part of a great fleeing mob. I received a confused impression of voices and smells and it was suddenly as though I were back there in ancient Pompeii. The dawn sky overheard was blackening with ash and the world was disappearing in a vortex of reds, ochres and yellows. My eyes fluttered and the canopy of my lids was a cool green. The blood flowing from my shoulder looked almost black, flowing in a stream over the snowy whiteness of my exposed arm. How strange, I thought, to die in such a terribly beautiful palette.

XXII

END GAME

AND yet, gentle reader, (as I'm sure you've gathered) I did not die! A long week later and the great shuddering roar of that eruption was like a strange dream to me. After the removal of Unmann's bullet from my shoulder and much rest I had been re-established in my room at the Santa Lucia where I was at least able to sketch a little. An easel was optimistically set up but I found myself quickly exhausted and it was far easier to drift off into sleep after some of Charlie's nourishing soup than to work. It was fully a fortnight before I was able to receive visitors.

First came Joshua Reynolds, on a rare foreign trip, bearing the profound thanks of HMG and whispers of medals, which I nobly refused for fully two minutes until he started taking me seriously and I had to beg for them.

The next day brought the newly liberated Christopher Miracle. He looked a little drawn (but not badly drawn, ho-ho), as well he might and he beamed at me with what looked suspiciously like renewed respect.

'I owe it all to you, old man,' he said with a catch in his voice. 'Flush would have strung me up if you hadn't intervened. I'm most awfully grateful.'

I gave a heroic but modest smile. 'We still don't know quite what happened that day, do we?'

'Ah, yes,' said Miracle. 'We do. If you're not too tired, dear Lucifer, there's another guest who is most anxious to speak to you.'

Charlie showed in the extraordinary apparition that was Mrs Midsomer Knight, once more swathed in veils and sporting a rather splendid new gown of deepest emerald. She took a seat by my blanketed form and inclined her head in greeting.

'Mr Box, how do I begin to thank you?'

'Please don't even try,' I said manfully. In truth I didn't have the strength to be gushed over. 'It's reward enough to know that my friend here is exonerated and that you and the professors – well, a quorum of them at least – are out of danger. That and the fact that a dangerous lunatic's plans have come to nought.'

'Ah yes,' mused Mrs Knight. 'My unfortunate son.'

I sat up on one elbow, wincing slightly. 'It would please me greatly, however, if you could clear up one or two points in connection with this matter.'

'Anything.'

'Perhaps I can help you there,' came a booming voice from the doorway. The massive frame of the Duce Tiepolo emerged from the shadows.

'Your Grace,' I said quietly. 'I fear I have done you a grave disservice. For I thought you behind this whole mad scheme.'

'I *am* guilty,' said the great man. 'Guilty of a mad love. For this wonderful woman.'

He took Mrs Knight's hand in his. 'It was so long ago,' he croaked. 'It is not an easy thing, Signor Box, to know that you have been born into wealth and privilege then see all that swept away. I was a hunted man. One day I arrived in Naples and I met a girl. She was only sixteen or so, and a little frightened of me. But I knew at once that I loved her . . . Loved her!'

'But she was married.'

The Duce nodded bitterly. 'With a child. The husband, Morraine, was a good man, an honest man, but we could not help ourselves, could we, my dear? It was like a fire, the passion that burned within us!'

Mrs Knight sighed. 'At first it was easy to see each other in secret. My husband, Maxwell, thought only of his work. He and his colleagues laboured from dawn to dusk. But finally our secret was betrayed! Maxwell was mad with jealousy. I went to see him. To tell him I must leave him . . . I found him in his laboratory. Told him that the Duce and I were in love. At first he seemed not to hear me. He was burning his papers after some scientific disappointment. He threw more and more paper on to the fire until suddenly it was out of control and . . .'

Mrs Knight pressed her hand to her mouth and sobbed. 'It took away my youth, my beauty . . .'

The Duce clamped his huge arm around the delicate woman's shoulders. 'And I knew nothing of this for years. The authorities caught me and I was deported. I found out about the fire and believed Kate to be dead. How was I to know that she had been spirited away from Naples and was back in England? Years passed. I never expected to see my lover again.'

'But you did.' I drawled, taking a slow drag on my cigarette.

'I did! Can you imagine it, Signor Box? After all that time? I have roamed Europe like a vagrant. I was passing through London and, one day, as I was walking through the park, you saw me, didn't you, my pet?'

He turned to his lost love, his weathered face wreathed in smiles.

Mrs Knight continued. 'Even after all these years I knew him at once.'

'And you felt the same?' I asked the Duce.

'Once I knew it was her, of course! What did I care for her scars? Her "ugliness"? She was my darling girl. Restored to me when I thought her long dead.'

The Duce's noble head bobbed low on his breast, then he raised it again, tears welling in his rheumy eyes. 'I bought the silence of my companion and we spent the whole afternoon together. There were secret letters, stolen moments. And then I hit upon the drawing-class scheme. We planned to elope. Elope! Like star-crossed lovers!'

'That night, the night of Miracle's ball, she was meant to steal away and meet me in the gardens. But she did not come! And then I heard about the body – oh! A second time she was taken from me!'

He groaned like a wounded beast. 'And so I came here. Home. To Naples. In secret, of course, and seeking – who knows what? Peace?'

I pulled myself up on the pillows. 'And what of that day in the Mechanical Institute, Mrs Knight? I gather you had already suspected you were under observation?'

The veiled woman placed her hands in her lap and sighed. 'That I had. But I thought they were sent by my husband, and that our scheme was impenetrable. I little thought what they might have in mind until that day. Miss Frenzy and I had just switched places when two men burst into the lavatory. At once they grabbed poor Miss Frenzy but she fought valiantly, biting one of them upon the hand.

'Of course I could not simply hide in the cubicle and leave Abigail to her fate but their faces were a pretty sight when they were suddenly confronted by two identically dressed women! As time was obviously of the essence, they bundled us both from the place and took us to some low lodging house where the truth was forced from us. One of them, a man called Bowler, decided that fate had put in his way a serendipitous event. They had come to abduct me, how much better if I were thought to be dead!'

She tailed off and gave a little sob. 'From that moment poor Abigail's fate was sealed. I was quite unable to protest as they gave me the first of those hideous injections and I was scarcely sensible from that day on.'

Tiepolo laid his big hand over hers. 'It is over now,' he said in a reassuring tone.

I sank back. 'And what will you do now, my dear? If you'll take the advice of an impecunious artist . . .'

'Thank you, Mr Box, but I do not need it! I am resolved to change my life while there's still time.'

The Duce Tiepolo grunted his approval.

Miracle frowned. 'And what of your husband?'

'I'm afraid he shall have to get used to it,' trilled Mrs Knight, almost girlishly. 'For the Duce and I are . . . well . . . eloping tonight.'

I wished them both well, confident that, in the fullness of time, I might receive massive financial reward for services rendered.

Miracle ushered them out then returned to my side.

'Well?' he demanded. 'Have you heard from her?'

'Heard from whom?' I said, all innocence.

'Why from Miss Bella Pok, of course! You have been in here fully two weeks! Has she not been to visit you?'

I shrugged lightly. 'I have received a note or two enquiring after my health.'

Miracle leaned forward in his chair. 'And when do you see her?'

I laughed sharply, making my injured shoulder twinge, unable to keep up the pretence a moment more. 'Tomorrow morning! But now I am most awfully tired, Chris. You must let me get my strength up for the great occasion!'

He left me, promising dinner at Maxim's, showers of gold and all the tea in China once I was fully recovered.

A happy peace had settled over my routine. Charlie had turned himself into an excellent nurse and his bedside manner was more than admirable.

That night I slept heavily, my head seeming to pound in time to the eruption of Vesuvius as I found myself back there, the sky behind me a strange, lurid red. But suddenly I knew it was not the sky at all but the canopy of my own eyelids. I blinked once. Twice. And the pounding roar of the volcano resolved itself into an urgent knocking at the door of my hotel room.

I glanced down at the bed. Naked, Charlie lay sound asleep at my side, his bruised body lightly covered by the cool cotton sheets. Suddenly I remembered.

'Bella!' I cried.

I jumped to my feet, immediately regretted it and flopped back on the bed. I looked wildly about.

'Up!' I hissed, slapping Charlie on the side. 'Up!'

He half opened his very blue eyes. 'What?'

'Get yourself up, Charlie boy. We have company.'

He groaned and shook his head. 'Tell them to sling theirs. *I'm* your company.'

I leant down and pinched him savagely on the nipple. 'Get yourself up, Mr Jackpot or you'll be sorry.'

Yelping in pain, the boy sat up and flapped his hands at mine. 'All right, all right, you swine!'

Still befuddled by sleep, he looked dumbly at his nakedness and began to get dressed.

'Quickly!' I hissed. 'It is Miss Pok.'

He struggled swiftly into his trousers and threw on his shirt.

'Now, after you've shown the lady in, you must make yourself scarce.'

'You ashamed of me?'

I sighed. 'You're my servant, Jackpot. It's time you started behaving like one instead of bleating away like the Little Match Girl.'

'Lucifer?' came Bella's muffled voice from beyond the door.

'All right,' said Charlie, sloping sullenly off towards the door. He dragged it open and ushered Bella inside with ill-concealed contempt.

'Miss Bella Pok,' he muttered.

'Thank you, Charles,' I said between gritted teeth. 'You may take the rest of the day off.'

'Oh!' he cried, clasping his hands to his bosom. 'May I, sir? Oh, how kind of you, sir.'

'That will be all, Charles,' I said firmly. He went out and slammed the door.

'Bella! How wonderful to see you! Pray accept my apologies for him. It is so devilishly hard to find good servants these days that one accepts even the most rough-edged and bothersome.'

'I thought he was rather sweet,' she said sunnily.

I was slightly breathless and my head ached. 'Well, well, no doubt that is your pleasant disposition. I fear I do not appear at my best . . .'

She took in my tousled appearance and sleep-shocked hair and waved away my apologies with a yellow-gloved hand. I took it and kissed it fervently.

'You are safe! That is all that matters!'

'You got my note, then? It was a foolish thing I did. To risk my life when I had so much to look forward to.'

Smiling indulgently, she lifted the white veil from her face. I felt my pulse quicken at this renewed view of her beauty. 'You are very bold, Lucifer,' she said quietly.

'I have offended you!' I groaned. 'It is only that I had hoped so much that when I got back to England we might . . .'

She sat next to the bed and took my hand in hers. 'Rest assured, dear Lucifer, that I have not forgotten you.'

I smiled happily.

'Now,' she said, settling herself. 'How on earth did you come by these dreadful injuries? I want to hear all about your adventures!'

'Oh?' I said wearily. 'Really?'

Impressions of the extraordinary events of the past weeks began to crowd my brain, all of them tinged in a volcanic glow. I thought of coming up with an entirely neutral version of events, concerned with sketching trips and abandoned canvases and amusingly dreadful restaurant fare but Bella deserved better than that. She knew I had some dark secret.

'Lucifer?'

I opened my eyes. 'Was I drifting?'

'So it seems,' she said concernedly. 'Are you quite well?'

I winced suddenly and she moved to my side, noticing, beneath my dressing gown, the bandages that swaddled my chest.

'Oh you poor, poor darling.'

I made a stoic face. 'It's nothing, really.'

She shook her head. 'I shall fetch you a drink.'

'Well, it is the hour for vermouth,' I smiled.

She took my hand and squeezed it. Moments later she had returned with two glasses.

I took the one she proffered gratefully.

The glass was almost at my lips when I suddenly felt curiously uneasy. It was not the ache in my shoulder, nor the fatigue of having so many visitors, nor even the effort of my recent tumble with young Charlie. It was a strange, indefinable something and it caused me to set the glass down on the counterpane. 'Think I'll save it for a moment. Don't want it to go to my head.'

Bella shrugged. 'As you please.'

I looked at her steadily and nodded towards the glass. 'Aren't you joining me?' I said lightly.

The young woman shook her head. 'No, thank you.'

She seemed to become aware that I was staring at her. Bella's pale, slender throat made a noticeable undulation and she looked down at me, smiling. Then her face changed with the suddenness of a mask falling away. She balled her hand into a fist and punched me hard directly in my wound.

I gasped in pain and shock and fell back against the pillows. At once, Bella had picked up the whisky glass and was prising my mouth open. My head swam with nausea as I felt her fingers stealing into my mouth and the edge of the glass tapping against my teeth.

'Drink it!' she hissed. 'Drink it, you bastard!'

There was nothing but steel in her voice now and the lovely eyes had turned cold.

I pushed at her but I was so weak that she forced me back on the bed. Risking some kind of fearsome rupture, I rolled off the bed and fell to the floor.

Bella at once stalked towards me, holding the glass in both hands.

'What the hell are you doing?' I screeched. 'Are you mad?'

'Drink it, my dear. It is prussic acid. There will be a little pain but soon you will be insensate.'

'Bella!' I cried, trying desperately to stand. 'What is wrong? It is I, Lucifer Box!'

'*Pauvre petite*,' she murmured. 'You pursued me like a goat from the day we met, didn't you? And never once did you guess at the truth.'

'Truth? What truth?'

She put down the glass and from her dress produced a dainty pistol which she levelled at my chest. She laughed. It was that gay, musical laugh I had grown so fond of. 'You remember a chase by coach through London?'

'Of course.'

'I drove that coach! I! I sent the venomous insect to your home! I did it all, to get my revenge on *you*!'

'On me?' I said, all innocence.

'I believe I once told you I am Dutch by birth. That is not quite true. I am Afrikaans. I lived in Pretoria till I was nine. Just me and my beloved father. Everard Supple!'

I shook my head desperately. '*Who?*'

'Can you have forgotten so soon? The man you gunned down in cold blood! I know, Mr Lucifer Box, I know all!'

Everard Supple? Everard Supple! It seemed incredible. The old fool I'd killed all those weeks ago as a routine assignment. But how could she have found out? This was just the sort of thing Joshua Reynolds was meant to protect me against!

'Supple was your father?'

'Yes! A great man. A man whose feet you were not worthy to kiss!'

I wasn't having this. I struggled to my feet, tears of agony springing to my eyes. 'A dangerous anarchist!' I yelled. 'I despatched him because he planned to assassinate the foreign secretary!'

Bella's eyes blazed in fury. 'I will not listen to your lies! I only know that I have spent these last weeks planning how best to despatch *you*, Box. I was not sure, at first, despite my information, that you were responsible.'

'Information?'

'My father's *diplomatic* contacts.'

'Ah,' I gasped. 'Spies.'

'I had no idea how I might engineer a meeting and then your little advertisement came along. It was too perfect. I came to your studio and I confess I could not believe you to be a killer. And then . . .'

'Then?'

'There, amongst the paints and brushes, I saw it. My father's glass eye!'

'Ah –'

'And then my heart hardened, Mr Box. I swore I would destroy you!'

'You didn't manage very well, did you?' I piped up, eyeing the door. Despite my weakened state I was going to make a break for it. Fool! Why had I sent Charlie away? There were hotel staff about. But could I make it in time? If I could but raise the alarm . . .

'Unlike you, Mr Box, I am not a professional murderer.'

I looked at her with as much stoicism as I could muster. 'What do you want me to do?' I asked. 'Beg for my life? I won't do it, my dear. You must know me well enough by now. I may be a cad but I'm not a coward. I stand by what I did to your father. I should do it again.'

'Ha!'

'You must understand, that I am a servant of His Majesty's Government. I never kill without taking the greatest pains to ensure that what I'm doing is right! Of course I feel for you and your loss but you must believe me when I say your father was a dangerous fanatic.'

'And what does that make you! The fêted artist, the dashing dandy. But by night – philanderer, sodomite and assassin!'

As a thumbnail sketch of me that wasn't half bad.

Bella aimed the revolver at my face and cocked it. 'And so . . . farewell . . .'

Then things moved very quickly. I sprang forward, throwing the deadly contents of the whisky glass towards Bella's face. Her arm shot up defensively and the liquid splashed harmlessly over the sleeve of her gown. An instant later she fired the revolver, but I had already thrown myself to the floor and, gasping in pain, rolled over and behind my easel.

Bella skittered towards me. I grabbed at a pot of brushes and flung it at her. The glass shattered against the wall and the pistol spat fire again.

I scrambled under a chair, the pain of my wound making me giddy, and struggled to think. I would never make it across the room alive.

'Come out, come out wherever you are!' cried Bella with a kind of dreadful gaiety.

She dragged the easel aside on its squealing castors and my ludicrous hiding place was exposed.

'What an ignominious end, Mr Box!' she crowed. 'Now, Papa! You shall be revenged –'

All at once, and to my utter astonishment, the bedroom door flew open and Charlie launched himself on to Bella's back.

The two of them careered around like a carousel, Bella's skirts sending painting materials flying. She bellowed alarmingly and began to twist her arm from Charlie's grip so that she might get a clear shot at him.

'Lucifer!' cried Charlie. 'Quick!'

I needed no prompting. I dashed out from under the chair, grabbed at a half-finished canvas and cracked Bella viciously under the jaw with it. She toppled backwards and Charlie fell from her, the gun grasped in one hand. He threw the weapon to me and I had raised it ready to fire when I stopped dead.

Bella had fallen back against the dresser and now stood stock still. Her shaking hands flew to her back and came away bloody. She sank to her knees, seemed to pause for a moment, and then pitched forward on to her face with an awful gurgling moan.

Stuck in her back was the lance of that frightful spelter statue she had drawn so prettily on the first day of our acquaintance.

Charlie dashed to my side and lifted my head on to his knee. Fatigue and nausea were washing over me. 'Charlie . . .'

We both watched as a torrent of blood as red as lava began to flow from Bella's back, drenching her gown. Then her eyes turned glassy and she lay still.

'This is meant to be my day off,' said Charlie. 'Who do I talk to about overtime?'

I looked him directly in the eye and managed a smile. 'Charlie, what can I say?'

He stroked my hair with uncommon gentleness. 'All part of the service.'

'Well, I'm glad you mentioned that, Charlie,' I murmured, managing to prop myself up on one elbow. 'You know, my pal Beardsley always said that his indisposition made him frightfully horny. No doubt one is not quite in control of oneself when one's glands are up.'

I smiled what my friends call, naturally enough, the smile of Lucifer.